Tales Most Strange

Jeremy Hayes

ISBN: 0991864263
ISBN-13: 978-0991864263

This book is for my Mom and Dad, who allowed me to watch and read whatever I wanted to fuel my imagination. When I was young, I loved to watch The Twilight Zone but I was too afraid to watch it alone. I could only watch it if my Mother was in the same room. Thanks Mom!

Other Books By Jeremy Hayes

The Stonewood Trilogy

Book I: The Thieves of Stonewood

Book II: The Demon of Stonewood

Book III: The King of Stonewood

The Goblin Squad
Coming Soon

Northlord Publishing
Visit us at: www.northlordpublishing.com for news about upcoming releases or to contact the author.

Website/Logo: Cody Kotsopoulos www.kotsysdesigns.com

CONTENTS

THE VAMPIRE PAPERS

Tendrils of lightning reached across the night sky as thunder rattled the shutters of my window. The wind howled like some otherworldly beast and the draft from under my apartment door caused the candles on my desk to dance about, threatening to wink out of existence at any moment. It was a dreadful night, but oddly, the most perfect atmosphere to begin my writing.

I felt that everything I had learned in the past eight years needed to be recorded, so that it may be of some use to others in the future. I know things, intimate details, that should not remain locked in the dark recesses of my mind. Would it not be a sin to hold such knowledge and never share? I thought so.

I only wish that more comprehensive writings had existed and were accessible to me eight years ago, so that I may have made better judgment and also saved myself so much trouble. But alas, everything I had learned, I had to learn myself, the hard way. To study the elusive creatures of the night, I needed to get close to one, befriend one, and that was no easy task. Vampires were not trusting by nature. My quest for knowledge was fraught with dangers that lesser men would shy from.

I first learned of vampires as a young lad from reading old books of folklore. They were mysterious villains, linked to the deaths and disappearances of many, though were seldom seen. The stories had hinted at their existence but provided no solid evidence. When strange things happened it seemed a simple thing to blame it on the doings of a vampire.

Folk feared the night and hung garlic and crosses on their doors, for no other reason than that someone else told them it was a good idea. Reading the stories when I was young frightened me and yet intrigued me all at the same time. I sought more books, more stories, I became obsessed with learning everything I could about these malevolent undead. I needed to know whether the tales were true or not. Did they exist, or were they just creations of our minds used to frighten children and adults alike?

As I got older, my curiosity led me away from the pages of books and soon I was visiting the sites of these vampiric encounters. I began talking to locals, hearing their accounts and their take on the tales, gathering what information I could. The more people I spoke with, the more I believed these stories to be true. After a year and a half, my laborious investigations eventually led me to, Maximilian Decker.

My unwavering determination was rewarded, though for a time, I questioned whether a reward it truly was, for I saw horrors that no living being should have to bear witness to, and my mind, and even my very soul, still suffer to this day. They say time heals all wounds but those who say it, have never met Maximilian Decker. No, time can do nothing for me now; I shall carry my psychological wounds for eternity and beyond. I have been damaged beyond which there is any hope for repair.

Thunder boomed overhead and drew me out of my internal musings. I dipped my feathered quill into the inkwell and then placed the tip of my writing utensil upon the blank parchment that lay stretched out before me. I began to write.

Are Vampires evil incarnate? Devils born of darkness whose sole purpose in life is the destruction of mankind? To this I say, no. Are they capable of committing horrendous atrocities which any decent person would deem unimaginable? Most assuredly. But Vampires are not spawned in hell, then unknowingly unleashed upon us. They were human once, flesh and blood, born of this world. They lived, they breathed and they possessed a soul at one time. All this and more, I learned from Maximilian Decker.

I leaned back in my chair as I recalled our first meeting. He was a most charming man, well-spoken and educated. Max could disarm you with a smile and then freeze you in terror with but a stare. His eyes could penetrate; peel away your skin until your very soul lay bare before his scrutiny. Try as you might, there is no secret you could withhold from this man, if he set his mind on extracting it.

I shudder still, when I think back to that night when he discovered my true purpose in seeking him out. Where by sheer force of will, he made me relate to him of my fascination with vampires and my quest to learn all that I could about their kind. He invited me to live with him in his mansion home, so that he might indulge my curiosities and show me things that no man had ever seen and lived to tell, or should ever see.

Max was terrible and kind, concurrently, and his mood could change with a moment's notice. The staff that lived with and served him knew this all too well. They lived their lives, day to day, in a perpetual state of nervousness. For the most part, Max treated them with respect and decency, but woe to those who angered him. Fear kept them from fleeing his home; fear of being brought back for punishment.

While I still walked about on eggshells, Max afforded me no reason to fear him. I was treated differently from all other humans who had dealings with the wealthy lord. Dare I say, he even enjoyed my company. I believe he truly relished the idea of recounting his life to someone for the first time. And I absorbed every word; every tidbit he chose to share with me, for this had been my lifelong dream.

Now, eight years after setting out on my quest, I felt it was the right time to chronicle all that I had learned. I glanced around my smallish, one-room apartment, which was littered with books featuring stories or accounts of vampires. But these books, every one of them, would pale in comparison with my writings when I finished; mine would eclipse them all. I would expose the falsities contained within those yellowed pages and reveal the frightening truths that were made clear to me during my stay with Max.

I leaned forward again and continued to write.

Maximilian was not born evil; his mother and father had not been demons or devils. He was born into a normal, albeit wealthy family, and from his retelling, lived a most average life. But was he now a monster? Oh yes, indeed so, most undoubtedly. The insights I sought though, were, what made the man into a monster? Did the conversion from life to undeath alone cause madness? Did one lose one's soul after becoming undead? What made the Vampire capable of ghastly acts which would have been repugnant to the same person in life? The first and simplest answer to this, was of course the most basic, and not unique to the undead, hunger; the instinctual need to feed. Humans had been slaughtering animals for food in gruesome ways since the beginning of life itself, and yet we did not label ourselves as evil for doing so. Vampires too, needed to eat to survive; only, they required the blood of humans. Max made the point of stressing to me that he at first did not relish this new life. He was horrified by that which he was required to do in order to survive.

A door slammed shut down the hall giving me a start. My noisy neighbor to the right must have just arrived home for the evening. Nobody would have dared slam doors as such in the home of Maximilian Decker. At times I missed the peaceful silence that shrouded the mansion. Of course there were times when that silence was shattered, the times when Max fed. But for the most part, you could have long uninterrupted moments alone with your thoughts.

For the longest time during my stay, I could not readily adapt to Max's schedule and spent much time alone during the day while the undead master of the house slept. We would talk long into the night until I could no longer keep my eyes open and sleep would claim me. My time alone during the day allowed me to reflect on my nightly conversations with Max, to ponder everything that I had been learning.

Much of the things I had learned about vampires in my books were myths and I had to chuckle at the things which some people believed would keep them safe. When I inquired about their aversion to garlic, Max continued with a tale of his youth, while casually fidgeting with a garlic clove he retrieved from the kitchen. And what of crosses nailed to doors? I had asked him. He did admit to me a weakness to crosses and to many things holy. But a cross nailed to a door did nothing; the item needed to be held by someone of unwavering faith to have an effect. Of wooden stakes, he would not speak.

I shook my head; my thoughts were straying from my task at hand. I again placed quill to paper.

Was hunger alone, enough to make a man into an unconscionable monster? Max did relate to me that he was horrified at first by what his cravings had forced him to do. So then, what changed him? Max's uncomplicated reply to this was mankind. He blamed us. Whether one viewed it as a blessing or a curse, Vampires were immortal and could exist for an eternity. Max was already close to a thousand years old when I had met him. He told me that mankind was capable of far more terrifying things than any Vampire, and the longer he spent with people, he saw them for the monsters that they truly were. He said that I had not lived long enough to completely understand his meanings, but were I to spend hundreds of years among my own kind, I would soon learn the truth of our nature. He claimed that he had not just simply become desensitized to murder, but had eventually developed a love for punishing wicked humans. And a love for it he certainly possessed. Many a night I stood rooted in horror, as I was forced to watch the man feed; carnal pleasure clearly written all over his pale-white face. Max had used certain words when describing the feeling he got as he sunk his fangs into the neck of an unfortunate individual and drank the blood of his victim.

I was attempting to recall his exact description when a knock at my door interrupted my thoughts. The storm still raged outside and I had to wonder if it was the elderly woman who lived to my left, seeking company as storms generally unsettled her.

I didn't need to unlock my door as I never bothered to lock it in the first place. I opened it a crack to peer into the hall. To my surprise, it was the always-noisy neighbor to my right. He had a grubby appearance; his clothes invariably bore holes and stains. The man had an acute fondness for drink and my nostrils were assaulted with the distinct smell of cheap alcohol.

"Might I trouble you for a spare candle or two? It appears I have burnt my last to the very base," he asked with a slight slur to his speech.

"Very well," I replied and motioned him to enter, closing the door behind him.

"You are writing, I see. Did I interrupt?"

"It is alright, I was momentarily paused, stuck on recalling the proper words to continue."

"What are you writing about? Perhaps I could help."

"Yes, perhaps you could."

His eyes went wide with horror, as I revealed razor-sharp fangs which were now visible as I smiled. I lunged forward with great speed and clamped down on his neck; his oh so warm and inviting neck. I drank his most delicious blood while spilling some onto my clothing and carpet. I devoured every drop until the man was quite dead and then allowed his lifeless body to slump to my dirtied floor.

Ah yes, I thought to myself, those were the words that Max had used to describe his feelings. I sat back down at my desk and continued to write.

WRITER'S BLOCK

I resisted the urge to yank out all of my hair. How could I, me of all people, suffer from writer's block? I have created possibly my greatest work, a thrilling tale that is sure to be loved by all, young and old, but I cannot think of a proper ending.

I was made famous with my classic yarns, *The Turning of Winter*, *The Grand Adventure*, and of course who could forget, *The Bird People.* Sales from my amazing tales bought this gigantic old mansion. This house was to inspire me to new heights in my writing, having such character and history.

Oh, but if these walls could speak, the stories they would tell. Lavish parties, scandalous meetings, political back-room dealings. But that was in the past. Now all that these walls bore witness to was the tap-tap-tapping of a lonely man on his typewriter. A boring, middle-aged writer, who could not even finish the most fantastic story he had yet written.

How many times had I wrote, then rewrote, then rewrote again, my final chapter, before tearing it out and placing it in a most unpleasant manner into the waste paper basket? Countless! That's how many times. And here I still sit, staring at a blank page, save for the heading, which reads:

Chapter Twenty-Four

Abraham's Return

But what on earth did Abraham return to? The true worth of a good story rested solely on its ending, of this I firmly believed. I built my career on it, in fact. A twist, an unforeseen event, anything the reader did not see coming, left them with a sense of awe and ensured they would talk of the story for years to come. Twenty years after I wrote *The Panhandler's Will*, people still debated and discussed that heart-wrenching conclusion.

It had been nearly ten years, though, since my last great work. For a while there were rumors of my retirement, my demise even, and now, there were not even rumors at all. I was becoming forgotten, no longer in the spotlight.

My latest story, the thrilling adventures of an explorer named Abraham, was destined to be my best yet. Well, if I could only finish this damnable last chapter. Was it a month now, that I had been stuck? Longer? God only knew. Hours turned into days and days into weeks. I do not even recall my last meal. I do not even feel hungry, so consumed am I with finishing this book.

Bah! I stood up in frustration and paced around my small writing room, causing candles to flicker and create dancing shadows on the walls. Rain pelted the large window that dominated the north side of the room, providing a soundtrack for the dancing shadows with a steady rhythm.

It was well after midnight but the exact time I could not tell. The ancient clock that leaned against faded wallpaper had ceased working and I had been too distracted to bother having it repaired. I tended to write throughout the night and sleep throughout the day. I had maintained that pattern for years, living as a night owl. I did my best work while most everyone else was sound asleep. I preferred the mood, the atmosphere if you will, of the night.

I needed a break from Abraham's adventures and decided to place a record on the phonograph. The Dorchestian Orchestra could always chase away my stress and worries, for a short time at the least. I picked up a feathered quill and walked about the room waving my arm around as if I was the conductor leading the band.

Requiring more space for my mock performance, I wandered into the dimly-lit hallway, continuing with my tomfoolery and becoming lost in the music. Down the corridor I went with a skip in my step, passing by several chambers which I had not even entered into for years. My house was quite immense, especially for one lonely writer, with only two women employed as cleaning staff whose chambers rested on the main floor.

A younger version of myself had explored this house at great lengths, looking to unearth any vanished secrets. If there had been any, the house guarded them carefully, holding them in close, not willing to share with its new owner.

Reaching the end of the hall, I whirled about, working my arm in the air frantically as the phonograph spit out a grandiose crescendo. Then it went silent, spoiling my performance.

Most curious, I stalked back to my writing room to investigate this mystery. To my surprise, I found the plug resting on the floor, removed from the socket. I poked my head back out into the hallway but there had been nobody who had come and gone from the room. I had been in the corridor the entire time, albeit a little distracted, but still I would have noticed the presence of another.

I replaced the plug back into its socket when I heard a door slam shut, just nearby. Odd, how could a door slam shut if none on this floor of the house had been open in the first place? I raced back into the hallway with a candle in my hand.

"Hello? Who is there? Greselda? Gertrude? Hello?"

The sound had come from the right and could have been any of the five doors located on that end of the hall. They led to rooms seldom used or visited. Thunder cracked overhead and I wondered if it had been the work of the wind from the nasty storm that continued outside. Some draft from a window, I convinced myself. The cleaning staff did not work at night and would not venture up to this floor at this hour.

Sensing the sun was soon to rise, I decided to retire to my bedchamber. My brain had overdosed on Abraham and I would continue my quest for a suitable ending later this evening.

As per usual, I slept the entire day through and awoke to a dark chamber, feeling quite refreshed. I quickly changed into my crimson smoking jacket, and foregoing a bite to eat, proceeded directly to my writing room, lighting candles upon arrival. I sat myself down in front of the typewriter and again stared hopelessly at the blank page that awaited my creative genius.

It seemed that it would have to wait awhile longer, as no thoughts came to my idea-depleted mind. As magnificent as the story of Abraham was, it was nothing without an equally astonishing ending.

Minutes became hours and then I stood with a growl, yes an actual growl, akin to an angry dog. I thought to relieve some of my rising stress levels with a little music and turned to my phonograph. Strangely, the record would not spin. I looked to the socket and again found the plug on the floor. The cleaning staff had been told years ago to never enter my writing room, that I would look after its care alone. And they had always obeyed that one and only house rule.

My attention was suddenly drawn to the sound of footsteps from the hall. Good, I thought, now I could speak with the staff and get this matter cleared up. I marched out of my writing room to find the corridor outside empty, devoid of anyone at all. Nobody could have walked that quickly, to reach the stairwell down before my entry into the hall. I had not heard any of the doors open or close.

"Hello? Who is up here?"

This was ridiculous, I thought, and stomped my way downstairs, past the living room, past the library, to find the guest quarters where my staff slept. I was about to knock on Gertrude's door when I stayed my hand. All was quiet and all was dark. It did not appear as either of the two women had been up and about. I decided it was too late to disturb them and most likely they would not be decent.

I sighed and strolled back to my library, particularly admiring the shelves that contained all my works. I was about to pick up *The Unremembered Soldier* when I heard those same footsteps above. I froze in place, listening.

Someone walked from one end of the hallway to the other, then back, as if patrolling.

"See here now! You stand still up there!" I shouted, as I ran with all haste back to the stairs and straight up.

To my surprise, I found the hallway once again to be deserted. This time my skin prickled as I scanned each of the doors to find them all closed. This silliness needed to stop.

Beginning with the first closest door, I opened it wide and stepped into the room, inspecting for occupants. I found the chamber with one lone window to be vacant, so I proceeded to the next room and entered. Also empty.

Two doors down I heard the sound of breaking glass, as if a vase had been thrust towards the floor. Ah ha! Caught you, I thought, and I rushed down the hall and forcibly threw the door open. I did indeed find a broken vase with pieces strewn about the floor. This had been a sitting room at one time and was occupied by several comfortable old chairs. I had decorated the mantle with several knick-knacks that I had acquired over the years. The particular vase, which now lay in ruin, was a gift long ago from one of my aunts.

Again my skin prickled upon the realization that the room was empty of living beings. The window stood closed and the latch was firmly held in place. No storm, no wind, no thunder from outside. How then did the vase just suddenly fall? And who was the owner of those footsteps I had most assuredly heard and not imagined?

A door slammed shut and I swear I nearly jumped through the roof. If there was a mirror in front of me, I am positive my face would have been visibly paler.

I dashed into the hall to find it empty, of course. That was enough for me. I can admit to feeling thoroughly unnerved and retired to my bedroom. As unsettling as this evening had been, I found sleep came easily enough.

I awoke the next night to find that the vase had been cleaned up. All traces of its existence now gone. My staff had been instructed to leave written messages slid under my bedroom door with any questions or concerns that they might have. This way I would not be disturbed but I could still keep up with the goings-on of my house.

Curiously, I found no messages. I would have thought my staff might inquire about the fate of that vase at the very least. I thought to go downstairs, but again, it was late, perhaps I would leave them a message before I retired.

Instead, I turned on my phonograph and sat down at the typewriter, continuing with my nightly ritual of staring at a blank page. Why? Why? Why, could I not think of a proper ending? Abraham had been gone a long time, so what did he return home to? I was not known for endings where everyone lived happily ever after; it was not my style. So what sinister fate awaited Abraham upon his return?

While pondering that question quite deeply, I heard the sound of someone running up the stairs, loud enough to be heard over the phonograph. I leaped to my feet and ran to the doorway. I found nobody belonging to those footsteps in the hall, so continued on to the stairwell, which was also quite clear of human traffic.

Before I could storm down the stairs, my music ceased playing again. I sprinted with all speed back to my writing room, nearly sliding right past the door on the smooth hardwood floor. I grabbed the door frame to halt my progress. Breathless, I scanned the room for the culprit behind this misdeed. I found the plug removed from the socket but nobody occupied this room but me.

Hairs stood on end as I considered the possibility of spirits, rather than a human suspect, much like my story, *The People of the Attic*. That thought disturbed me and I returned to my bedroom and hid under the covers. I was not tired and I was admittedly frightened, so sleep did not come to me for several, painstakingly-long hours.

The next night when I awoke, I did not go to my writing room, instead I opted to remain in bed. I lay there, as quiet as a field mouse, listening. There were of course the customary "house noises" that all houses were wont to make. But as the hours passed, I heard those footsteps again from out in the hall. I held my breath as they went from one end of the hall to the other, then back again and down the stairs.

As they faded away, I exhaled and trembled. I was in no mood for writing and spent the remainder of the night in bed. Approximately two hours after hearing those first steps, they returned and patrolled the same route. Shortly thereafter, sleep must have claimed me and I awoke the next night.

This time, as I lay there pondering these ghostly events, an idea struck me like a brick to my skull.

"That's it!" I actually spoke aloud, sitting straight up.

The ending of my story came flooding into my mind, as if the dam that had been holding it back all this time had finally collapsed. Ghosts! That was it, ghosts! Abraham returned home to find his house occupied by ghosts.

Forgetting about my own ghostly problems, I flew out of bed and raced to my writing room. Not wishing to waste time with candles, I turned on the lamp that stood next my typewriter and typed away. That last chapter just flowed through me and onto the paper.

I spent several hours perfecting my ending then collapsed back in my chair, mentally exhausted. I did it; I finished my story, my greatest story of all. Just wait 'til my publisher gets ahold of this, I thought, with a childish grin. Satisfied, I went to bed and slept soundly with that same smile displayed on my face.

The moment my eyes opened, I quickly ran to the typewriter to proofread my marvelous conclusion. To my horror, a blank page stared back at me with no words upon it, save for the chapter number and title. In a crazed state, I turned that room upside down in search of the missing chapter. It was nowhere to be found, no trace of it at all.

I was about to go question my cleaning staff, when I sat down and began to type. I figured I had better write it again, while the ending was still fresh in my mind. After a handful of hours, I had finished and was positive it was as close to the version I had written the night before as I could get. This time, I locked the door to my writing room with the only key in the house before going to sleep.

The following night I was awakened by those same ghostly footsteps. I did not move until the patrol was finished and the steps faded back down the stairs. Then, despite the fear that gripped me, I ran to my writing room. I found the door locked just I had left it, so produced the key and proceeded in towards my typewriter.

My heart stopped beating for a moment. Blank! The page in the machine was again, blank! Desperately, I sat down, my fingers tapping away again at the keys, trying to recall exactly what I had written. Sweat dripped from my brow as I typed in a feverish panic. Tap-tap-tap-tap-tap-tap-tap-tap-tap-tap-tap-tap-tap-tap.

When I finished, I was certain that my words had not been exact, my original ideas having become hazy since last night. But I was still satisfied that it was a well-written ending, worthy of the story. Feeling drained, I wrapped my arms around my typewriter and decided to sleep right here, right on top of the machine. Let's see someone try and take my chapter now, I thought, victoriously.

I slept soundly throughout the day and I awoke to find myself in the exact same position I had been in when I fell asleep, draped across my typewriter. I smiled at my cleverness and sat up to inspect my page.

BLANK! The page was blank! I let out a maddening roar. Teary-eyed, I again began typing. Tap-tap-tap-tap-tap-tap-tap-tap-tap-tap-tap-tap-tap.

* * * *

"Now if everyone will just follow me into this room, we can see where Francis did a lot of his writing," the female tour guide said. "There is the exact typewriter that he used. That stack of paper there beside it, is said to be the greatest story that he had ever written, though sadly, he never completed it. It is believed that his frustration at being unable to think of an ending is what drove him to take his own life. The staff that knew him at the time said he was deeply depressed at being afflicted with writer's block. Even today, the security guards that patrol the house, and the cleaning staff that work here, claim that sometimes they can hear music playing from that phonograph, and other nights, they hear the tap-tap-tapping of the typewriter."

THE DESERT OF DISAPPEARANCE

I was drenched in sweat when I awoke. My clothes clung to my body as if I had just stepped out of the shower. I spit out something…dirt? Why was my mouth full of dirt? No wait…sand! I must have been on a beach but how on earth did I get to a beach?

My mind was muddled. I felt disoriented, like the feeling of awakening from a long nap. I had no idea where I was or the time of day but I apparently lay face down in sand with something resting on my back.

A sharp spasm of pain shot through my right side as I sat up into a kneeling position, a cushioned chair sliding off my back. A chair?

In a panic, I looked about. Stretched out in front of me appeared to be miles and miles of sand dunes. My god, I was not on a beach, I was in a desert! Behind me lay the answer to the multitude of questions that had suddenly forced their way into my foggy mind. My heart sank to the most lowest of depths upon viewing the wreckage of the airplane, and then, I remembered.

Many hours ago, the plane had taken off from the Big City; its destination was the far eastern side of the globe. My boss and I were traveling to attend a business conference. I glanced down and noticed I still wore that silly tag on my buttoned shirt, *Hello my name is Julia.* My boss thought it would be a good idea to wear the name tags for when we landed at the airport and met those who would be waiting for our arrival.

I was struck with a sudden pang of sorrow, realizing my boss was most likely dead inside the wreckage of the plane. I never particularly liked him, or enjoyed putting on a fake smile and pretending to laugh at his stupid jokes, but he didn't deserve to die like this.

I realized I must have been ejected from the plane before impact, as I sat several yards from the wreckage, my seat in the sand next to me. I remembered the captain's voice over the speakers ordering everyone back to their seats as the seatbelt signal lit up. I had been returning from the restroom when the first of the turbulence began, sending me into the lap of an elderly gentleman. Under different circumstances he may have welcomed a young woman on his lap, arms draped around him, but the violently shaking plane only sent panic through the several hundred passengers.

I promptly returned to my own seat to find my boss pale and visibly shaken as he was not a fan of flying to begin with. I wasn't quite fond of it myself, though I was less nervous about the whole process than he.

The plane shook for several long, tense minutes, and

then stopped. There was a collective sigh of relief along with some cheering and clapping, but it was short-lived. The plane suddenly dipped and I left my stomach somewhere far above in the clouds. Oxygen masks dropped from a compartment in the ceiling and then I knew this was bad, real bad.

I secured my mask and turned to my boss whose fingers were dug deeply into the armrests of his seat. I smiled weakly, an admittedly poor attempt to downplay the seriousness of our current situation. The plane then rolled and my memories stopped there. Now I sat in the sand, blistering heat beating down upon my golden locks.

A quick inspection of my body miraculously revealed no major injuries. The right side of my body was sore and most likely bruised, but considering the state of the plane, I would gladly accept some bruising. How I survived was beyond my knowledge. I wasn't known for having an abundance of good luck. Though, looking around at my surroundings, I wasn't so sure if this was good luck or not.

We must have crashed somewhere in the Great Desert, since I was aware that our route to the east would have taken us over the vast ocean of sand. The desert was so immense that it was simply unavoidable.

How long had I been lying here unconscious? Was a rescue effort on the way? Would they even be able to find me in the middle of this wasteland? All these questions I could not answer but I hoped for the best.

The heat from the blazing sun was near unbearable but I could find no respite. I dared not enter what was left of the plane to seek shade, fearing its collapse, on top of what I would be certain to find inside.

I stood up to better assess my surroundings and

found I had lost one of my heels at some point, so kicked off the remaining shoe and propped up the seat that lay in the sand. With little else to do, I sat myself down and waited.

It took several long hours before the sun began to set and I felt awash with dread that no sign of rescue had come. I was almost certain that they would cease their efforts with the coming darkness, to renew in the light of the morning. That meant a long lonely night by myself.

With the dark came an uncomfortable chill that I would not have expected to feel within a desert. The sleeves of my shirt were fortunately long, though my legs grew cold as I wore a knee-length skirt. I was certainly not dressed for this drop in temperature. What a horrible place this was! It was too hot during the day and too cold during the night.

Between the biting cold and the despairing thoughts of my current predicament, sleep did not come easily. Try as I might, I managed only a few minutes here and there, nothing significant. The desert was unnervingly silent and the darkness played tricks on my eyes, spotting movement where there must have been none.

As the sun rose in the morning it could do nothing to chase away my foul mood. How long would I have to wait for a rescue to arrive? Surely the demise of our flight would be known by now. My parched throat cried out for a drop of water and if a rescue did not come soon, dehydration would be the end of me. Just my luck, I thought, to survive a plane crash only to die of thirst while waiting to be rescued.

I sat cooking in the baking sun that day and shivered all through the next night. By the following morning, I decided to take a walk around the entire wreckage to see if there was anything thrown from the plane to eat or drink, without having to venture into the nightmare within. My stomach was in pain, requiring nourishment soon.

On the opposite side of the plane I found myself vomiting into the sand. Someone else had been thrown from the plane, much like myself, but they were not whole. Debris was strewn about, but sadly, no food or drink.

Then I spotted something curious up ahead and approached for a closer look. There, in the sand, were footprints leading away from the wreckage into the vast wasteland. Several pairs of feet if I was not mistaken. I mean, I was no tracker, and was not the outdoorsy type, but the prints varied in size. It was most curious. The tracks led away for as far as I could see, disappearing over a distant dune.

There must have been other survivors, I came to realize. They must not have found me, or perhaps thought I was dead. But for some reason, they decided to trek further into the desert. To what purpose? I wondered. Surely a rescue party would be in search of the plane's wreckage, so staying near to the plane made the most sense to me. So why leave it?

Then the thought struck me. What if one of the other survivors was familiar with this part of the world? Maybe an outdoorsman. Or, what if one of the pilots survived? Perhaps they had known our general location before the plane crashed and they knew which direction to travel in order to find civilization. In that case, might it then be wise to follow the tracks?

I wouldn't dare to just venture into the desert, choosing a direction at random. The tales were many of people who had vanished in the Great Desert, never to be seen again, with no trace of them ever found. But I had a visible trail to follow and I would very much like to be in the company of others.

So my mind was made and I quickly took to following the footprints left in the sand. I figured I could always follow them back to the wreckage, if the need arose.

Within an hour, I found myself questioning the wisdom of my decision. The sun began to blister every inch of my exposed skin and the sand burned the bottoms of my feet. I had never in my life felt heat as brutal as this and soon felt dispirited. The desert appeared endless and each dune I passed brought me no closer to those I followed.

Several hours into my trek I was on the verge of collapse, when a sight up ahead gave me hope. With renewed vigor, I ran as quickly as I could in the burning sand towards a large pool of water. I had heard of oases before and counted myself lucky to have found one. Strangely, the quicker I ran, I could not get any closer to the oasis. As I moved closer, it moved farther away.

After an hour of chasing the phantom body of water, I did collapse in despair, realizing it had been a trick of the sun. As the sun disappeared, so too did the elusive oasis.

As chilly as the night was, I welcomed it this time, desperately needing a break from the heat. Though soon enough, I was shivering again. I could not follow the footprints in the dark, so pulled my knees to my chest and attempted to rock myself to sleep. Sleep did not come this night and I cried.

With the arrival of the sun in the morning, my body

resisted my attempts to stand and continue with my quest. I was sore and I was weak but I had to get up and move on. Somehow, I managed to find the strength and as the hours passed, my movements became more sluggish and I stumbled several times. Every direction I looked, water taunted and teased me off in the distance. I cried most of the day but still continued following the trail. The one good thing was that the footprints continued, so the others were still alive and had also made it farther than this. If they could do it then so could I.

As night fell, I was rocking myself to keep warm. I was completely exhausted and severely dehydrated. My stomach had given up complaining about food, thankfully, but I could not last much longer, this I knew. I found myself wondering if rescue parties had discovered the wreckage yet and contemplated turning back. No, it was too far to go back now. My fate would be decided by the footprints that I followed.

I was on the verge of crying again when I noticed something unusual in the blackness of the night. There was some sort of faint light source, emanating from over a distant sand dune. Of course I had to wonder if it was another trick played on my eyes but soon curiosity was winning out. If I risked following this strange light, it was possible I would lose the trail of footprints and find myself hopelessly lost come sun up. But the light could have been coming from a campfire or a city even, so my decision was made.

I forced myself to stand and fumbled about in the dark, making my way towards the dune and the strange source of light. The dune ended up being much farther away than I had anticipated but I drew hope from the fact that the light did get closer, instead of keeping its distance like the oasis had.

I was soon crawling up the sand dune on all fours to peer over the top. My heart skipped a beat and then I exhaled with elation. Before me lay a deep valley and a large bonfire burned somewhere near the center. Around the fire I could make out many dark forms milling about.

Forgetting my exhaustion, I half-stumbled and half-rolled down the opposite side of the dune into the valley, crying out for help with my parched throat. The dark figures stopped moving, frozen in place by my unexpected arrival. As I got closer, my skin prickled and the hairs on my neck rose. I was assaulted by a strange feeling, a feeling of dread. When the figures became visible by the light of the fire, I understood that feeling.

The figures were not human; of this I was most positive. Nor did I think they could have ever been human at one time. They stood like humans but their limbs were spindly and unnaturally elongated, with skin as black as coal. Their heads were bald with no hint of hair, and their eyes milky white, quite large and pupiless. I would have guessed them aliens, from some distant planet, but I got the feeling that this valley was their home; much like the Big City was mine.

Despite their nightmarish appearance, it was their voices that I have to say unnerved me the most. They gibbered to each other with indecipherable words, for gibbering was the best description I could assign.

After gibbering to one another for several moments, they turned on me, grabbing me roughly and forcing me closer to the fire. I was then thrown to the ground beside two others who were most definitely human, with my hands bound behind my back. My inhuman captors then walked away, leaving me alone with the two men, one of which wore the uniform of a pilot.

"You survived the plane crash too, huh?" the pilot asked me.

"Yes, I followed your footprints away from the wreckage. My god, what are those things??"

"Your guess is as good as mine," he said. "But I don't think they are friendly, whatever they are."

"You were the pilot of the plane?"

"Co-pilot, yes. I knew that being rescued in this vast desert was no certain thing, so Winston here, and I, decided to take our chances on finding our way out. That didn't turn out so well, as you can see."

"What are they going to do to us?" I wondered aloud.

Neither man answered, but as it turned out, we didn't have to wait very long to find out. Two of the creatures soon approached, gibbering all the while, and grabbed Winston, hauling him to his feet. He struggled briefly and then was dragged towards the fire. To our shock and horror, he was thrown into the fire and I will never forget those screams. They will haunt me until the end of my days. Dozens of the creatures danced around the fire, whooping with delight.

I yelped out loud as something grabbed my bound hands.

"Sssh, be silent," the co-pilot whispered, as he began sawing at my restraints with something sharp.

"What are you doing?" I asked.

"I have been carrying a piece of metal from the wreckage, hoping to signal any passing planes by reflecting the sun. I think I can cut through these ropes."

And he soon did, freeing my hands.

"Give it to me, now. I will free you," I suggested.

"No point, we both cannot escape. I am going to attract their attention while you attempt to slip away."

"Nonsense! Let's both run, right now. I don't want to be alone again."

"We both cannot escape, they would be on us in no time. No, my dear, I will lead them away from here while you make a break for it. I will not argue with you. One of us needs to get out of here to hopefully tell the world what we have seen."

"I will die in the desert alone."

"Better to die out there, alone, than be burned and possibly eaten here by these things."

He had a good point there, so I nodded. I was about to ask his name, when he rose and ran, screaming for attention as he went. The horrendous creatures whirled about and gave chase. Fortunately, none of them paid me any attention, so taking advantage, I ran in the opposite direction and was soon scrambling up the side of the steep valley wall.

I cried out as something suddenly bit into the back of my right leg. Reaching back, it almost felt like the shaft of an arrow protruding from my skin. I felt warm blood begin to trickle down my leg. With a grunt, I managed to snap off the shaft, then ignored the pain and continued to climb.

I did not stop when I reached the top and I did not even hazard a glance back. I ran blindly into the night and did not stop until the sun had risen the next day. It's amazing what the body can do when fueled by absolute terror. But I eventually collapsed, my tank having run dry.

There was no sign of the valley I left behind and I was again surrounded by an endless sea of sand dunes, for as far as my eyes could see. My leg ached and continued to bleed. This was it, I thought, I could not continue any further. I was going to die here in this spot, or get dragged back to the valley come nightfall.

I gave into despair and lay in the sand, unmoving, until the sun began to set. Before the darkness could envelope the desert completely, I noticed some bobbing lights descending a large dune. I couldn't say for sure if what I saw was real. My eyes could have been deceiving me, or perhaps, it was the strange valley-creatures coming to bring me back.

Were it the latter, there was nothing I could do. I no longer possessed the strength to even sit up. As the bobbing lights drew closer, I thought I heard voices; human voices and not the mad gibbering of those otherworldly nightmares.

"Captain, look!" I heard someone say. "That must be one of the survivors."

"I believe you are right. Radio for the helicopter."

I was soon surrounded by several men in military fatigues. I smiled weakly and then blacked out.

The next time my eyes opened, the scenery had drastically changed. There was no longer a blazing sun overhead and there were no more dunes of sand in every direction I looked. I was in a bed, half sitting, propped up by several pillows. An IV line was attached to my left wrist.

As my eyes finally focused completely, I realized I was inside a hospital room. I could hear two voices speaking just outside in the hallway.

"Dr. Manning, how is our lone survivor doing?"

"She will be fine with plenty of rest and liquids."

"It's just incredible that she managed to survive not only the crash, but days in the desert."

"Incredible indeed. She was suffering from severe sunstroke when she was found and babbled constantly about a valley of dark creatures and that the co-pilot could be found there."

"Did they ever find the co-pilot's body?"

"Strangely, no. All bodies were accounted for except for the co-pilot and another passenger named Winston Bentt. There has been no trace of them at all."

"Well I would say she is quite lucky to walk away from a plane crash, suffering only from sunstroke."

"She was bleeding from an injury when she was found. I removed a foreign body from her leg."

"Debris from the plane?"

"Oddly enough, no. It was not metal, it was stone. And if I didn't know better, I would have said it was some kind of ancient arrowhead."

SCARECROWS

I received the call around noon on Friday. It looked like I would be spending the weekend in the country. Not that it mattered overly much; I do not have a family and had no real plans. Probably would have sat around my one room apartment with a bottle of whiskey, staring aimlessly at the picture tube.

I had nothing else on the go at work either, having successfully closed my last case the previous day. It had been fairly simple, took me all of a week. It's always the jealous husband. Were I to write a book about such things, that would be the shortest chapter. Chapter heading reads, *Murdered Wife*. Chapter text reads, *It's always the jealous husband.* End of chapter.

I had some papers to file away in the office before running home to pack a bag and make a quick corned beef sandwich. I grabbed a coffee from a corner shop and headed off for Bridgeway, an eighty mile drive south of the Big City.

I assumed the local sheriff's department was not used to handling such calls; it was most likely a rarity. Dealing with chicken thieves or the odd break and enter was probably the extent of the crimes in that rural area.

I wasn't sure if my boss gave the call to me because I had nothing else on my plate, or whether he thought I was best suited for the scene I would find there. I had been fairly successful in a few serial killer cases over the years and I had spent one year undercover, within *The Children of Darkness* cult. Boy, I had seen some things there that would give the hardest man goose bumps. Many details had to be left out of my formal report as they had no scientific explanation. I couldn't have my bosses thinking that I had gone mad.

Lord it was a hot summer day. The sun beat down on my car like a magnifying glass held over an ant. I was surrounded by cornfields and there were no trees to provide any shade to this lonely country road. At one point, I was forced to pull over and remove my jacket and loosen my tie. Even with all the windows rolled down, I could not get any relief from the sweltering heat.

Shortly before reaching my wits-end, I saw the police barricade up ahead. I turned down a narrow side road and was motioned to stop by a local deputy. I pulled up beside him and held my badge out the window. "Detective Edward Kane."

He nodded. "Is it just you, sir? Or is anyone else following?"

"Just me."

"You can park your car over there on the right with the others."

For now it was just me. My partner quit only a few

weeks ago. We were investigating a string of grisly murders. In one particular house we found the victim, well, maybe that's better left unsaid. My partner was deeply affected by the scene and quit shortly thereafter. He was a clever fellow but inexperienced. I worked better alone anyways, always had.

I decided to leave my jacket in the car. To hell with formalities, it was too damned hot. I didn't even bother to tighten my tie. My shirt was soaked underneath the straps of my shoulder holster.

I approached a group of grim-faced men that were standing amidst a cornfield and nodded to the sheriff. "Sheriff."

"Detective," he responded with a nod of his own.

The group of officers parted, leaving me with a clear view of the crime scene.

"Nobody has touched him or moved him in any way. We have been waiting for your arrival."

I stood and silently stared at the spectacle before me. When he noticed no reaction on my face, the sheriff spoke again. "I don't know if this kinda thing goes on all the time up there in the Big City, but around here, this just doesn't happen."

While I certainly had seen worse, this was still quite disturbing, and a new one for me. Before me was a middle-aged man with a slightly heavy-set build, tied to a t-shaped wooden post. His arms were stretched out to the side in some grim mockery of a scarecrow. Upon closer inspection I noticed his lips were sewn shut and his eyelids forced open. Straw was stuffed down his shirt and pants. He had probably been dead a day only.

"Do we have an ID?" I asked.

"Tom Willoby," the sheriff replied. "A farmer. Lives about three miles east of here. Good man, no enemies. Wife reported him missing about a week back."

"Why would someone kill him, then drag him out here to display him like this?" a deputy wondered aloud.

"He wasn't killed then dragged here," I answered.

"Huh?"

I got a little closer, squinting at some marks I noticed on the post and also on the man's skin. "I would say he was hung here while alive. See these marks on the post and the ones on his skin? It appears as though he had been struggling here for a time. He was possibly hung here while unconscious and then awoke to this nightmare."

"What killed him?"

"Dehydration would be my initial guess, as I do not see any wounds, aside from a little blood on his head. Probably knocked unconscious from a heavy blow," I figured. "Who found him?"

"Another farmer named Dan Burrows. While Tom does own his own cornfield, this one here belongs to Dan. Found him early this morning and called us immediately."

"I will need to speak with this Dan, then."

"Of course, Detective. He was told to remain on his farm for further questioning."

"You don't suspect this Dan?" I asked.

"He is an older man. Kind ole' fella. Doesn't have a violent bone in his body and certainly wouldn't be strong enough to do this," the sheriff assured me.

"This looks like something satanic, if you ask me. You think this could be a cult's doing?" inquired a deputy.

I thought on that a moment before answering. "Hard to tell at this stage if we are looking for a deranged lone killer or a cult acting together. But I mean to get to the bottom of it."

I followed a trail on the ground which indicated the farmer had been dragged to this spot before being hung on the post. The trail led out to the main road and stopped there. Further investigation of the immediate area revealed no other signs. I spent another hour widening my radius, and when nothing more could be found, I decided to pay a visit to farmer Dan.

I was not aware of any cults that operated in this region, but then, I admittedly was not too familiar with Bridgeway and the surrounding townships. My initial instinct was a lone killer. A dispute over farmland perhaps? An argument in a bar? There were several possible scenarios but I would need to speak with a few people that knew the man first.

I found Dan Burrows standing outside his house, wiping sweat from his brow with a dirty red handkerchief, and then returning it to his back pocket. As the sheriff had described him, Dan was a frail-looking, elderly man. His land looked overgrown and not well-tended at all. Dan had probably gotten too old for the upkeep, and as I soon learned, lived alone with his wife and had nobody around to help.

"So, you don't know anyone that had any recent altercations with Tom, for any reason at all? Anyone that didn't like him?"

Dan scratched the few wisps of white hair left on his otherwise bald head. "No, sir. Tom was a kind soul. Everybody gets along in these here parts."

Had to be about business or land, I figured. "I noticed everyone around here has a cornfield. They are everywhere. I imagine there is a lot of competition then, with selling corn, am I right?"

"No, no, I wouldn't say that. Selling corn to you folk in the Big City is big business. Plenty to go around for everyone."

Dan was ruled out as a suspect and when he offered nothing more of value, I decided to head back to the sheriff's office where Tom's distraught wife and sister were waiting. The two women were a mess and that was even with being spared the details of the crime. They were only told that his body had been found. The sheriff felt they didn't need to know any more at this point.

I got the same stories from them, kind soul, no enemies, no disputes over land. His wife said he had gone out in the evening to put away some tools and never returned. I figured I would visit their place first thing in the morning and take a look around.

It was getting late and I had not eaten anything, aside from that corned beef sandwich several hours ago. I thought to go check-in to a local motel a few blocks away from the sheriff's office, when a deputy called into the station sounding frantic.

"What is it?" I asked curiously, walking over to join a group of officers.

"Grab your coat," the sheriff replied. "Another body has been found, same as the other. Hung like a scarecrow."

I left my car at the station and rode with the sheriff in his squad car, sirens ablazing. We found the second *scarecrow*, approximately two miles away from the first, in a secluded part of a cornfield. The scene was exactly the same, the work of the same killer.

I found it amazing how frightening these fields could

be at night. The moon was high in the sky and the sounds of chirping crickets was nearly deafening. The darkness of the night chased away the heat from the day and I was glad I grabbed my coat before leaving the station.

The gruesome scene before me only added to the already eerie feel of the cornfield. The victim here was younger, possibly in his twenties. Slim athletic build. Not old enough to own his own farm. A farmer's son, or hired help, was my guess.

"Do we know the victim?" I wondered.

"The man who found him says the victim works two farms over. He is not from around here but works the fields for a summer job," a deputy replied.

"Where is this man?"

"Right over here, sir."

Indeed the man, with his dog, stood mere steps away but visibility was non-existent among the tall oppressive corn stalks. One could easily become lost within this living maze.

The man was older, forties, slim build. His dog was a shepherd mix of some sort. "How did you come to find the victim? We are a little far from your farmhouse, aren't we?" I asked.

"Yes, and I seldom make it out this way at all," he replied. "But something had Mindy here all agitated this evening. She kept running from window to window, barking. We couldn't rightly sleep with that racket, so I put on her leash and out we went, to see if I could find what was bothering her. She headed straight for the cornfield, so I grabbed a lantern and let her lead the way. Never seen her behave like this before. She led me right here to this spot. Mister, I ain't never seen a sight like that and I hope I never do again, for as long as I live. I am gonna be havin some nightmares you can bet on that."

"Did you hear anything at all? Did you see anyone in the area? Any cars perhaps, on the road?"

"Nary a thing. There is little traffic in this area after dark. Didn't see no one, didn't hear a thing."

"Thank you."

I walked back to the scarecrow and turned to the sheriff. "Have your men cordon off a large section of this cornfield. We will have to return in the morning to search for clues. It's too dark now, too easy to miss something. I would also like as many people as you can get to do a sweep of these fields. I have a feeling there may be more than just these two that we have found."

The sheriff shook his head in disgust but nodded in agreement.

"And before we head back to the station, we will need to visit the farm where this gentleman worked," I added.

The next day was just as hot as the previous. I sat in my car, which felt no different than an oven at this point, just off the main road and surrounded by cornfields. I was listening to police chatter over a radio. Officers from several of the surrounding townships were spread out and scouring the cornfields in search of more scarecrows.

Our second victim, Bill Clover, had also gone missing several days ago. The farmer he worked for said he was a drifter type, just doing seasonal work. He figured Bill had just decided to quit and leave and didn't think anything of his disappearance.

As with the first victim, Bill was dragged through the cornfield, most likely unconscious at the time. But even with the light of day, I could not follow the path to any particular destination of note and there were no other clues to be found.

I was fairly sure it was someone acting alone and not a cult. Probably someone living on their own, reclusive, even by Bridgeway standards. A large man most likely, strong enough to lift these victims in order to hang them in their macabre poses.

I was just about to pull away and start canvassing the closest farms when I heard over the radio, "We have another scarecrow."

By the end of the day, another was found, bringing our total to four. All men who worked in the fields, all displayed in the exact same way. The sheriff and his men were visibly shaken. They couldn't recall the last murder in Bridgeway and now they had four in the span of a couple days. They were looking to me for guidance and answers but I hadn't yet had anything solid to offer.

I spent the entire next day canvassing farms and speaking with people in town. News in these little towns spread fast and folk were spooked. Many would not readily answer their door to a stranger and I would need to hold my badge up when I could see movement behind curtains.

So far, there had been no signs of struggle in any of the victim's homes. They had to have been attacked outside.

I asked around about any particularly odd folk, someone maybe seldom seen in town. A common name thrown about was, David Borden.

"Gives me the creeps, he does," someone said.

"Don't often see him in town much and I tell you that is still too often for my liking," one store owner told me.

"Never looks you in the eyes, that one. Not right in the head," another said.

The descriptions I received of David, very large man, mid-forties, extremely reclusive. After enjoying a fantastic fried egg sandwich for lunch, I decided to pay David a visit.

I approached his farm which was set about two miles off the main road and I parked in front of a wooden gate. I could have easily unlocked it and drove further onto his property but elected to just climb the fence and continue on foot. I pulled out my revolver from its shoulder holster to double check that all six chambers were full, just in case, and then returned it.

The pathway leading up to the house was overgrown with grass and weeds. It was clear that it was seldom used. Folk did say that David was rarely seen, and in fact, nobody even knew if he had a family out here living with him. Not one person had ever visited his property.

I could see a large house, several sheds, and a barn. The entire property was surrounded by tall cornfields and chickens just wandered around everywhere, going about their business.

As I approached the front door to the house, I noticed its state of disrepair. Shutters hung at odd angles, a few windows were broken and it was desperately in need of a paint job.

I wiped sweat from my forehead and then knocked. When there was no response, I knocked again, more aggressively.

"Hello?" I shouted. "Hello, anyone here? I am Detective Kane, I just want to speak to the owner of the house. Hello?"

Nothing. I tried the door handle and it was locked. I walked the perimeter of the house but could not make out anything beyond the dark curtains that were draped across each of the windows.

I decided to check out the barn and found two horses inside, along with several more chickens. I spotted some fresh blood on the floor, but this was a farm, many farmers killed livestock for food, so I couldn't just jump to any conclusions. For all I knew, it was just animal blood.

Nothing appeared out of the ordinary, though this David was not an organized fellow. Tools were just haphazardly strewn about the property. He had clearly not cut his grass in a very long time and didn't seem to care much for keeping up appearances. While that alone was not enough to make the man guilty of these crimes, I did get a strange feel about the place. I felt I was being watched, though could find no evidence of it.

"Hello? Hello?" I called out a few more times.

I walked back to my car and figured that I would return later this evening. Perhaps David had made one of those rare visits into town this afternoon.

Back at the sheriff's station I learned that a fifth scarecrow had been found by officers. They were clearly on edge, panicked by these frequent discoveries. I got the feeling that if the killer were to be found, he would never make it to trial. These officers were hell-bent on dealing out their own kind of justice. I can't say as though I blame them. We were definitely dealing with a sick mind here and this man was not about to stop anytime soon.

After visiting the fifth crime scene, and finding it just like the previous four, there was no time to return to

David's house. It had gotten too late in the evening, so I went back first thing in the morning.

I parked my car in the same spot and hopped over the fence. Motion caught the corner of my eye as I trudged up the overgrown path. A large man emerged out of the cornfield and lumbered along towards the house. He must have stood about six-foot-four and easily weighed upwards of two-hundred and sixty pounds. He was heavy-set but not muscular, with unkempt brownish hair and a straggly beard. He wore dirty, disheveled clothing, with mud-caked rain boots.

"Hello? David Borden?" I called.

The man stopped and turned, regarding me with cold eyes, but did not answer. I held up my badge.

"I am Detective Kane. I am looking for a David Borden, just want to speak with him. Are you him?"

He slowly nodded, coolly scrutinizing every inch of me.

"Oh good. I have been talking with all the other farmers in the area. You were the next on my list but I must have missed you yesterday. I stopped by in the afternoon but I guess you were not home."

"I was sleeping," he said, looking away.

"Oh, during the middle of the day? I hope I didn't disturb you then?"

"I find it too hot to work in the middle of the day. I work mostly at night. And no, I did not even hear you," he replied in a monotone voice.

"That makes complete sense to me, this sun out here is deadly. And speaking of which, it's already getting uncomfortably warm, may we speak inside?"

"Is this about them scarecrows?" he asked, still

keeping his gaze elsewhere.

"Yes, as a matter of fact, it is."

There was a long moment of silence as he hesitated, I sensed an internal struggle waging inside of him. Then he nodded and proceeded to the house. I felt the hairs on my neck rise, so I adjusted my shoulder holster and followed the giant inside.

My nostrils were immediately assaulted by the smell of mold and sour milk, combined. We had entered into the kitchen and its state of disarray astounded me. The sink overflowed with filthy plates and glassware. Flies buzzed around everywhere, sampling crumbs and scraps of food that littered the countertops and tables. I did my best to maintain a composed face, not wishing to offend with my level of disgust.

"What have you heard about the scarecrows?" I finally asked.

"Just the whispered conversations of folk in the grocery store, is all," he replied, looking everywhere else but at me. He fidgeted with an egg whisker which he had picked up from the counter.

"Have you seen anyone strange in these parts of late? Maybe heard anything out of the ordinary at night?"

He slowly shook his head, no.

"Did you know any of these men at all, the ones that died?"

"Seen them in town from time to time, is all," he said with that same monotone voice.

I paced back and forth within the large kitchen area. I appeared to be deep in thought, thinking of my next question, but I was scanning every inch of the room, looking for something, anything, out of the ordinary.

"Do you keep any scarecrows yourself, out in your fields? The real ones, of course."

"Everybody does, you have to. Them damned crows will eat your crop to the last kernel of corn without them."

Then I spotted something on a table near a doorway. Several sewing needles with two spools of thin yellow yarn.

"Are you married at all, David?" I inquired. "Live here with your wife, maybe?"

"I am not married. I live alone."

"Parents?"

"My parents are gone. It was their farm, now it's mine."

"No siblings?"

"No."

Looking to the kitchen table I thought I noticed something etched into the top but it was obscured with a dirty plate.

"That's an interesting portrait," I said, diverting David's attention to the other end of the room.

As he glanced over to the wall I shifted the plate aside to reveal the message carved into the table beneath it. *God has forsaken us*, it said.

"That was Granny," he said in reference to the portrait. "She is also gone."

"Ah," I said in response. "Well I appreciate you taking the time to speak with me, David. I need to visit a few other farms this morning, so I won't take up any more of your time. I am sure you must be ready for bed."

David nodded and I excused myself. Before I made it outside he spoke again. "This town is cursed."

"Pardon?" I turned to face him again, and again his eyes were averted.

"The town is cursed," he repeated.

"Cursed? How so?"

"Them witches that were burned so long ago. They cursed the land within this town. God has forsaken Bridgeway. The people are doomed."

"Doomed in what way?"

Nothing further would he say, David stood as silent as a statue, staring off into oblivion. I nodded and left the house, walking back to my car.

Instead of driving back to the sheriff's office, I returned to my motel room and took a nap. I had been keeping late hours the last few nights and it had finally caught up to me. I was asleep the moment my head hit the pillow.

Several hours later, I was studying a map of the surrounding region which I had taped to the wall of my tiny, nondescript room. I began pinning thumbtacks to the map to represent the crime scenes. The five human scarecrows formed a circle around David Borden's farmland. The creepy giant had unnerved me with his demeanor and comments about a curse. So, David liked to work at night, did he? I planned to drop by later this evening to find out what he was up to.

I couldn't tell the sheriff about my suspicions. I couldn't risk him and his men rushing in to make a hasty arrest. He was under a lot of pressure from his superiors to find this killer as quickly as possible and they were all chomping at the bit to grab someone. This required a little more patience. I informed the sheriff I was following up on a lead tonight and to stand by and await my call.

After speaking with my boss over the phone, and assuring him I was getting closer to finding the killer, I got into my car and headed back to David's place. I turned off my headlights a half-mile away and parked about a ten minute walk from the gate to his property. I took a flashlight and a portable radio with me, in case I needed to call the sheriff for backup. Remembering I had one in my trunk, I stuck a flare gun in the back of my belt. Backup wouldn't do me any good if they could not find me.

Stealthily, I climbed the fence and used the full moon to navigate my way around the property. I had gotten a strange feel from this place in broad daylight; it only intensified as I crept about in the darkness. The only sounds were chirping crickets.

I noticed there were lights on within the house and I snuck up to one of the back windows. I could hear faint music playing, with the distinctive scratching and popping sounds of a record player.

I crouched down behind a wheelbarrow and watched as David came out a side door, whistling while he lumbered towards a large shed. He went inside and closed the door behind him. Taking advantage of the situation, I quietly entered his house through that same side door, taking care that it did not slam shut behind me and make any noise.

I found myself in a living room and it was no less disorganized than the kitchen had been. A musty smell hung in the air so thick I could taste it. Dirty dishes and glasses littered the room, and the stained furniture was on the verge of collapse.

My eyes shifted immediately to a message scrawled on the wall, *Where is God now?* Was it written in blood? No, maybe red paint. Must have been paint, it was too bright.

I found a similar message carved into the top of an

end table, right next to a lamp. *Death awaits us all, in fields made of corn*, it read. I put down the flashlight and switched on the portable radio, I had seen enough. Static. All I got was static.

That was when I heard it. A blood-curdling scream from somewhere outside. A male voice. I drew my revolver and raced outside, goose bumps forming along the skin of my arms. Frantically, I looked about for the source but could find nobody. The door to the shed where David had entered was wide open. I raised my gun and cautiously approached the dark shed.

Rustling noises behind me caused me to whirl around with a start. Something was moving in the cornfield, something large. I didn't have time to retrieve my flashlight, so decided to dash headlong into the foreboding maze of cornstalks.

Upon entering, the darkness closed all around me, tightening its eerie grip. I had to rely more on my ears, than I could with my eyes. Something was being dragged through the cornfield, or likely, someone. It was close, so I continued to fumble my way around in pursuit.

"David!" I shouted in the darkness. "David, this is Detective Kane! I need you to stop!"

The rustling sounds continued moving away from me into the depths of the cornfield. I attempted to use the radio one final time but still heard only static. Frustrated, I dropped the radio and followed the sounds, my gun held in front.

The chase lasted a few minutes more before the sounds ceased. I stood completely still, listening for any movement at all. My eyes had somewhat adjusted to the gloom and they darted back and forth, scanning for my target.

A soft moan to my right had me moving again. I burst into a small clearing somewhere within the vast cornfield. A short distance in front me stood a dark figure, its back towards me. It appeared to be tying someone to a t-shaped wooden post. My heart skipped a beat. I caught the killer red-handed.

"David! Turn around slowly with your hands in the air," I commanded.

No reply. He continued with the ropes.

"I will only say this one more time, turn around slowly and keep your hands where I can see them."

Nothing.

BLAM! A perfect shot behind his right knee.

No response.

BLAM! A perfect shot behind his left knee.

No response. Incredible.

"I said turn around! Turn around now!"

Nothing.

BLAM! A perfect shot to his right shoulder.

Then he turned. My god those eyes, those red eyes! Bright red eyes glowed in the darkness. The figure lurched towards me with jerky movements, like a newborn fawn testing out its legs for the first time. As it got closer, I realized it was a scarecrow. A scarecrow??

BLAM! BLAM! Two shots in the chest. It never even slowed.

BLAM! Click…click…click…click…oh damn.

It struck me in the head with a fist that felt like stone. My world went black.

* * * *

I awoke as my head was jostled to and fro. My eyes were open and yet I could not see. I was surrounded by blackness as dark as pitch. What happened? Where was I? Had I been dreaming? Wait…I was moving. I was being dragged. Someone held me by an ankle and was dragging me.

I attempted to lift my head and was rewarded with searing pain. Then I remembered it struck me. But what was *it*? A scarecrow? A real scarecrow with glowing red eyes? Is that what I had really seen?

Whatever it was let go of my leg and I stopped moving. Clouds suddenly shifted aside and my vision returned with the arrival of moonlight. I propped myself up on an elbow and saw that dark figure in front of me dig a t-shaped post into the ground. I was still within a cornfield and it looked as though I was to be the next scarecrow.

It turned to face me and again those glowing red eyes sent chills down my spine. Something was digging uncomfortably into my back, when I remembered the flare gun.

I pulled the gun free of my belt as the monster walked towards me on unsteady legs. I had only one shot. I steadied my hand and pulled the trigger. My aim was true and the flare struck the scarecrow dead center in the chest. Its body exploded with an inhuman shriek that nothing born of this world could have possibly made. The scarecrow's head, arms, and legs, landed in a heap and caught fire. As the flames consumed what was left of the creature, the red eyes slowly faded and disappeared entirely.

I am not sure how long I sat there, attempting to

digest all that I had seen this night, before finally getting to my feet. Was I really to believe that an actual scarecrow was the serial killer here? I know what I saw and it had not been some bizarre dream.

I attempted to orient myself by looking to the stars. I had to find David. I believed he must still be alive, tied to that post as a scarecrow. The man who was my suspect turned out to be the next target. To all appearances he was the craziest individual in this town but he may have actually been the wisest. The land was cursed indeed.

Well, I figured, as I set off, I could not explain this night to the sheriff or my superiors. My boss would have my badge and recommend me for a psychiatric evaluation. I supposed *The Case of the Bridgeway Scarecrows* would be filed as unsolved.

THROWING VOICES

It is tough trying to make a living in the Big City. Without an education and without knowing the right people, your options are quite limited. The city is very unforgiving.

I am a struggling entertainer, a ventriloquist. For a time I had hit rock bottom and was near penniless. I didn't have the right chemistry with my last dummy and my performances suffered because of it. People were not filling the seats and club owners were becoming less interested in hiring us.

Recently, though, I found a new dummy and started a new act, *Sullivan and Micky*. I didn't mind allowing the dummy's name to be used first; my ego was not inflated enough to worry about such things as that. I was getting more gigs than before and that was all that mattered.

We went everywhere together, Sully and I. Parties, bars, restaurants, hell, even the picture show. People just always expected to see us both. Walking down the street we would get stopped by those that recognized us.

"Hello Sully," they would say.

Or, "Nice to see you, Sully."

The dummy always got the attention; everyone preferred to speak with the dummy. Club owners would even talk business with Sully. I supposed they found it remotely amusing to get the dummy's signature. As long as we made money, they could talk to Sully all they liked.

We lived in a tenth floor room at the Carville Hotel, two blocks from the theater district where we did most of our performances. It was a seedy part of town and the dilapidated hotel left much to be desired, but it was cheap, and we needed cheap.

"We have almost paid the hotel all the money we owe them but that still leaves us with quite a bit of debt. It gives us a roof over our heads, for a little while longer anyways," Sully said to me, as we stood in front of a mirror practicing one of our acts.

"We have three shows booked this week," I replied. "That should get us square with the hotel. We can worry about the others later."

"The others worry me more than the hotel, Micky," he said.

He had a point. We had borrowed money from the wrong sort of people, people who were not very forgiving about owed money and missed payments. Because of that, we were confined most nights to hiding out in the hotel. Our favorite pool hall was off-limits since it was a hangout for many of the gangsters and the malt shop was too close to the pool hall.

Anyhow, that gave us more time in front of the mirror to work on our act. People abhorred a ventriloquist who moved his lips. It was a disappearing art form that needed to be perfect.

A knock came at our door and Sully and I exchanged nervous glances.

"Who is it?" I finally risked asking.

"It's me, Dorothy, come on let me in."

Dorothy was a struggling actress who performed in a play at one of the theater's Sully and I occasionally worked for. She was a decent dame, one hell of a looker, just not so bright.

We unlocked the door and let her in.

"Aww, there's my Sully," even the women all loved the dummy. "Where have you been hiding, huh? I don't see you around the malt shop no more."

"Ah, you know, just working on our act and stuff. Micky and I got three gigs this week," Sully answered.

"Oh, hey Micky. That's good for you guys, I am happy."

"Hey Dorothy," I said.

"Look, me and a couple of other gals are going by Lana's tonight. It's that swanky new joint that opened at Royal Square. Why don't you come with us? I have told my friends about you two, they would love to meet you."

"Not sure we are up for that tonight, baby, but thanks for the offer. I think we are just gonna hang here tonight and work on our act," Sully replied.

Dorothy pouted and then pinched Sully's cheek in a ridiculous gesture. "Don't be such a wet blanket."

"I am serious, we are just not in the mood for crowds tonight, right Micky?"

"What he said," I replied.

"Alright, alright. Well if you change your mind you

know where to find me, ok?"

"Yeah, sure babe," Sully said as he locked the door behind her.

"She likes you," I told him.

Sully laughed.

"I am serious, she really likes you."

"It's you she really likes," Sully countered.

"Oh please, she never talks to me, she always talks to you. It's like I am not even in the room sometimes, unless she wants us to do an act for her."

Sully put on his best smile. "Well, what can I say? The ladies find me charming. I am bushed. Why don't we just turn in early tonight, eh?"

"Sounds good to me," I said. "We gotta be fresh for our show tomorrow night."

The following night, Sully and I sat restlessly in one of the dressing rooms at the Golden Cabana nightclub. On stage, we could hear a barbershop quartet entertaining a sold out crowd. I tapped my leg nervously, as this would be the most people in attendance that we had performed for yet.

"I think we should start with the bus stop bit," Sully said, breaking the silence.

I shook my head. "That is a good closer. We need to open with the grocery store bit that we practiced last night."

"We need to grab this crowd's attention right from the start. Let's go with the bus stop," he insisted.

"We never start with the bus stop. We gotta lead up to that one!" I replied, raising my voice.

"What the hell is going on in here? Who are you arguing with?" asked Denny, the club's owner, who had just entered the room without notice.

"Just working on our act, is all," I replied.

The large man just shook his head. "Look, you are on in ten minutes, just be ready."

As promised, ten minutes later, Denny took the microphone on stage and announced, "Now, for the first time at the Golden Cabana, I present to you, Sullivan and Micky!"

We took to the stage with a deafening round of applause from the audience, who were mostly intoxicated by this point. We bowed to the crowd, then the dummy waved with his goofy grin and we took a seat.

I made the decisions here, not the dummy, so we opened with the grocery store bit to a mixed reaction. Luckily, more people were laughing than sitting silent. We picked up better momentum as we went along and soon we had much of the room in stitches. They were laughing hysterically, pointing their fingers and slapping their knees.

Some people did get up and leave in disgust; apparently our brand of humor did not sit well with their sensitive sensibilities. Oh well, we could not please everyone.

As planned, we closed with the bus stop bit and people could still be heard laughing as we left the stage and returned to the dressing room. Each of us smiled, that was a great performance.

Shortly after, Denny visited the room wearing a perplexed look upon his face. "Are you for real?"

"Pretty good, eh? They loved us," I said.

He stood for a moment in silence, struggling to find the right words to say in response. "Alright, I promised you guys three shows. You be sure you do better for the second show. You hear me?"

"Of course, Denny, you can count on us," I assured him.

He left the room shaking his head.

"I would say the crowd enjoyed themselves, aside from the few who left," Sully said to me.

"I agree. We certainly practiced enough. But you know these club owner types, they expect standing ovations from every single act. We'll show him on Friday."

Friday night came and again it was a sold out crowd at the club. This time we followed a dark-skinned woman who sang with the voice of an angel, Clara was her name. She left the stage with a roar of applause and whistles. The crowd called for her to come back and sing one last song but now it was our turn.

Tonight we opened with a bit about me taking Sully to the doctors for a checkup. This time we received a few chuckles but the majority of the audience was silent. Ok, whew, tough crowd. We moved on to the grocery store bit and now a few people began to get up and walk out. There were even a couple boo's!

We nervously fumbled through the third bit, even messing up the punchline.

"Get off the stage, you bum!" one drunkard shouted from a table near the back of the room.

I decided that we should jump straight into the bus stop bit, seeing as that was probably our best. But it was too late to salvage this performance, the people booed and hissed and we didn't even get to finish the bit before the curtains dropped in front of us. Thank god, I thought, I didn't wish to spend another moment in front of that unruly crowd.

Sully and I sat in silence within in the tiny dressing room, when the door burst open and a red-faced Denny stalked inside. He did not look happy.

"I thought we had an understanding? You were supposed to give a better performance tonight. I am lucky I booked the Four Imbeciles so they can go out there and appease that angry crowd," Denny said, referring to a slapstick comedy team of four brothers.

"I don't know what went wrong, those bits are good bits," Sully then said.

"No, they are not good bits! I thought you were going to try harder tonight?"

"Probably a picky crowd tonight, is all," I added. "We'll do better tomorrow night."

Denny pointed at both of us. "Stop that, alright? Just stop that. We are not on stage here, so I don't want to hear both of you talking to me, gives me the heebie-jeebies, it's creepy. You are not going to be performing tomorrow night."

"What?" I shouted, maybe a little too loud. "You promised us three nights."

Denny shook his head in disgust. "I am not letting you on stage for a Saturday night crowd. I will honor the three nights but lord knows I shouldn't. You can have Monday night, then I don't want to see you again, you hear me?"

He slammed the door so hard the giant mirror behind us nearly fell to the floor and now hung at an odd angle. I couldn't really understand what happened tonight. We used the same bits as the night before and those ones seemed to have gone over well enough. I glanced over to Sully but he just shrugged his shoulders.

We walked home that night in silence, giving the pool hall a wide berth. We went to bed fairly early, considering it was a Friday night. I lay in bed attempting to conjure up some new bits that we could try out for Monday night. We had one last chance to redeem ourselves. If we bombed again, no other club would have us and we would be back in dire straits, yet again.

I managed to think of some funny new bits and Sully and I spent Saturday and Sunday in front of the mirror practicing. We even ignored a message from the front desk that was left by Dorothy, wishing us to join her and some of her friends Saturday night.

"These are pretty funny, Micky," Sully said to me, in reference to the new additions to our act.

"Thank you, Sully. I hope these will bail us out of trouble tomorrow night."

"Yeah, without the money from Denny, we can't pay the hotel what we owe them, let alone the gangsters from the pool hall," he reminded me.

I nodded. I wasn't a godly person but I prayed for luck on Monday night.

Monday night came and Denny was on edge, pacing back and forth behind the stage. Monday was usually the slowest night of the week but it appeared there was even less of a crowd than expected. Denny had not booked Clara or the Four Imbeciles tonight. Tonight there was only two acts and we followed a magician who called himself, The Great Fazoo.

I took a deep breath and we walked onto the stage. The room was less than half full and only a few people clapped at our arrival. It was as if the rest sat on their hands. Alright, I thought, let's open with the bus stop bit then. The crowd remained silent.

Sully shifted uncomfortably next to me as we both could feel the distaste among the audience. It lingered in the air, thicker than the cigar smoke. Ok, I decided it was time for a new bit, the funniest one I had thought of the other night. It involved us visiting an army base so that Sully could enlist.

Now the silence was replaced with the odd boo and the sound of chairs scrapping against the floor as people got up and left. I stuttered and stammered, ruining the beginning of the next bit, anxiety getting the better of me. The curtains dropped and my heart sank. We were done.

This time Denny did not visit us in the dressing room and Sully and I found him sitting in his office. We shut the door behind us and took a seat opposite him at his cluttered desk. The club owner looked at us both and then snickered.

Sully was the first to speak. "So, ah, sorry tonight didn't quite work out as we intended."

"No kidding," Denny replied.

"We will just collect our pay then and be moving along," I added.

"What did I say about both of you talking to me at the same time? Huh? I will pay you half of what I owe you, and believe me, that is still being generous," Denny shouted.

"Half?" I risked shouting back. "That's not fair! We still did our three performances. That was our deal!"

"You will take half and be happy you got that much," he responded and tossed an envelope on the desk in front of us. "Now get the hell out of here. I don't want to see either of your faces again, especially yours," he pointed at

Sully.

"Denny, without the full amount you promised us, we will lose our room at the hotel. We will have no place to live," I said, my voice sounding frantic.

"Not my problem. Beat it."

"But Denny…"

"Scram! Now! Before I really lose my temper."

I closed my eyes and slowly exhaled. I could not return to a life of poverty, not again.

BLAM!

"Jesus Christ, Micky! What did you do?" shouted Sully.

Denny fell back in his chair, a bullet hole in his forehead, and slowly slumped lifelessly to the floor.

"We need that money, Sully. We are not leaving here without it."

"You can't just murder someone like that! Where the hell did you even get that gun??"

"That's of no concern at the moment. We need to grab whatever money this greedy bum has stashed in that desk and get out of here quickly."

We ransacked Denny's desk, finding enough loot to pay off the hotel, the gangsters, and still leave us with some extra cash. Then we dashed out of the office, passing several astonished-looking stagehands, and returned to our hotel room.

I placed the small revolver on the table next to me and considered my next move. My partnership with Sully had proven to be disastrous. He was a good dummy, people did like him and he was personable, but we didn't possess the chemistry that I had initially thought. I figured it was time for a new dummy.

"What the hell are we gonna do, Micky? Huh? People know it was us that killed Denny. Oh my god, I feel so sick. We are in a lot of trouble."

"I am afraid, I am just going to say that it was you who did it," I replied calmly.

"Me? You pulled the trigger! For the love of god, I didn't even know you owned a gun!"

"This is the way it has to be, Sully, I am sorry. I am not going back to a life of poverty on the streets, begging and borrowing money from violent gangsters."

"This isn't fair, Micky! We are partners! I thought we were friends! You killed Denny, not me!"

"Our friendship ends tonight, sorry Sully."

In desperation, the dummy grabbed the gun off the table and pointed it at me with trembling hands.

"If it's gonna end tonight, then it's gonna end with a bullet in your selfish head. I can't believe you would just toss me aside like this and then blame me for a murder you committed."

Suddenly, and without warning, the door to our hotel room flew open, kicked in by a large police officer. Four of them in total rushed into our room with guns drawn, all aimed at Sully.

"Drop the gun, now!" commanded one of the officers, as they all looked back and forth between Sully and myself, confused by the bizarre scene in front of them.

"He did it," Sully told them. "He shot Denny. I didn't even know he had a gun."

"Place the gun on the floor and nobody else needs to get shot this night. Got it? Drop the gun."

Now I am not sure if Sully had meant to drop the gun on the floor, or if he had decided to raise the gun at me once more and finish me off, but the police were not happy with his movements and all fired their weapons. In total, Sully was hit with six bullets and fell to the floor, never to move again. I sat in my chair, head slumped with sadness.

One of the officers chuckled. "Well, I have never seen anything like this before."

"It's Sullivan and Micky. You guys never heard of Sullivan and Micky?" another asked. When the other officers shook their heads, he continued. "They are a ventriloquist act. Terrible! I saw them not that long ago and it was the worst performance I ever seen. At first people found them funny, like a novelty. I mean a ventriloquist's lips are not supposed to move at all, right? It's supposed to look like the dummy is talking. Not this act, no, it was the other way around. Like I said, at first it's kinda funny, but when it continues for the whole act, I mean come on, that's awful."

One of the officers addressed another and pointed at me. "Grab the doll, it's evidence. I'll write the report."

Doll? Did he just call me a doll? I will show them what a doll is capable of!

CHANNELING EVAN MUNROE

I wish now that I had never heard the name of Evan Munroe. As good a friend as he was, I would have been much better off never having known him. Could I manipulate time and erase him from my memory, I surely would.

I suppose I could begin this tale on that dreadful Saturday evening in August, when Evan and myself, along with our boorish friend, Willard Barnes, spent the evening in Willard's basement playing cards and throwing dice.

A more ill-mannered person than Willard, I swear I had never met. I did, however, grow up with him, and as a result, counted him as one of my closest friends. Evan moved into our neighborhood two years past and became the third member of our trio.

I felt bad for Willard at times and I supposed my intimate knowledge of his home life led me to better understand him than most. To everyone else, he was a wicked bully with a cruel streak, and each of those things was correctly attributed to the large teen.

His mother was a neglective gambler, spending most of her waking hours at the bingo hall, and his father was an abusive drunk, contributing to a most foul behavior in their only son. Willard was a normal child when we had first met at the age of six; his change was gradual over the passing of many years. By the time his personality had become insufferable, it was too late for me, and we had already spent much of our lives as best friends.

In becoming our friend, Evan had little choice in the matter, having moved into the house between ours on the outskirts of town. His options for friends were limited in the beginning, living a good bus ride from our college and the rest of the town.

College was out for the summer and we did what most boys do; stay up all night long and sleep away most of the day. Willard's parents were rarely home, and even when they were, they cared little for what their son and his friends got up to, so we spent most of our time in Willard's basement.

Most people had a strong distaste for Willard, so Evan and I were guilty by association, and therefore rarely ever received invites to parties and gatherings from fellow classmates.

Evan, though slightly smaller than Willard, was a bit of a tough guy with strong opinions, which led to his butting heads with Willard quite often. The two could argue ceaselessly at times, as I looked on with only a shake of my head. I dared not insert myself into their debates, even when solicited by each to side with one over the other. I found it best to remain neutral; it lessened the headaches.

Their disputes were always petty and nonsensical in nature, much like the one that was fast escalating that Saturday night in August. They were embroiled in a difference of opinions over the origins of the particular card game with which we had been playing. I was positive neither of them had been correct but each of them was quite adamant in their stand.

More than once they attempted to drag me into the middle of their quarrel but I was having none of it. As their incessant fighting increased in volume and reached a fever pitch, I had decided I needed to step outside for some air.

It was a beautiful summer night. There was a slight chill to the air but it was comfortable, especially considering the oppressive humidity that dominated much of the day. Willard's house backed onto a sizable field which was quite dark, given the absence of street lights in our neighborhood. Even the radiance from a full moon did not afford me much vision in the darkness of the field.

My hopes had been to clear my aching head and listen to the sound of crickets but that was not to be. Even from out here, the muffled voices of Willard and Evan continued to pursue me, and to top it off, their voices were now joined by Willard's parents, who began their own verbal disagreeance from upstairs in the house. It sounded as if some plates might have been hurled against a wall and then out stumbled a thoroughly intoxicated Mr. Barnes from a side door. He somehow managed to navigate his way down the driveway and out onto the street without falling.

I shook my head and concentrated on what I believed was a deer running through the field. I was not entirely sure if it was in fact a deer though, or merely a trick of the eyes in the darkness. In any event, imagined or not, it helped calm me down and I was finally able to enjoy the silence and the sound of crickets.

Wait a moment, I thought, silence? The fighting in the basement had finally come to an end and I truly was left with only the sound of crickets. How serene that felt indeed. With a sigh, I figured I should go find out who won, or if both just agreed to disagree, as was usually the case, with neither willing to give in to the other.

"So, what's the verdict?" I inquired, while descending the steps back to the basement.

Strangely, I was met with only silence.

"Don't tell me you both fell asleep? It's too early."

I then saw Willard rise up from behind a long, chocolate-colored sofa; his face as pale as a ghost. I knew immediately that something was amiss.

"H-he made me do it. He left me with no choice."

"What are you talking about, Willard?"

"You know how he is. He made me do it."

I remembered my skin began to prickle. "What did he make you do?"

Speechless, Willard backed up and then sat himself down in a comfy chair which matched the sofa. Tentatively, I approached the sofa and peered over the edge, my heart nearly stopping at the sight which had greeted me. There lay Evan on the floor, very still, red marks around his throat, his eyes wide open in one final look of horror.

I promptly determined that our friend was dead and

my legs almost gave out from under me. I am quite sure I turned a shade of pale to match that of Willard's now pallid appearance. I had never before seen a dead body and it is something that will haunt me until the end of my days.

"He made me do it," Willard repeated.

My mind reeled. I was always the rational thinker of our group, the logical one, the problem solver, but in this instance, I had no idea how to proceed. As my stomach twisted into knots, I came to the conclusion that I needed to call for the police.

I turned to leave but Willard must have somehow read the intentions on my face. "Where are you going?"

"Willard, I need to call for help."

"No point, he is beyond help now."

"Regardless, someone needs to know. It's the right thing to do."

"They will put me in jail or hang me."

Yes, they most assuredly would, I thought, but kept that sentiment to myself. I continued to the stairs and Willard's tone changed drastically, his words stopping me in my tracks.

"Maybe you didn't hear me? I said they will put me in jail or hang me."

"Yes, I heard you but this is not right. I need to call for help."

"I told you already he is beyond help. The only person you need to help now is me. I am your friend, remember?"

"Yes, I am your friend. But so was Evan."

"Evan had that coming. We have been friends longer, you and I. You cannot betray me now."

"Betray you? Willard, you just murdered Evan!"

"With your help."

"Pardon me??"

"You stood there and watched and allowed it to happen."

"I did no such…"

"I will tell them. I will tell them you helped me."

"Why you evil son of a…"

"Careful, friend. We need to calm down if we are to get ourselves out of this predicament."

"We??"

"Yes, we. You and I. I think we should bury him in the field and claim he was never here this evening."

I stood there, my mouth agape, unable to formulate a response. I was the only friend he ever had and he would think to treat me as such? The ungrateful bastard.

"They will never believe you," I said, after finding some courage amidst my rising anger. "Look at the size of you over me. How could I have possibly stopped you? I wasn't even down here when you did it."

Willard rose in a flash, his pale skin turning a shade of red. "You wanna join Evan?"

"Pardon me? You are threatening me now? Your only friend?"

"I am not going to jail and I am not going to hang, not for him. Do you hear me? But if that happens, you will pay for it."

"If the police arrest you, how do you plan on killing me from prison?"

"I will tell my Uncle George that you did it and framed me, his favorite nephew. He will kill you."

Willard's Uncle George was a dim-witted hillbilly with the mind capacity of a child. How he survived on his own living in a cabin in the woods, I will never know. But Uncle George would believe anything Willard told him and I had no doubt that the simpleton would come after me and kill me. George was a hunter and shooting things was one of the few tasks he was actually good at.

My conscience nagged at me but I believed Willard's threat. "We bury him in the field then and he was never here this evening."

Willard smiled that wicked smile and nodded. "Grab his legs."

As repulsed as I was, I did grab his legs, and the two of us struggled to carry Evan's body out into the pitch-black field behind his house. As I mentioned, I had never seen a dead body before this night and now I had seen more of one that I would have ever cared to. I never imagined Evan could be so heavy and sweat dripped from my forehead as we finally found a secluded spot a fair distance away from the house.

Willard returned to fetch a shovel, leaving me alone with Evan, his dead eyes still wide open. I turned my back and sat on a stone, facing the opposite direction. I could not believe what I had just been a party to. There was no going back now; I was indeed an accomplice. I felt ill.

Willard promptly began to dig upon his return. When he grew weary, he handed the tool to me to continue, and gave me a look that told me that it was not open for debate.

An hour and a half later, with the moon high in the sky, our grim deed was completed. We had done our best to cover the hole and indeed it looked as though nobody had been digging in the first place. Nothing appeared out of sorts, and with luck, Evan would never be found.

We spent the rest of the night in the basement corroborating our story, that Evan had other plans this evening and had gone someplace else.

Not twenty-four hours later, Evan's parents began to worry and made phone calls and visits all over the neighborhood. That night, police began canvassing the area, and of course, came to speak with Willard and I, seeing as how we were Evan's closest friends.

As nervous and as sick as I felt, we both stuck to our story that we had no clue where Evan had gone that evening. The neglectiveness of Willard's parents, for once, provided benefit. They were home that night in question, but cared little to check in on their son, and therefore had no idea that Evan was ever downstairs. They told police that Willard and I were indeed home the entire evening by ourselves.

Days turned into weeks and weeks into months. The heat was off and soon life returned to normal and Willard and I were back in school. Evan was treated as a runaway, despite the protests of his parents that he would never have done such a thing. I tried my best to occupy my mind with my studies and think about that night as little as possible. I even tried to avoid Willard as much as I could.

Despite my attempts to forget, Evan haunted my dreams and sleep did not come easily for me. Guilt feasted away at my conscience, but my fear of prison or the hangman's noose, kept my feelings to myself.

It was October 31st, Halloween night to be exact, when I was invited to a classmate's party. It was to be a grand event with about thirty other students invited. To my surprise, and regret, Willard was also invited. Try as I might to avoid him, he was not well liked, and thus he followed me everywhere.

As the night wore on, a pretty girl named Edna entered the living room carrying a game board of some type.

"Hey everyone, I have a nifty idea. It's Halloween night, the night when our world and the spirit world come together and spirits walk the earth. Let's try using the Ouija board to contact some spirits."

A few people groaned, jesting that the board was just a foolish toy. Some others grew pale, obviously frightened at the prospect of inviting spirits into the house. The majority thought it was a fun idea and the majority won over.

Edna excitedly set everything up on a dining room table. Walter, who was hosting the party, turned off all the lights so that the room was illuminated with only four candles.

"Ok, who should we try to contact?" Edna asked of the full room.

"Erika Blayne," someone suggested, referring to a woman who had been burned as a witch, a century gone by.

"Horace Pickleton," another blurted, who had been a serial killer and hung for his crimes.

"Evan Munroe," a third person shouted, and the room went silent.

Willard and I exchanged glances, and I hadn't even realized I was holding my breath, until I was forced to inhale a gulp of air, lest my face turn blue from holding out too long.

"Evan isn't dead, he just ran away," Willard said nervously.

"I never believed that for a second," replied the boy who had made the suggestion in the first place. "Someone killed Evan, I would bet everything on it."

"I think so too," another boy added. "How is it that the police never found him anywhere? I think he is buried somewhere."

Edna smiled. "Evan Munroe it is then. If he is dead, we can call upon his spirit and ask him what happened."

Edna explained that four people would be required to each place one of their hands on the Ouija board, in an attempt to channel the spirit of Evan Munroe. She would participate, along with Walter, then she invited over Willard and I.

"You and Willard knew Evan the best, so you both should be involved."

As you can imagine, the two of us were both quite hesitant, but everyone agreed that we two were the best choices and did not cease in goading us over to the table. Alas, we relented.

I never possessed much of an opinion on the Ouija board. I was undecided about the possibility of an afterlife and what became of a person's spirit after death. I questioned the validity of the board, which could be purchased in a toy store of all places, for a nominal amount of money.

Reluctantly, Willard and I took a seat at the table with the others and placed our right hands upon the Ouija board, joining hands with Edna and Walter. A nervous sweat began to form on my forehead and worst of all, I was forced to relive that horrible night in my mind.

Edna wasted no time. "We here at this table, call upon the spirit of Evan Munroe. Evan, if you have died, come join with us now. Guide our hands and share with us your fate. Help us find closure in your mysterious disappearance. Please, Evan Munroe, come to us now."

Willard snorted with contempt right before the loudest clap of thunder I had ever heard boomed outside, shaking the house. Everyone jumped and a few of the girls squealed out loud. There had not been any storms in the forecast.

As everyone calmed, the candles on the table began to violently flicker, threatening to extinguish, despite the fact that every person in the room, sat or stood, completely still. My heart began to race as a breeze tickled my cheek, as if someone had passed closely by.

Suddenly, Edna yelped, and indeed I nearly did as well, as a tingling sensation flooded into my hand which touched the Ouija board. It was evident by the others faces that we all felt the same sensation.

"Evan, is that you?" Edna asked, in a nervous squeaky voice.

The board under our hands felt as though it moved of its own accord, for surely I had no part in pushing it. The Ouija board circled the game board several times before stopping over the word, *Yes*.

"Evan, were you murdered?" she asked next.

Again, the board came to rest over the word, *Yes*.

"Do you know who murdered you?"

Willard and I both held our breaths, as the board once again stopped on, *Yes*. There was a collective gasp among the others who huddled around the table now. Even the skeptics were leaning in closely for a better view.

"Evan, can you tell us who murdered you?"

My jaw dropped open in a silent scream as the

tingling sensation from my hand began to creep its way up my arm. A moment later it overwhelmed my entire body and suddenly I felt a presence within my mind. I don't know how to explain it exactly, but without a doubt, Evan Munroe was inside my body.

Involuntarily, I let go of the board and lunged towards Willard. He shrieked in terror as my hands wrapped themselves around his throat. Willard was much bigger and stronger than I, though he was helpless to break my stranglehold. Somehow, I had been imbued with great strength. Strength from beyond the grave it would seem.

To the absolute horror of everyone present, I choked Willard to death right there at the dining table. His eyes bulged and stared at me with disbelief, as his life slowly slipped away. My actions had not been my own, and as death claimed Willard, I felt Evan leave my body and I was left in control once more. I slumped to the floor sobbing while others ran about in a panic.

I can't say for sure how long I actually sat there before police arrived and took me to their station in handcuffs. During my questioning, I broke down and told them of everything. Of course I tried to plead my case that I had not been the one who killed Willard; that Evan's spirit had inhabited my body, but of course, the authorities wouldn't believe such a thing.

After my display of strength in strangling Willard, the police were unsure of my story that Willard had been the one who killed Evan. To them, both deaths were the same, so therefore, I could have been responsible for both.

I somehow avoided the death penalty and wouldn't hang but now I sat in a cold dark cell where I would spend the rest of my life. Every day I curse the name of Willard

Barnes and I am forced to remember that horrendous night, when we channeled the angry spirit of Evan Munroe.

IN THE COURT OF THE JESTER

The immense ballroom was filled nearly to capacity, as revelers milled about laughing and drinking and sampling a decadent array of foods. King Christophe II had only recently defeated his hated enemies to the north and took over their lands, effectively expanding his ever enlarging kingdom. So today was a day of celebration.

Every lord and lady and wealthy merchant in all the lands was invited to partake in a day of feasting and general debauchery in honor of the King's great victory. They traveled from near and they traveled from far, whether they cared for the usually quite arrogant and unpleasant King or not. And why wouldn't they? The King spared no expense to provide the most palatable of foods and the most potent of drinks. And of course, who could forget the entertainment?

"Where is my Fool?" the intoxicated King bellowed

over the raucous crowd and the sweet sounds of a lute being strummed in a corner. "Fool? Fool, where are you?"

"Over here, sire," I answered most dejectedly, as I was about to sample my first bite of the fine assortment of edibles.

"Drop that food instantly, it is time to perform, I am in the mood to laugh," he commanded. "Wouldn't everyone like to see the Fool perform for us now?"

There was a chorus of cheers and applause in agreeance from the throng of partiers. Folk cleared a path for me to shuffle my way towards the King's raised dinner table; the bells hanging from my fool's cap jingling all the way.

Shuffling is what I had to do, as my left knee was twisted inwards since birth, preventing me from walking normally. Life might not have been so harsh, were that my only abnormality, but alas, the gods had truly cursed me, and for what purpose, I know not. My right arm hung significantly longer than my left, I was hunched over from a lump that protruded from the back of my spine, and I suffered from a lazy eye; my left eye chose to roam around, rarely if ever in sync with my right.

Freak, some called me, and others referred to me as a goblin. In any case, I was a sideshow to be mocked and laughed at by those more blessed than I. The King utilized me for his personal amusement and to entertain his guests. I supposed I should feel fortunate, being afforded a chance to live in the court, instead of being cast aside or put to death like others who suffered from similar deformities.

The crowd quieted as I now stood in front of the King's dinner table, all eyes on me. I cleared my throat.

"Ah…yes…well have you heard the tale of the bard from Fallhaven? No? Neither have I, he no longer possesses as head…heh heh," I was referring to a city in the north, where the previous ruler was obsessed with beheadings.

I only received a mild reaction from the crowd on that joke, so jumped straight into my new material concerning the defeated northern King. Sweat was forming on my brow as King Christophe yawned.

I suddenly yelped out loud as a tomato struck my face and splattered its juices upon my gaudy shirt. That sight received a warm welcome from the partiers as they burst into laughter.

"Heh, heh, yes sire, your aim is remarkable," I complimented the King.

"Oh, Fool, what is that you dropped there?" the King asked, after tossing a copper coin onto the floor behind me.

I knew where this game was headed and had to play along. "Where, sire? I don't recall dropping anything."

"Turn around, Fool. There on the floor, behind you."

I turned around and bent over to pick up the coin, bracing myself for the kick in the behind that was surely to follow. I was not disappointed, as the King's spoiled nephew planted his boot forcibly into my buttocks, sending me sprawling to the floor with an explosion of hysterical laughter. One particular slovenly merchant nearly choked on a mouthful of quail at the apparently uproarious spectacle.

"Oh my, I am so clumsy," I said, as I attempted to rise.

A second kick to the same spot, which had now left a considerable bruise I was positive, sent me back to the floor face first. The guffaws continued and Lord Bently, a middle-aged man with an inflated stomach, actually fell from his chair.

I accepted two more kicks to my hindquarters before the King tired and ordered some minstrels to begin with a little music. I was given a reprieve and finally struggled back to my feet.

Much later, as dessert was served, I received a cream pie to the face and a bowl of pudding poured down my trousers; a most successful party.

The following morning I found myself in the empty throne room, sweeping up from the previous night's celebrations. I enjoyed my time spent alone but it was not to last. I frowned as an all too familiar voice entered the room and broke the silence.

"Fool, look at this mess. How long must I suffer the sight of it?" asked the King.

"Not much longer, sire, nearly finished in this room," I answered.

The King shook his head in disgust and took a seat upon his most luxurious throne. He was strikingly handsome, with a neatly trimmed golden beard and a full head of matching hair. His eyes were a sparkling blue and his chin chiseled. Women swooned over him, especially since he was still single; never taking a wife after the Queen died many years past.

Yes, the King was a fine specimen indeed, and from the portraits I had seen, the Queen was a beauty with no equal. So why then was their son so hideous?

"What are you brooding over, father?" I dared to ask.

"Do not call me that!" he barked in response.

"My apologies, I only thought that since we were

alone…"

"Do not think! You are my fool, you are not here to think. Anyone could have walked in at any time. You will never call me that."

"Y-yes, sire."

"But to answer your question, I await news from Sir Brandolyn, who is on a most important mission for me. He should have returned yesterday but he has not."

"What mission? I thought the northerners were all defeated?"

Sir Brandolyn was the King's greatest knight, the fiercest and bravest of all the kingdom's warriors. If he had been sent on a mission, then it was quite important indeed.

"This does not have anything to do with the north. For years I have consulted old tomes in search of an ancient buried treasure. At last, with the aid of that blind old hag from Sulphur Swamp, I believed I had determined the treasure's whereabouts. I dispatched Sir Brandolyn and five of his most loyal men into the Valley of Mists to retrieve it."

"What kind of treasure?" I wondered in fascination.

"Not for a fool to know, now finish cleaning up. I feel my mood turning sour and will need you to make me laugh shortly."

Two days passed and there had still been no word from the knight. The King was entertaining envoys from a southern kingdom, so as usual, I was present and once again receiving a boot to my arse from the spoiled nephew. The guests found it quite amusing and tears streamed down their bronzed faces from laughter.

Just before I was about to be poked with the blunt end of a spear, a messenger hurried into the throne room to whisper words into the King's ear. His face significantly brightened.

"Everyone out! Now! Leave immediately!" he ordered, leaving no room for debate. "Not you Fool, you may stay," he added as I had turned to quicken myself away.

The two of us sat in silence for what felt like an awful long time. I dared not ask any questions. Then, Sir Brandolyn entered the room, his always-gleaming armor dirtied and dusty. Black smudges dominated the parts of his face that were not covered with his bushy brown beard. In his hands he carried a small black box, similar to a lady's jewelry box.

Sir Brandolyn knelt before the King and extended his arms, presenting him with the black box. "My King, we found the tomb as your map had been quite accurate. That witch had been right and we found guardians inside. Skeletons rose up and fought us as we attempted to access the crypt. Myself, and Sir Malek, are the only survivors, but we found that which you sought. I offer it to you now."

"Marvelous, marvelous indeed! You have done well!" the King glowed with excitement as he accepted the black box. "Did you open the box?"

"No, sire. You commanded me not to. It has remained sealed and always in my possession, 'til now. I know not what is inside."

"Excellent, excellent. Now go clean yourself up, there will be a dinner in your honor this evening. Once again, you have proven yourself to be the greatest of my men."

"Thank you, sire," the knight said, before taking his leave.

I watched the King stare at the box for several long

moments. I was most anxious to see what important treasure was contained within. With shaking hands, he eventually opened the lid of the box to reveal a long, thin, purplish bottle, sealed with a cork. My mind swirled with possibilities. A magic potion, perhaps? A priceless liquor from some forgotten age?

The King wasted no time in removing the cork and I jumped back in fright as a white mist streamed forth from the open end of the bottle. It snaked its way out and pooled near the foot of the throne. I was on the verge of shouting a warning, that it was possibly a poisonous cloud, when the words caught in my throat. My jaw hung open in awe and I had to wonder if what I saw was even real.

As the mist cleared, there now stood a large man with purplish skin, who was oddly clothed and wore a strange hat, similar to those worn by the desert nomads of the south. He bowed towards the King.

"Thank you for releasing me from the bottle. My name is Al-Zorashan, a genie, and I grant unto you three wishes."

The King nearly fell from his throne, so taken with feelings of ultimate joy. The priceless treasure he spent years trying to locate was now his. His mouth was dry and his palms were sweating as his mind raced through the list of all his grandest desires.

"Gold," he blurted. "I want my entire bedchamber filled to capacity with gold coins."

The King's bedchamber was the largest room in the castle, occupying the entire top floor.

The genie snapped his fingers. "It is done."

The King called for a page, whose eyes nearly popped out of their sockets at the sight of the purplish genie, and commanded him to run to his bedchamber and return with news of what he saw. The young boy ran from the room with great haste and soon returned, thoroughly breathless and eyes wide with wonder.

"My King, I could not even see into your chambers as my view was obscured by mountains of gold!"

When the King finally finished roaring with laughter, he dismissed the page and sat back in his throne in silent contemplation. His eyes then lit up as he reached a conclusion.

"I am handsome, and strong, and in the peak of my life. I wish to be immortal. So genie, I wish that from this day forward, I shall never age another year."

The genie nodded his head and snapped his fingers. "It is done. You shall never age again."

The King beamed with delight, as a tingling sensation was felt all over his body. I looked on quietly, truly amazed by the entire scene. A genie! A real genie granting wishes! The King was surely blessed.

Then to my utter shock and astonishment, the King said something that at first, I thought I had only imagined. I was prone to vivid daydreams and assumed I was having one at that very moment.

"I am now wealthy beyond imagining, more so than before. I am also now immortal and shall remain my handsome self for an eternity," the King proclaimed. "So, my son, I will give the third and final wish to you, so that you may wish away your unsightly deformities and return to this court as my long lost son, sent away for tutoring, or some other such excuse."

"Sire?" I could not believe my ears.

"Yes, you heard true. At this moment you are the

only child I have. So go ahead, wish yourself normal, so that I might now introduce you as my son and prince without embarrassment and shame."

I was rendered speechless. It wasn't a daydream at all. After a lifetime of humiliation, serving as the King's fool, I was now offered the opportunity to change my life and wish for a normal body. I was beside myself with glee.

The purplish genie turned to me and smiled. "Is that what you wish? Speak it and it will be done."

* * * *

I sat uncomfortably in the large chair as hundreds of lords and ladies gathered for a celebratory dinner. Sir Brandolyn was to be the guest of honor for his bravery in completing his most important quest. Without the courageous knight, the incredible genie bottle would never have been recovered, and thus, our three wishes never granted.

As the crowd appeared restless, I felt it was time for the entertainment. "Where is my Fool? Fool? Fool, where are you?"

"I am here, sire," the Fool answered, emerging from behind some gathered guests to stand before me.

He was a strikingly handsome man with a neatly trimmed golden beard and sparkling blue eyes. His matching golden hair was mostly obscured by his ridiculous-looking fool's cap with the jingling bells. He had shuffled over awkwardly wearing shoes four sizes too large.

I shifted on my throne as the hunch in my back impeded my posture. Well, I figured, as King I would just have a new throne built that would better suit my unshapely body.

I tossed a copper coin to land on the floor behind the fool. "Fool, what is that you have dropped on the floor there behind you? Go on, pick it up."

MARS-FOUR, CAN YOU HEAR ME?

I awoke to another dreadful day on this desolate red planet; the excitement of actually living on another world had long ago worn off. Most days now just felt very long and quite monotonous. You don't realize how much you take walking outdoors and breathing fresh oxygen for granted, until you can no longer do simple things as that.

Suiting up to step outside our home base is a one hour process. And you do not wish to rush that, as one small misstep could mean your doom. Even then, you are viewing the world around through the glass of a fishbowl that you are constantly wearing on your head.

Not that there is much to see, aside from mountains and a wasteland of red dust. The landscape on Mars did not differ much from certain regions found on Earth. There was nothing uniquely alien about it. It reminded me of post-apocalyptic movies, where much of the Earth was now devoid of any types of life.

We were hoping to change that; it was our mission here on the red planet. I had come here to the fourth planet from the sun with five others to begin the colonization process. We were supposed to make a livable and sustainable base here, allowing for more people to eventually join us. So far, we had been quite successful in the eight months since our landing. We had our home base, which sat nestled in the valley between two mountains, Vesta and Maia, as well as three greenhouses, where we managed to grow fruits and vegetables with the aid of solar panels.

Our mission was given the green light once scientists developed a method for us to extract water from the Martian soil. It was not a simple process but it worked. Every few months we received supplies from Earth as well, which did include extra water. The fact that water crystals were found in the soil was a good sign. We had hopes of one day unearthing some underground lakes or springs, which we firmly believed must still exist.

The future of life on Earth was becoming ever uncertain. Mankind was running the planet into the ground, much as we always had been. The impact on the environment in the wake of World War III was catastrophic. Many of our natural resources were dwindling to dangerously low levels and most disheartening to me, was the extinction of many of our planet's more common species. It saddened me to think that future generations would never know the joy of hearing a bird sing; that they would have to learn about our feathered friends from history books alone.

Humans needed Mars if our species was to survive.

Not only was it our neighboring planet and the easiest to reach but it was the most hospitable for our kind. Scientists truly believed that Mars was going to be the new Earth. My team and I were here to pave the way for future colonists.

"Martin, you're finally awake, I see," said Captain Lewis Prawn, our mission's leader.

I nodded and shook the cobwebs from my befuddled mind. "I am. I had trouble sleeping again."

"Well grab yourself a coffee and ungrog yourself. I need you, Vivian, and Dmitry, to get out there and secure those loose solar panels on Green-Two this morning."

"Why this morning?" I asked. "We have all day to do that."

"We don't, actually. Samantha has detected a very large dust storm headed our way. It should arrive this afternoon and the high winds could actually rip those panels off the roof if we don't get them secured this morning."

Great, I get to spend my entire morning doing repair work, and then the rest of the day will be spent twiddling my thumbs as we hunker down for a dust storm. On Earth I was an explorer, or an Archaeologist, if you will. I had salivated at the thought of coming to Mars to explore a new world. So far, I hadn't had much of a chance for exploration; we were too busy growing food and endlessly repairing things in the wake of the hostile storms that raged across this planet. And storms here just didn't last a few hours; they could go on for days. The longest lasted a month, but thankfully, that was just prior to our arrival.

I grabbed a mug of awful coffee and sat down at a table with Vivian, a stunningly-attractive woman of Asian descent. She was a genius mathematician.

"Any news from Earth?" I asked her.

"Not since Tuesday," she replied. "But the captain is scheduled to make contact this afternoon, if that storm doesn't interfere."

Which it probably would, I figured.

"Doesn't sound good over there, though," she continued. "Tensions are rising again between countries. Central Control worries about another war."

I shook my head in disgust. Of all the amazing things that humans had achieved since the dawn of time, destroying each other is still what we excelled at the most. And there seemed to be no end to that in sight. Our hatred for our own kind has ruined much of our planet, which is why we are forced to turn to Mars and seek a new home. As dreary as life was here on Mars, at least I was far away from those war-mongering barbarians on Earth.

After an hour of suiting up, then double and triple checking that everything was in proper order, myself, along with Vivian and Dmitry, stepped outside our base and began the ten minute walk to our second greenhouse, or Green-Two as it was called.

"Mars-Three, check," I heard Vivian say from the speaker inside my fishbowl helmet.

"Mars-Seven, check," Dmitry followed suit.

"Mars-Four, check," I then said.

"This is Home-One, I can hear you all loud and clear. Proceed to Green-Two," Samantha prompted.

Green-Two sat in a flat expanse of land away from the shadows of the two mountains. It was important that it received as much sunlight as was possible. We reached the large structure, which was responsible for producing most of our vegetables, and hurriedly got to work. Three of the largest solar panels had come loose during the last violent dust storm and we would most likely lose them if they were not secured before the next.

Dmitry, who was a mechanical engineer, quickly climbed to the roof to begin the repair process. I handed him tools as needed, while Vivian walked the perimeter of Green-Two, inspecting for anything else that required our attention.

"How does it look, Mars-Three?" I asked Vivian.

"So far so good. No visible structural damage that I can see," she replied.

Good, I did not want to be out here longer than we had planned. Dmitry's work was tedious enough as it was. It was very difficult to perform precise repairs while wearing the bulky gloves that were a required part of our space suits. Something that might have only taken twenty minutes on Earth, became a two to three hour job on Mars.

As one hour became two, Dmitry was finally working on the last of the three panels. Vivian waited impatiently nearby, having completed her inspection long ago.

"Mars Team, this is Home-One, please hurry. That storm is blowing in much sooner than expected. You do not have much time," we heard over the speakers.

Vivian paced nervously behind me.

"Mars-Three, go on back to base, there is nothing left for you to do here," I suggested.

"You're sure?" she asked.

"Of course, go on. We'll be right behind you. How is it looking up there Mars-Seven?"

"Curse these gloves, I hate them," he replied.

"How much longer?" I wondered.

"Ten minutes."

About twelves minutes later, I watched Vivian enter the base off in the distance. "Alright Mars-Seven, it's been over ten minutes."

"Five more minutes."

I shifted nervously from foot to foot as the sky grew darker and a distant mountain vanished behind a haze of red dust.

"Mars-Four and Mars-Seven, this is Home-One, I need you both to return to base now. Abort mission. The storm is closing in fast. Do you copy?"

"We copy, Home-One," I responded. "Come on Dmitry, let's go. Losing one panel won't be so bad."

"Two minutes."

"Forget two minutes, let's go! We have a ten minute walk back!"

Dmitry relented and began to climb down, mumbling to himself. As I glanced around, the dust clouds had cut the distance in half from the last time I looked. We headed back towards the base as swiftly as we could walk in our cumbersome suits.

Four minutes into our trek back, I cursed, having forgot the bag of tools on the ground beside Green-Two.

"Dammit! Mars-Seven keep going, I forgot the tools. I gotta go back," I said, angry at myself.

"No time, buddy. Forget them."

"We can afford to lose one panel but we can't afford to lose those tools. I will be quick."

Before he could argue further, I turned around and marched determinedly back towards the greenhouse.

"Mars-Four, this is Home-One, what do you think

you are doing?"

"I forgot the tools, I have to go back."

"Turn back this instant, that's an order! That storm is almost upon us. We can always replace those tools, we can't replace you."

"I am almost back at Green-Two anyways, I can see the bag. Won't be long."

As I reached the greenhouse the winds were already whipping around me, raising the red sand into a blinding fog of particles. This was not a good situation at all and I soon gave in to panic.

"Mars-Four, this is Home-One, get inside Green-Two and wait out the storm there."

I dreaded the idea of spending the duration of the storm alone in that uncomfortable greenhouse. After all, it could last days or weeks. No, I was determined to make it back to base. I picked up the bag of tools and marched onwards.

"Mars-Four, get inside Green-Two!"

"Negative, Home-One. I have secured the tools and I can make it back. See you all shortly."

Stubbornly I strode through the blowing winds. Visibility was steadily decreasing and I soon figured that I should have just stayed at the greenhouse. My pace slowed as strong winds now worked against my efforts.

"Mars-Four, this is Home-One, how are you doing? We have lost visual on you. Are you close?"

"I believe so, Home-One, five minutes away."

Then to my dismay, a particularly strong gust of wind forcibly pushed me several feet back and my boot caught on a rock, sending me tumbling to the dusty ground.

Regrettably, I dropped the bag of tools and now

could no longer see it, as a cloud of rust-colored dust spun around me in a mini-tornado. In fact, to my horror, I could no longer see our base or the greenhouses. I could barely see my own white glove in front of my face. Worst of all, my tumble had disoriented me and now I was not even sure which direction I had been traveling in.

"Mars-Four? Mars-Four? *SZZZZRRTTTTT* your status?"

"Say again, Home-One?"

"*SZZRRRT SZRRRRT* copy?"

"Home-One, I cannot see the base. I am waving my arms in the air, can you see me at all? I need you to tell me which direction to travel."

"Mars-Four, *SZZRTTTTTT* can *SZZZRRRRT* me?"

"Please repeat, Home-One."

My breathing began to rapidly increase and my heart raced.

"Mars-Four, can you hear me?"

"Yes, Home-One, you are breaking up but I heard that last transmission. I need you to tell me which direction I need to go in, please."

"Mars-Four, *SZZZZRTT* can you hear me? Hello? Mars-Four?"

Frustrated, and in a state of panic, I picked a direction and plunged forward. I played the odds since I had a fifty-fifty chance. West would bring me to our base and east would bring me back to the greenhouse. North or south meant doom but I was doomed anyways if I just stood still.

"*SZZRRT* Four, can you hear me?"

"Hello? Home-One?"

"*SZZZZRTTT SZZZZZZZZZRTTTTTTTTT.*"

"Hello?"

"*SZZZZRT* you *SZZRT SZZZZZZZRTTTTT.*"

My heart sank as over ten minutes had passed and I had yet to touch the outside of either structure. The wind blasted me with constant force and again sent me tumbling to the ground. The Martian Mother Nature was looking to punish the foolish human who thought he could outrun the storm. Perhaps she did not like colonists and was testing my mettle to see if I was worthy to call this planet home.

I struggled to stand and then marched for another twenty minutes or so before walking headlong into something very solid. I was pushed along at a great speed with the wind behind me and was fortunate not to crack the glass of my helmet when I collided with this object.

Feeling the jagged surface in front of me, I determined that I had reached one of the mountains. Whether it was Vesta or Maia, I had no way of knowing. Either one meant I was way off course and there was no way for me to place the location of our base. My best bet now was to seek some form of shelter from the storm within the mountain. We knew that some caves did exist but Captain Prawn had not allowed me to explore them yet. His priority was the stabilization of the colony first, exploration had to wait.

I no longer heard static from my speaker as all transmissions had gone completely dead. They would have been unable to help me at this point anyway; my only chance now was to find a place to hide.

My visibility was still almost non-existent and I was forced to feel my way around the base of the mountain. To my elation, I soon found a deep crevice where the slope downwards was not too steep. I decided to descend and was rewarded with relief from the buffeting wind. I took a seat to rest my weary limbs and calm my frail nerves.

What a fool I had been. I lost the tools and quite nearly lost my life because I didn't wish to be uncomfortable, spending time alone at Green-Two. And I was still not out of this predicament. Who knew how long this storm would last and I only had so much oxygen in my suit.

I activated the two powerful flashlights that were mounted on the top of my helmet and peered downwards into the crevice. It appeared to go quite deep, beyond the reach of my lights, and the slope was manageable, if I wished to investigate deeper. The explorer in me won the internal struggle and down I went, albeit quite slowly and cautiously.

The angle of the slope told me that I was now traveling underneath the mountain, and soon I was surrounded by pitch-darkness, with only the lights from my helmet to guide me. It wasn't long before I could not even hear the winds of the storm from above.

Curiously, I pressed onwards, further underground. I was fortunate to be able to stand to my full height within the tunnel as it leveled out and continued on, and a tunnel it appeared to be. The rocky walls looked strangely smoother down here and even the floor was less jagged.

The fear of being lost in this storm was soon replaced with the excitement of exploring this most curious tunnel. This is what I had signed up for in the first place; I was no farmer.

Further and further I went, when I noticed some bizarre markings on one of the walls. I couldn't be sure if they were alien in origin or just caused by natural erosion, so I approached for a closer inspection.

So focused was I on the wall markings that I did not notice the immense gap in the tunnel's floor, and I soon felt the terrifying experience of falling, as the floor disappeared from under me.

I landed heavily with a crunch and a scream escaped my lips. I was no doctor but I was positive I had just broken my right leg. I cursed at my lack of awareness. Now I had really gone and done it. Even if the storm ended soon, I highly doubted my radio would work this far underground to send or receive any transmissions from Home-One. I also figured that the dust storm would erase any tracks I had made on the ground, therefore rendering the others useless in determining the direction I had traveled.

Despairingly, I looked about at my surroundings and found I had fallen into a large cavern; so large that my light could not reach the walls. Then my heart skipped a beat, as I noticed I was lying on…what? Papers? It appeared that I lay atop several dust-covered papers. Newsprint by the looks of it. Newsprint, with writing! And writing…in English!

My hands shook with excitement, momentarily forgetting about the agonizing pain in my leg. I fumbled about with my bulky gloves, attempting to pick up one of the papers several times before I was finally rewarded. I lifted a newspaper up in order to read the headline on the first page, for a newspaper it most assuredly was! My mind reeled at the implications that I clutched some ancient Martian newspaper.

I was stunned by the headline that I read aloud.

"Politicians scoff at the notion of colonizing Earth."

This particular article went on to discuss how mankind was destroying Mars at a rapid rate and would soon become extinct if they could not find a way to colonize the monster-infested blue planet, called Earth.

So we destroyed Mars and moved to Earth. Now we were destroying Earth and were looking to move to Mars. Good lord, we were destined to be caught in this vicious cycle for eternity.

THE INHERITANCE

The cab driver carefully navigated the narrow winding road as we ascended the dark hill in the pelting rain. Winds threatened to force the small vehicle off the road, and on more than one occasion, I found my stomach caught in my throat, as I gazed out the window to a steep drop below. It would have been a frightening drive on the best of days and this horrendous storm only made it worse.

Even when lightning lit up the sky, it did little to improve our view, as thick weeping trees leaned over the road, reaching with gnarled branches to brush the vehicle as it passed.

I breathed a sigh of relief when we eventually reached the hill's summit and the gravel road evened out. That relief was short-lived though as I beheld the sight of that most sinister-looking house which sat at the end of the road. To think that this house was my destination was enough to cause my skin to crawl. It was akin to those mansions that were most often portrayed in horror pictures.

Soon I stood in the driving rain, looking up at the front door which was shrouded in darkness. The cabbie graciously dropped my bags beside me and hastily returned to the vehicle.

"Thank you, my good man. Now what do I owe…"

I never even finished my sentence as the cab sped off and was soon out of sight. I stood momentarily dumbfounded, until the rain was soaking through to my undergarments, so I grabbed my bags and dashed for the cover of the porch.

The two-story house, while looking ancient by its architecture, was in fairly good shape, considering it had not been occupied in at least a year. The glass of the windows seemed to be all intact; untouched by vandals. Though I supposed, despite its spooky appearance, it was not the most accessible of places for trouble-makers or squatters. Why would my father have chosen to live here, in such a remote and forbidding location?

The wind picked up again and with it carried a biting chill. The rain began to blow sideways and soon the porch offered no protection whatsoever. I fumbled about in the pockets of my overcoat to locate the keys that were presented to me from the lawyer. The key to the main door was large and looked no less ancient than did the house. It added character, I figured.

With a rewarding, "click", the heavy front door unlocked, and I rushed inside, dragging my bags behind me as quickly as I could. My eyes could not readily adjust to the blackness of the lobby and I was soon rummaging blindly through one of my bags in search of my electric torch. Luckily I had thought to bring it, as I had been informed that the aged house possessed no electricity at all.

With a push of a button, my vision returned, revealing a grand, spiral staircase, leading upwards, with several doors dotting the large greeting room in which I now stood. An old coat rack hovered to my right, but the chill air from outside had followed me in, and I thought to keep my coat on for the time being. I did, however, do my best to shake off my rain covered coat, before proceeding further into my new house.

Or soon to be new house, I figured I should say. In an odd move, my father had stipulated in his will that his house would only become mine, after I spent at least one night inside of it. It had taken me nearly a year, after the news of his death, to eventually travel to our old town and meet with the lawyer. I was a busy man and had to see that my endeavors at home would be well looked after in my absence.

Regrettably, my hectic work schedule did not afford me much family time and I had seen very little of my father over the years. He meant well, I am sure, but I found I could only handle him in small doses. Father was a veteran of the Great War, and if allowed, could prattle on with an endless supply of war stories and heroic tales of friends long gone. I might have found the stories more engaging to listen to, if it wasn't for my father's terrible stutter; it required great effort for him to finish a complete sentence. The stutter was the result of an old war injury that he suffered from an explosion of some kind and subsequently made conversations with the man quite painful.

I rarely visited the old fellow who lived alone since my mother died over thirty years past. Father did press the issue, from time to time, but I usually had one excuse or another for not being able to make the trek. He was a hard-working tradesman his entire life and I don't think he approved much of my becoming a writer. Not that he ever said so, but I am sure he thought a man's hands were put to better uses than tapping the keys of a typewriter for hours on end.

Though, looking back, I figured I should have visited more often. He was my father and my only immediate family member, as I was an only child. I guess I figured he would have lived much longer, so there was no pressing need. I mean a bomb in the Great War, along with a tumble from a third-story roof, couldn't kill him, I just thought the reaper would have had a more difficult time in claiming him. And by god, that horrible stutter effectively repelled me.

Affected now by a slight feeling of guilt, I decided to head upstairs and find the master bedroom, where I might set down my bags and make myself more comfortable. Each step I took on the grand stairwell creaked quite loudly, as if a small rodent was hidden beneath each one and squealed as I brought my weight down upon it. There would be no stealthy burglars taking me by surprise in this house, I chuckled, albeit nervously, to myself.

The house was fully furnished and the décor matched the ancient-look of the architecture. It was reminiscent of visiting an old museum or historical building of some importance. My father had a love of all things antique, from ages long past.

The house would require a good cleaning though, as

dust and cobwebs covered much of the furniture and trinkets found on shelves. I stopped briefly to admire a portrait that hung on a wall at the top of the stairs. It was of an elderly gentleman whom I did not recognize as a family member. Just some anonymous piece of art father must have liked. Goosebumps rose on my arms as I felt the eyes of that portrait follow me down the long corridor.

Thunder cracked outside and I quite nearly jumped out of my shoes, seeing as how I was still frazzled by the disturbing eyes of the portrait. Navigating this dark house with only the light of my electric torch did nothing to help calm my nerves.

Spotting a set of double-doors at the end of the hall told me that I had most likely found the room I had sought. The doors creaked open to reveal the master bedroom as I had expected. Antique tables and chairs filled the room, and the king-sized, four-postered, canopied-bed, looked quite inviting. Like the other areas of the house, there was a layer of dust everywhere, accompanied by an old musty smell. Three tall windows would have provided sufficient light, were the sun shining outside.

Above the bed hung a portrait of my mother, exactly how she looked before she had died. As I walked about the room, I was assailed by that same creepy feeling that the eyes were following me. Thunder boomed again and I almost dropped my light.

A little while later, I had gotten comfortable and had a fire roaring within the bedroom's fireplace; a nice touch indeed. I had changed into something more suitable for sleeping but still kept me warm. I lay on the bed which I had thoroughly dusted and shaken and found it very soft.

I had decided to explore more of the house in the morning, when it would have a much less chilling atmosphere. The warming-heat of the fireplace was causing my eyelids to droop and soon I was beginning to nod off. A loud crash from somewhere down the hall forced my eyes wide open and I sat up straight in a panic.

Had I imagined it, perhaps? Some noise that only existed in my subconscious mind? But then I heard something else, the sound of some object rolling across the hardwood floor. I was surely awake now, so firmly believed that what I heard was real. The question now was, should I investigate? The storm could still be clearly heard outside, so it was possible that whatever may have fallen was just a result of the wind or the wall-rattling thunder.

Curiosity won and I reached for my electric torch which I had kept within close-quarters on an ornately-carved wooden end table. I slipped into some fuzzy slippers and crept to the double doors. Try as I might, there was no opening them without causing such a creaking-racket that could have awakened the dead. Instantly regretting that last sentiment, I shook the thought away and crept down the hall, attempting to discern the direction the noise had come from.

Even tip-toeing as I was, the aged floorboards still creaked, revealing my approach to any ears that cared to listen. Being a writer, I had a healthy imagination as one might expect and my mind unwantingly conjured all sorts of spine-chilling images.

The eerie rolling sound continued anew from behind a closed door, directly to my right, and if someone had been looking at me, I was most certain my hair would have been standing on end.

I approached the door, as the eyes from the portrait down the hall followed my progress, and pressed my ear against it, listening intently. Of course the sound would cease upon my efforts of discerning its source and I found myself inching the door open to shine my light inside.

I was somewhat relieved to find a long candle holder resting on the floor, where it must have fallen from a nearby mantle. Further inspection of the somewhat small room, though, revealed a most curious décor. I entered the room after deciding it needed a closer examination.

I shone my light all over the four walls of the small den, which were almost completely covered with photos and paper clippings. A single window looked out over a fairly steep drop down the side of the hill that the house sat upon. Lightning from outside would periodically light up the room as bright as day.

To my surprise, every photo in the room was a photo of me; various shots taken during book tours and book signings. The paper clippings were from reviews or articles concerning the many books I had written. A wooden table sat next to a plush reading chair and the tabletop contained a copy of each of the books that I had written. The entire room appeared to be some kind of shrine dedicated to me and all my works. And all this time I never thought father cared.

I slid open the one drawer under the table and found several handwritten letters inside. I skimmed through the contents of a few letters and found them to be correspondences from a good friend of my father's. From the replies in the letters, it would seem that my father would incessantly brag about his famous author son.

My eyes teared up at that moment. All these years my

father was my biggest fan and I had not the slightest clue. And I shied away from having contact with him and made excuses to never visit. What a fool I was. I wondered, if in the end, he had actually hated me.

As I stood there facing the window in my moment of self-loathing, a strange light seemed to be emanating from behind me; I caught the reflection in the glass. I spun about in a panic, thinking an intruder stood behind me, also carrying an electric torch.

My heart stopped beating altogether and I stood there with my jaw hanging low; hairs standing on end. Before me, hovering in the doorway, was a ghostly specter, glowing with a pale-white radiance. The most unsettling aspect of this scene, was that this spirit resembled my father, complete with his small round spectacles and beard. It was also dressed in a suit and tie; father was rarely seen without one on.

Was I dreaming? Surely this could not be an actual ghost hovering before me. Then it spoke, or rather, it attempted to, and I fell back in fright, sending copies of my books from the table to the floor.

"I-I-I-I-I-I…" it stuttered.

"Good Lord!" I cried out in horror.

The glowing spirit floated closer; its arms extended towards me. "I-I-I-I f-f-f-f-f…"

Without a second thought I darted around the ghost and raced from the room. It seemed that my father had returned to not only haunt me with his ghostly presence but with his horrendous stutter as well. I accidently dropped my light and sprinted straight back to the master bedroom, slamming the double doors shut and locking them with a latch.

I was panting to catch my breath and running the situation over in my mind. I wondered if my father had planned to haunt me all along. He left me his house in the will and specified that I would have to spend a night in it in order to own it. He wanted to lure me here, to what purpose? Perhaps to shame me for never visiting him, to express his unhappiness at my admittedly poor behavior? I figured he must have knocked over that candle holder so that I would discover the room-turned-shrine.

My heart pounded in my chest and it sounded like drums beating in my ears. What would I do? Where could I go in this storm? My thoughts were interrupted as my father drifted effortlessly through a bedroom wall to enter the chamber and stare at me.

"I-I-I-I-I f-f-f-f-f-fo…"

I screamed with dread as it reached for me once more. I bounced off the doors, forgetting in my panic that I had locked them. With trembling hands, I unlatched the doors and dashed away, eluding the spectral hands that were nearly upon me. I couldn't be sure what would happen if the ghost touched me but I had no desire to find out.

I had dropped my electric torch back in the other room and decided to retrieve it. I scooped it up and turned to find the doorway completely blocked with the frightening specter. He had me trapped, right in the very room he had planned.

"I-I-I-I-I-I-I-I-I-I-I f-f-f-f-f-f-for…"

Seeing no other option, I leaped through the glass of the room's window to plummet down the steep drop with a scream.

The ghost drifted over to peer down through the

shattered glass.

"I-I-I-I-I-I-I-I-I f-f-f-f-f-forgive y-y-y-you."

BEFORE THE GATES OF ST. PETER

As my eyes opened, I felt an immediate sting from the brightness. It took the better part of a minute before I was able to open them fully. Wherever I was, it was foggy, and I couldn't quite pinpoint the source of the light; it came from everywhere and nowhere, all at once.

I could make out no details of my surroundings, just thick fog everywhere I looked. I was not even sure what I was lying on but it felt soft and feathery.

I stood and wavered dizzily on unsteady legs, my head felt as foggy as my surroundings. Curiously, I noticed I was wearing a white robe of sorts; I have never owned a white robe. Where the hell was I?

I must have been dreaming, that had to be it. But everything seemed so vivid, so real. I pinched myself but felt no pain. Was that the evidence then to prove my dream theory? Surely you could not feel pain in a dream.

I tried desperately to recall my last memories to aid in solving this unsettling mystery. I remembered being in the bank, we were holding it up. I was watching the door while Hank and Eugene were collecting the money from the tellers.

I remember an argument, there was shouting, Hank was yelling at one of the tellers. Then, **BLAM!** Hank's shotgun went off and all hell broke loose. People started running in every direction and Hank and Eugene began executing them. We had agreed beforehand; no killing. But our plans had gone awry.

The moment I heard the first siren, I was out the door and speeding down the street on foot. The first two police cruisers on site decided to pursue me. I figured I had just bought Hank and Eugene some precious time before other coppers would arrive.

I ducked down an alley and soon heard the sounds of coppers pursuing me on foot. **BLAM! BLAM!** Two bullets whizzed over my head and struck the brick wall of a building. I turned the corner…then nothing. I can remember nothing after that.

Scratching my head, I exerted much effort attempting to put the pieces together after leaving the alley but that's where my mind goes blank. What happened? Did the coppers catch me? Not that it would have done them any good if Hank and Eugene got away. I didn't kill anyone and I didn't have any of the money on me. I would just say I was coerced into being a lookout for my two overly-violent partners. I would never give up their names. Not that I cared much about either of them but that was just the code on the street; you didn't rat on others.

I began walking and the ground beneath me felt so

soft. What a vivid dream indeed. I still could not see very far in any direction due to the thick fog.

Again I looked down to my robe, inspecting it closer. What happened to all my clothes? I opened the front of my robe and my jaw dropped in surprise. There were three strange marks on my chest; scars? Three small round scars. They looked almost like…bullet wounds.

Suddenly a new theory crossed my mind and I began to panic; my breathing became rapid. Was I dead? What if I turned that corner and those rotten coppers shot me? Shot me dead! Was that why I couldn't remember anything after that? Is that why I was walking around in this foggy haze?

Again I looked to my chest. Three apparent bullet wounds and no pain; I felt nothing at all.

"Hello? Hello? Anyone here?"

Oh dear god, I must be dead. I felt too aware for this to be just a dream. My hands began trembling and I ran about in circles. Everywhere was fog and it felt as though I must have been running on clouds. I was too young to be dead. Damn those coppers! Damn them to…hell?

Wait a moment; I was not surrounded by pits of fire. There was no wails of the anguished; no devils cracking fiery whips. Despite my life as a criminal, I made it to heaven. Was this heaven? Sure seemed it. White fog, soft clouds, very bright. I supposed that if I did have to die, at the very least I had made it to heaven.

A sound from off in the distance grabbed my attention. I turned to my left but could make out nothing amid the swirl of white mist. Cautiously, I crept ahead, following the sound of…paper? Someone turning the pages of a book?

I only had to walk about fifteen feet before a sight stopped me dead in my tracks. My jaw probably touched my ankles as I stood rooted in place. The fog had cleared enough so that I could make out a man seated at a small golden table. He wore a pure white robe, similar to the one I now wore. He had snow-white hair and a long white beard. Before him on the table, sat a gigantic leather-bound book, and the man paid me no attention as he leafed through the book, glancing casually at each page.

When I was finally able to gather my wits about me, I approached the man and cleared my throat to announce my arrival. He looked up from the book and those blue eyes seemed to peer straight through me.

"Ah, Stanley Goode, I see you have finally made it."

"Y-you, know my name?"

"Of course I do, I know all about you, Stanley. You were born in 1921, your father's name was Floyd and your mother's name was Angela. You had one older brother named Frank, who died in the Great War."

"Y-you are really St. Peter? The keeper of the gates to heaven?"

"Did Jesus not say unto me, 'I will give you the keys of the kingdom of heaven?'"

"Well yeah, I suppose he did."

"Yes, Stanley, I am St. Peter."

"So, I am not actually in heaven yet?"

"No, not yet, not until I deem you fit for entry."

"I-I am fit for entry. I mean, I have not led the most decent of lives but I never killed anyone. Not even in that bank, I was just the lookout."

"What happened in that bank, Stanley?"

"I don't know exactly. I was only watching the street

for coppers when I heard some arguing and then a gunshot. The other two men did all the shooting, I swear it. I ran after that."

"Who were these other two men?"

"Just guys, you know, old partners from the hood. I didn't even like them. Two real toughs."

"Stanley, you stand here in judgment. Now is not the time to lie or hold back information. If I deny you entry into heaven, you realize where you will go, do you not?"

"P-please you can't send me down there! I beg you!"

"Well the decision is really yours. Do you want to be cooperative? If you didn't shoot anyone in that bank, who did?"

"It was Hank Smith and Eugene Hale, I swear it. Please don't send me to hell! They both have killed many people. They are very violent individuals."

I didn't mind ratting out those goons now. I was dead, after all, they couldn't hurt me anymore. If ratting them out ensured my entry into heaven, so be it.

"If these two were not friends of yours, how is it that you partnered up with them? Where do you meet with them to discuss business?"

"The pool hall on West Addams Street. They hang out there all the time."

"Thank you, Stanley. I believe you are telling me the truth."

"I am, I swear. I wouldn't be fool enough to lie to you. Besides I have nothing to fear from them now."

St. Peter rose from behind his desk, closed his book, and then began to walk away.

"So, what now? Where are the gates? You are granting me entry, right?

"I am granting you entry alright, but not into heaven, Stanley. Instead you will be granted entry into a maximum security prison."

"Huh? What's going on here? Hey, where are you going?"

"Guards, Mr. Goode is all yours now."

* * * *

"So he cannot see us up here?"

"No, this window is concealed."

"Impressive show. You say this works every time?"

"So far the success rate is one hundred percent."

"Marvelous. Those bullet wounds…,"

"Courtesy of a makeup artist who works in this studio."

"And when he pinched himself when he awoke…,"

"The prisoners are injected with morphine to numb their senses. They almost always think they are dreaming at first. They pinch themselves or attempt to cause pain in some manner but they feel none."

"He gave up the names of his partners quite easily."

"Indeed. These criminals have a strict code about ratting out others. Without this deception, we might never have gotten the names of the two shooters who escaped that bank. I highly doubt Stanley would have given us anything useful."

"Incredible. Great work, Chief Williams."

SHOOTING BY THE LIGHT OF THE MOON

The night of October 31st, one year past, Halloween night to be exact, still haunts me to this very day. I still awaken some nights crying out in a cold sweat from my nightmare-plagued sleeps. You would think that I should be happy and content, as I have never been more sought after for the female lead in big pictures. I am famous and I am wealthy, but I am burdened with guilt over the horrific knowledge that I have buried away in my mind.

From the time I was quite young, I had always wanted to be an actress. I was in all the school plays and joined a theater group when I was a teen. By the time I was twenty-one, my dreams were coming to fruition, as I landed small roles in some feature films. I was mostly playing the waitress, or the bartender, or the attractive girlfriend to a fringe character, with only minor speaking parts. Sometimes I could display my long, natural, raven-colored hair, and other times I was required to wear blonde wigs.

I continued with those types of roles for several years, until that fateful day when I received a phone call from a casting agent in the employ of the famous director, Otto Friedhelm. That phone call changed my life.

I lived modestly until that point, in a small bachelor apartment on the south side of the Big City. The odd time someone would recognize me on the street. "Hey, you are that girl from that movie," though, they never remembered my name.

I always had enough money to cover my rent, and my bills, but there wasn't much left over for anything else. I can admit to having a weakness for flashy jewelry; diamonds in particular. When I hung up the phone that day from the casting agent, images of exquisite diamond rings and brilliant new dresses flashed through my mind.

By some sheer stroke of luck, Mr. Friedhelm wished to cast me as the leading woman in his latest picture. I was still required to do a reading first but by the sound of it, it was merely a formality. I was informed that Mr. Friedhelm was very impressed with my previous work and felt that I was that undiscovered star, just waiting for the right role to flourish.

I wasn't given many details of the film over the phone, only that it was going to be a dark drama, bordering on horror. A plane ticket was purchased for me and I was to fly to a small town in the Wallachia region of Romania. I could not contain my excitement. A leading role, my biggest paycheck, and a free, all-expense paid trip to Romania.

Immediately upon my arrival, I was given the star

treatment. A driver was waiting for me at the airport to take me to a lovely little town where I had my own room at a charming, picturesque hotel, near the base of a large mountain.

The hotel was owned and operated by the amiable and ever-accommodating, Ms. Verdi. The food was fantastic and my every need was seen to. I had a beautiful second-story view of a forest, where the autumn leaves were a variety of stunning reds, oranges and yellows. The room itself was furnished with wonderful hand-carved antique furniture. The hotel, and the town on a whole, looked as though it was stuck in time, a quiet little community, living much as it had in centuries gone by.

I wasn't in town for very long before I was finally introduced to Otto Friedhelm. He was a charismatic and talkative man, with salt-and-pepper hair and a greying beard. He bordered on eccentric and seemed to have an endless supply of energy. He continuously rambled on about one such thing or another without stopping to take a breath. Sometimes, he didn't even complete a thought before changing the topic to something entirely different.

I was relieved though, that he thought I would play the perfect Emily. He only had me read a few lines from my first scene before announcing that I was the perfect choice. I will never forget my feeling of joy at being treated like a star. I even had my own chair with my name on it that would get delivered to the site of each scene by one of the crew members.

Curious, I stopped to chat with the young crew member. "What is your name?"

"Thomas."

"Nice to meet you, Thomas. And what is it that you

do here, for Mr. Friedhelm?"

"I carry your chair from set to set."

"That's it?"

"Yes, that's it. You are the star. Someone has to be sure that your chair gets to where it needs to be."

I was indeed flattered that somebody's sole duty on set was to carry my chair around. I would be lying to say otherwise. I remember hoping that this was not going to go to my head.

I had now received the full script from Mr. Friedhelm and discovered that it was a movie about a tormented man who had been cursed to live as a werewolf. I played the love interest of the man who would become the werewolf but my character was not to learn of this terrible fact until the climax of the film.

On the first day we were to begin shooting, I met the male lead, Luther Miklos. He was a tall, handsome man, with dark hair and a thin beard. He had nice wide shoulders and spoke English with a thick accent. I had never seen Luther in anything before but I was informed that he was more of a local actor. Like me, this was going to be his first big break, thanks to Mr. Friedhelm.

A week of shooting went by and I was having the time of my life. Mr. Friedhelm was a perfectionist and most scenes we shot several times until it was just right. Though he was always a gentleman about it and would apologize constantly for wishing to try different angles, or adjusting stances and items in the background. He had an endless supply of energy and was a whirlwind around the set.

We had just wrapped up shooting the scene where my character, Emily, meets Luther for the first time. Emily travelled a lot as a photographer for a magazine and Luther was her guide through a fictional town in the Old Country. The scene was shot in a café and after Mr. Friedhelm yelled, "cut", and announced a break, I made my way back to my special chair. I noticed a different young man was standing nearby it.

"What is your name?"

"My name is Marko."

"Well hello, Marko. What happened to Thomas?"

"Thomas fell ill, so I was hired to replace him. And it's an honor to carry the chair of a famous movie star."

"I hope Thomas is alright. And thank you, but I am not really a famous movie star. Not yet anyways."

Weeks turned into a month and it was now nearing the end of October. We worked every day and we worked long days. The weather had been turning cooler, and as a result, was causing many crew members to fall ill. For example, I was now on my fifth chair carrier! They were all local young lads from the town who were more than eager to carry a chair around for whatever Mr. Friedhelm was paying them, which I had to imagine would not have been much at all.

Our work schedule had been intense and it was now time to film the final scene, in which Emily discovers that the man she has fallen in love with turns out to be a werewolf. This scene was to be shot in a forest under a full moon. I wondered how they were going to work the transformation scene, as I had been told the makeup process for Luther was painstakingly long.

As fun a time as I had been having, I was eager to shoot the last scene and get back home to see my family. I was informed we had to wait another four days until the moon was full before we could start filming. We could have just used some stock footage of a full moon but Mr. Friedhelm was always insistent that everything had to be authentic. As I said, he was a perfectionist.

After such a frenzied month, I have to say that I didn't mind relaxing for a few days. I didn't realize how exhausted I had been until I was given my first day with nothing planned. It gave me a little more time to explore the lovely little shops in town and pick up a few souvenirs of my visit.

As the sun set on the fourth day, a young man approached me as I was lounging near a large window in the hotel's lobby, enjoying the view.

"Pardon me, Miss. Mr. Friedhelm is ready to shoot the last scene and has asked me to fetch you."

"Thank you, I shall grab a few things from my room and join you shortly. I have not seen you around the sets before."

"Oh, I just started. I get to carry your chair to the next location."

I rubbed my chin. "Let me guess, the last young man fell ill?"

"Indeed so and lucky for me. It's very exciting to work on a movie set."

I paid the comment no further heed and grabbed a few things from my room before following Emilio, for that was the young man's name. I was fortunate that I had the foresight to bring my sweater as there was a biting chill in the air this evening.

I found my young escort appeared jittery and looked about nervously with every sound. I suddenly remembered that tonight was Halloween and found it strange that the town seemed deserted. The sun had not vanished very long ago and it was still early in the evening, so where were all the people?

"Do your people not celebrate Halloween at all, Emilio? I see some decorations around the town but no people."

"Oh yes, we love Halloween."

"Well, where is everyone then? Is tonight not Halloween?"

"It is Halloween but tonight there is a full moon."

"So?"

"Normally, nobody goes out on a full moon," he replied, his eyes shifting about skittishly.

I decided not to push the boy further and just followed in silence the rest of the way. We hiked a good twenty or so minutes into a dark forest and thankfully Emilio had brought a lantern with him or surely we would have become lost. I was becoming increasingly anxious before we finally found a clearing where the others were waiting on us.

I was a little surprised by the fact that there were not many people present. There was Mr. Friedhelm, of course, who was rambling a mile a minute, Luther, who was pacing back and forth near a large tree, no doubt going over his lines in his head, and two crew members, one to work the camera and another to hold a spotlight. My chair was already waiting for me as Emilio had been here earlier.

"There is my Emily," Mr. Friedhelm announced excitedly. "I hope you don't mind my dear but time is of the essence tonight and we must begin presently."

I was fine with that. I had the last four days to practice my lines and was fairly confident that I had everything down to memory.

Luther appeared agitated but was able to compose himself as Mr. Friedhelm yelled, "action." Luther was also the name of the character he played. Emily and Luther met in the middle of the clearing within the dark forest. The night was cloudy, and at the moment, the bright full moon was veiled behind a cluster of thick clouds.

Luther, the character, had been acting quite peculiar as of late, which had Emily concerned. He had been disappearing at night without a proper explanation as to his whereabouts. Sometimes, she even noticed strange wounds upon his body; cuts and bruises that Luther had no recollection as to their origin.

Luther had grown weary of living a lie, so out of his love for Emily, decided upon this late night meeting to reveal to her his nightmarish secret.

My character had yet to be involved with any scene concerning the werewolf, so I had not yet seen what Luther looked like in the makeup. I remember feeling somewhat excited by the prospect.

Luther was a fantastic actor. Real tears fell as he began to tell Emily of a dark secret that he had so far kept hidden from her. Normally, Mr. Friedhelm stopped us to shoot many different takes of the same scene. It was not so this time. He stood silent behind the cameraman, riveted by our performance, or Luther's, more specifically. The camera kept rolling as we continued uninterrupted.

"Luther, my love, what is this dark secret you speak of? I know you to be a good man and I cannot imagine that there is anything that you could say to bend my mind."

"Emily, I am not a good man, I am in fact, a

monster."

"A monster? Oh please. By whose definition?"

"By mine. By the townsfolk. And by yours soon enough, I do not doubt. I have been cursed, my dear. I am truly a monster."

"Stop this nonsense, Luther, I…"

My words were halted in midsentence as the clouds overhead opened up and the light of the full moon filled the clearing. Luther suddenly doubled over and groaned as if in immense pain. According to the script, our conversation was to continue on awhile longer but it seemed that Luther had jumped ahead. Mr. Friedhelm had not yelled "cut" so I decided to stay in character and finish the scene.

"Luther, what is wrong with you?" I cried with concern, my hands pressed against both of my cheeks.

He stood up straight, his arms reaching towards the sky and let out a hideous, feral growl. It was then, and I remember it oh so clearly, that I witnessed something that defied logic. I had often pondered how this scene would play out in terms of Luther's makeup. I had imagined a long pause while a team of people worked feverishly to effect his transformation. I had been wrong, quite wrong indeed.

A scream, a real scream and not play-acting, got caught in my throat. So horrified was I by the scene unfolding before me that I could not even expel a single sound. My mouth hung open in silent terror.

My body trembled as I watched hair, no wait, thick fur, sprout from all over Luther's body. His fingers elongated and ended with razor-sharp claws. His shoes split open and his feet enlarged and resembled large paws.

There was a blood-curdling howl as a snout replaced his otherwise handsome face and as he howled, he revealed two rows of menacing fangs. His ears had become pointed and in mere moments, Luther resembled more beast than man.

I knew immediately that this was no act and that I had just borne witness to something so utterly terrifying and most likely seldom seen and spoke about. I had no idea what to do at this point. The others were not shocked by this and continued to watch; in fact the camera kept rolling!

Luther, or whatever he was now, a real werewolf I supposed, returned his gaze to me and growled hungrily. I am not embarrassed to admit that my legs turned to jelly and I collapsed to the ground. I was paralyzed with fear and lacked the strength or courage to defend myself. I lay there an easy victim for the hideous beast.

Unfortunately for me, the horror was not to end just yet. Suddenly from out of the forest, ran Emilio, the chair carrier, dressed in one of the police costumes and carrying one of the prop guns. He waved it bravely at Luther before the werewolf turned on him.

What Luther did to that poor young man, I dare not speak of. The images of what I saw haunt my dreams and the mere thought of it brings tears to my eyes. It probably lasted mere moments only but felt an eternity to me at the time.

When Luther finished with Emilio, he turned his attention back to me. If the actor I knew was still somewhere behind those cold eyes, there was no trace of it now. As he advanced towards me, a deafening gunshot startled us both, echoing off the trees around the clearing.

Mr. Friedhelm finally stepped out from behind the cameraman and approached cautiously with a large pistol aimed at Luther.

"That's a cut, Luther. Our filming is at an end now. Our contract has been fulfilled and you have been provided the agreed-upon meals. You may leave now."

The werewolf cocked his head and growled, before taking another step closer towards me.

"No, Luther, she was not part of our deal. I know you can understand me. You know what kind of bullets are in my pistol. Each is coated in solid silver. Do not make me use it."

Somehow, in that bestial head, Luther understood those words. He howled one last time then lopped into the darkness of the forest and vanished from sight.

Mr. Friedhelm exhaled and lowered his pistol. "That's a wrap. Excellent performance my dear," he said, turning to address me. "Worthy of an award to be sure. You have to know, this was all necessary to capture the most realistic werewolf picture ever made. Sacrifices were needed. I had to…"

He rambled on and on and I heard nothing more, so traumatized was I. I was put on the first flight home the next day and spent weeks recovering from the shock, unable to even speak with my family. I couldn't be sure who was more the monster, Luther, or Otto Friedhelm. It would seem I sólved the case of the mystery illness which inflicted certain crew members and led to their eventual disappearance. All bargaining chips used to entice the werewolf into appearing in the film.

Many times I thought of running to the police to inform them of Mr. Friedhelm's crimes but who would believe me? What would they say when I confessed to witnessing a werewolf murder a young man? People would think me mad.

Not surprisingly, the picture was an instant success. Word spread quickly and theaters were packed the world over. My phone rang daily with agents looking to hire me for upcoming films. I did not return any calls as my feelings of distress had yet to subside.

A year later, I read a somewhat satisfying article in the newspaper. Mr. Friedhelm was found dead of an apparent strangulation near a pyramid in the Great Desert. As it turned out, he was researching his next monster movie which involved a mummy. The authorities were seeking the murderer but so far had no leads.

Of Luther Miklos' fate, I know not. I never seen nor heard tell of him after that Halloween night. He was given several awards for his outstanding performance in the picture, though of course, never attended any of the events to claim his prize.

SHADOW ALLEY

I gulped down the last drop of my mediocre coffee, left a dime on the counter for the waitress, and then proceeded straight to my car. A half hour earlier, I heard the call come over the radio about a body found in an alley of the Junkie Jungle. The Junkie Jungle was one of the nastiest neighborhoods in the bowels of the Big City. It was largely populated with junkies, of course, along with drug dealers, gangsters, and ladies of the night. All the undesirable types enjoyed congregating in that one area.

Normally I would not respond to a call in the Jungle, that was for the regular coppers. But I was in the area following up some leads on another case and the description of the body found in the alley piqued my curiosity. The average murder in the Jungle was carried out with your usual knives or guns. This one…sounded different. So I decided to drop by for a peek.

I parked my car as close as I could get to the police

cordon and locked my doors as I got out. I didn't need some junkie ransacking my car looking for nickels and dimes. A couple officers approached to intercept me so I flashed my badge. "Detective Edward Kane."

"Oh sorry, Detective, go on past."

"Thank you."

I continued on into an alley and nearly gagged from the smell of urine and feces. Graffiti dominated the brick walls and used needles crunched underfoot as I walked along. The alley was quite dark and about six people wide. I pulled out my hanky and held it over my nose to keep from vomiting. How did people live in these alleys?

"Stay awhile and you will get used to the smell," said Detective Banks, when he noticed my approach.

"No thanks, I don't think I want to be here that long," I replied.

"To what do we owe this honor? A visit from Detective Kane," asked Banks' partner, Detective Green.

"I was in the area," I said. "Heard the call on the radio and was curious to see what you got here."

"Well then, come and take a look. Bet you haven't seen this before."

I followed my two colleagues down towards the end of the alleyway where a police photographer was taking photos of the crime scene. That giant flash bulb blinded us with every photo taken. We kindly asked the man to return in ten minutes time.

Green was right; I hadn't seen anything like this before. "Death by a thousand needles, eh?"

"At least that. We haven't had them counted yet, but he was stabbed at least a thousand times with a needle."

"You have an ID on the victim?"

Banks nodded. "Harry Willis. Small-time gangster with The Jungle Cats gang. Needless to say, not a very nice individual."

"Wouldn't be such a travesty if the killer wasn't found," Green added.

"Any suspects?"

"Hmm, let's see here. Someone stabbed to death with a needle in the Junkie Jungle, so yeah, I'd say we have a few hundred suspects."

I didn't appreciate the sarcasm. I had known Banks for years; lazy detective. If the suspect was not standing a few feet away holding the smoking gun, there was a good chance that Banks wasn't solving the crime. He wasn't dim-witted, just lazy.

"No witnesses then?"

"None, or none that will talk anyways. Most folk down here tend not to speak out against the gangs. But you can be sure The Jungle Cats will also be looking for the killer. Street justice."

He had a point. Criminals like these usually dished out their own justice and were quicker at finding killers than the police. Perhaps some junkie got a bad batch of smack and took his frustration out on the dealer. In any event, it wasn't my case and what went on in the Jungle wasn't my concern.

I bid my colleagues a good evening and headed back to my car. It had been a long day and it was time to get home for some rest.

It was about a week later, I was at my desk in the office typing up a report, when I was approached by Detective Banks. He tossed a large envelope onto my desk.

"Take a look at these."

I opened the envelope to find a series of disturbing photos. Three different bodies in total; all appeared to have been stabbed to death by a thousand needle points. Just like the body I had seen for myself.

"These were all this week?" I wondered.

"Yes, each one about a day apart. The same alley for each murder."

"The same alley? Talk about brave. These all members of the same gang?"

"Yes, all Jungle Cats. This has to be some turf war between gangs."

"Since when did gangs resort to using needles as weapons? What happened to guns and knives? Those make a statement."

"Maybe the gang is trying to throw us off their trail? Make us believe it was someone else?"

"Since when did the gangs of this city begin to care whether we knew a murder was caused by them or not?"

"Maybe it's a smaller gang and they are not ready for an all-out war with the Cats just yet. So they are picking them off one by one."

"I doubt that. I think you have a serial killer here, Banks."

"Shhh, keep your voice down, I don't want the Chief to hear that. When it's gang members killing gang members, he doesn't particularly care. He starts thinking serial killer and he will be on my rear and fast!"

And there it was, lazy Banks didn't want to put much effort into tracking down a serial killer. All along he was hoping the gangs would sort this mess out amongst themselves. These were definitely not gang killings, in my opinion. I would be looking for a junkie turned murderer.

"If it's the same alley each time, have you staked out the alley?"

"I have had officers patrol the alley several times a night, for the last two nights. There has been no activity."

Of course there hasn't been any activity, I thought to myself, uniformed officers will keep the gangs and the killer lying low and out of sight. Banks left, taking his photos with him, and no doubt was going to stick to his gang war theory. Oh well, it was not my case.

The following afternoon, I was leaving my favorite sandwich shop, when I heard the call over the radio about another body found in the Junkie Jungle. Curious, I decided to stop by.

I was not surprised at all to find out that the body was that of a gang member, stabbed to death with a needle and found in the same alley. This time though, it appeared the victim put up a fight.

I approached one of the officers on scene and flashed my badge. "Question for you. Are you familiar with all the murders in this alley?"

"Yes, sir. Seen each one."

"Have the victims all been armed?"

"Yes, each one was packing a gun, but this guy here was the only one who got his out before he was killed."

"No signs that he wounded anyone?"

"Nope. Fired all six shots from his revolver and hit nothing. We recovered all the bullets and there were no traces of blood on any of them, nor any blood anywhere else in the alley."

The alley was not too large. Even if this guy was a terrible shot, I would think that one of the six bullets would have hit something. I also found it extremely odd that someone armed with only a needle, would risk attacking men armed with guns. Generally, that doesn't work out so well for the individual without a gun.

The first four men were killed before pulling their weapons. That told me that either they knew the killer, or they felt the killer was not a threat, such as some skeletally-thin junkie. Now the last guy emptied his gun before being killed. By this point the gang members would be jumpy and suspicious of everyone. He probably pulled his weapon upon first seeing someone in the alley. Not that it did him any good. He missed all six shots and was still murdered.

I stood there scratching my head in thought, watching the crowd that had gathered at the far end of the alley, just beyond the police tape. I locked eyes with a frightfully-thin man in a tattered grey coat, before he ducked out of sight.

I excused myself from the officer and quickly made my way down the alley and under the tape. I pushed my way through the gathered crowd and came out onto a street with a spacious park on the other side. A rusted old playground was in the middle next to a sandbox.

Frantically, I looked about for the man who wished to avoid my gaze and I caught a glimpse of a grey coat entering a building beside the park. I raced across the park and was disgusted as needles crunched underfoot. What kind of place was this for children to play? The city needed to do something about this and soon.

I used the sleeve of my coat to open the building door and found it led to a stairwell. I nearly gagged from the stench as I stood there contemplating whether to go up or down. A door slammed shut from below so I quickly descended the foul-smelling stairs. Another door led me to an underground garage. The garage, of course, was virtually empty; as people in this neighborhood could either not afford a car, or were not fit to drive one.

Fortunately for me, the man I sought sat cowering in a corner and the chase was over. He had short, salt-and-pepper hair, with facial stubble of the same color. His cheek-bones protruded from his face and I could tell most of his teeth had rotted and fallen out. He looked like a skeleton with skin, wearing a filthy grey overcoat.

"I would just like a word with you," I said after catching my breath. "Why were you in such a hurry to get away?"

"I don't like your kind," he lisped through missing teeth.

"My kind? What is my kind?"

"Lazy, good-for-nothing coppers."

"Good-for-nothing? What state do you think this city would be in without the police?"

"Ya do a lot of good here in the Jungle, don't ya? It's as lawless here as it was in the Wild West."

I supposed I could not argue his point there. Guys like Banks did tend to let the Jungle sort out its own problems.

"What do you know about these killings in that alley back there?"

The man spat on the ground. "Good riddance to all those vile gang members. Got what they deserved, they did."

"Who has been killing them?"

"Who cares, who? They are dead and that's all that matters."

"I thought the Jungle Cats controlled things for the

most part down here?"

"They do."

"So who would be brave enough to oppose them, using only a needle for a weapon?"

"Perhaps someone is sick of their evil ways. Perhaps someone didn't like what they did to poor Albert."

Ahhh, now we were getting somewhere.

"Albert? Who is Albert?"

"Albert Lockridge. And don't ya pretend like ya never heard of him."

"I am sorry, but I don't normally work the Jungle, I am not too familiar with the area. I have only popped in out of curiosity over these latest murders."

"Albert was my best friend," he replied, as his eyes became glossy.

"Albert was a junkie?"

"Albert was an unfortunate young man who ran into tough times."

So Albert was a junkie, I figured.

"What happened to Albert, then?"

"Those Jungle Cats, those animals, they killed him! Burned him alive, they did!" the man shook with rage.

"Why?"

"One of them stepped on a needle one day, got stuck in his shoe. He blamed Albert for throwing it there. A couple of them beat him near to death and then set him on fire."

"You witnessed this?"

"I sure did. Haunts me still, it does."

"Why didn't you tell the police who did this?"

"To what good? None of ya's ever listen to us down here. Ya never believe the words of a junkie."

"This happened in that same alley?"

"Sure did."

Ok, so we have revenge killings. Some upset individual, quite possibly the man sitting before me, is getting back at the Cats for killing this Albert fellow. My initial fear was that a serial killer could eventually leave the Jungle and continue his killings elsewhere in the city, becoming my problem. It did not appear that this would be the case here but I was thoroughly intrigued as to how this person killed five armed gang members thus far. The man sitting in front of me surely had the motive but hardly the strength. A single stab with a needle was not enough to take a man down. The moment a skinny junkie struck with the first attack, they could be easily subdued. As far as I knew, none of the victims had been poisoned.

"What is your name, sir?" I asked.

"Go to hell."

I took my leave and headed back to my car, avoiding the alley where Detectives Banks and Green were most likely present, inspecting the latest victim. I didn't care to speak with either of them; there really wasn't any point. Banks was determined to let the gangs sort it out and not entertain the idea of a serial killer. I had not been informed about Albert's death before, which of course, explained the recent killings to me perfectly.

Although it was not my case, curiosity did get the better of me, and I returned to the Jungle later that night. I replaced my normal overcoat with a ragged one I picked up from a thrift shop only hours before. I pulled the hood of a sweater I wore underneath over my head and carried an empty bottle in a brown paper bag.

I found two uniformed officers walking the beat

nearby the alley and flashed my badge. I told them I was working a special assignment and needed all uniformed officers out of the immediate vicinity. I needed the gang members and the killer to feel comfortable about walking the alley tonight.

The officers agreed and said they wouldn't be too far away. I entered the foul-smelling, shadow-haunted alley, and took a seat on the ground, resting my back onto a graffitied wall. I pretended to take sips from my empty bottle and just sat there, waiting.

After nearly two hours, my patience was rewarded, as three men entered from the far end of the alley. They spotted me and drew guns, then cautiously approached. I immediately regretted my poorly thought-out decision. Initially, my plan was to blend into the environment and appear as just another homeless man, to see what might unfold. But I suddenly realized the members of the Jungle Cat gang would not know who they were after, so they would target anyone found within this alley.

I cursed inwardly and my hand crept inside my coat to grip the handle of my revolver. I knew I was fast, just not sure if I was fast enough to take out three armed men before one of them got to me.

"You are one stupid junkie, you know that?" one of the three men shouted, as they cut the distance in half.

My suspicions were correct; they thought I was the killer. Even if I could convince them otherwise, they would kill me anyways. I made an amateur mistake in coming here alone.

"Stand up, junkie. Now!" another commanded, pointing his pistol at me.

"We ain't gonna make the mistake of getting close

enough for you to stab us with those needles. So you just stand against that wall there so we can fill ya full of lead," the biggest of the three said.

"You are making a big mistake," I said, and considered flashing my badge, for all the good it might do.

I did stand though, with my one hand still on my gun, quickly weighing my options.

"The mistake is all yours, coming back to this same alley," the biggest one continued. "Did you just think you were gonna keep killing our members and get away with it?"

"Let's torture him first," suggested one of the men with a red mohawk. "Killing him quickly is too good for him."

"You might be right," the biggest agreed, and he appeared to be the leader, of these three anyway. "Alright junkie, take that coat off, and slowly. No funny business or I will shoot you."

I figured the time to act was now at hand. I was about to drop my coat when a most curious sight caught my attention. The shadows behind the three gang members began to swirl about until they took on the shape of a man. I blinked several times thinking it was some trick of the eyes but there it stood. It was the form of a thin man but a man none-the-less.

Noticing the curious expression I wore upon my face, the three men hazarded a glance behind them. The man with the red mohawk didn't even bother to speak first and fired two shots into the shadowy form. It didn't surprise me that the bullets passed right through to strike the wall behind.

The shadow then rose up, elongating its body beyond

the size of a normal person, so that it towered over the men. It lifted its dark arms to reveal shadowy-hands, which ended not with black fingers, but with the shapes of needles. Indeed, ten needles sat where ten fingers should have been.

The shadow lunged forward and plunged all ten needle points into the chest of the mohawked gang member. The man fell and howled with a mixture of pain and terror. The creature, for I did not know what else it could be, raised its arms and drove them down again, repeatedly stabbing the man.

The two remaining gang members emptied both their pistols into the horrendous shadow-creature without consequence. Its needles apparently were real enough to cause actual harm, but otherwise, it was just an insubstantial shadow, spawned of the darkness itself.

As the screams of the mohawked man ceased, the shadow turned on the other two men and made living pincushions out of them before my eyes. They punched and kicked to no avail. They were better off attempting an escape, though, I imagine there was nowhere to run at night, when the shadows themselves were pursuing you.

Once all three of the men were lying still on the filthy ground of the alley, I instinctively drew my own weapon. I just witnessed how useless bullets were to this strange creature but force of habit had me pointing my gun at it regardless. I don't mind admitting that my hand trembled.

The thing before me made an odd motion, almost as if it saluted me, then it melted back into the darkness of the alley and vanished from sight. I am not sure how I knew this but I just knew; the shadow of Albert Lockridge had just claimed three more lives.

The alley soon flooded with uniformed officers, after having heard the gunshots and screams from nearby. I was forced to relate that the mysterious killer fled the alley and that it was simply too dark to get a description. What else could I say? That I witnessed the shadows themselves murder these three men? That it was the spirit of Albert Lockridge returned for revenge?

Nearly a half hour later, I finally extracted myself from the alley and was headed back to my car. I noticed Detectives Banks and Green headed my way.

"Kane, you saw the killer?"

"Your first instinct was correct, Banks, just let the Jungle sort itself out. You won't be solving these murders."

THE STEEP PRICE OF MAGIC

As time passed me by, people were becoming less and less interested in an aging magician and escape artist. There was a time when I was a much sought after act; filling some of the best theaters in the Big City. The last several years though, I was reduced to performing at children's birthday parties, where the name, The Great Fazoo, was no longer recognized, nor respected.

Where did it all go wrong? I supposed it might have begun with the arrival of Vlad Wasili, a young and cocky magician who started out by performing on the streets, dazzling crowds in the theater district. He was known for some revolting acts that thrilled and terrified at the same time. He could spend days trapped in various things, such as a block of ice, or a tank of water, in front of fascinated onlookers.

Somehow Vlad turned his street performances into a

successful stage show, and for the last decade, was a permanent fixture at The Four Aces Casino. As a result, he lived in a penthouse suite in one of the city's most affluent neighborhoods.

I could break out of a straitjacket in thirty seconds but that didn't seem to impress people any longer. I would need to appear to chew my own arm off during the escape, showering the front rows with blood, in order get people's attention nowadays. That was Vlad's style, not my own.

Being a magician was all I had known. As a child I had watched a live performance by Gary Ghostly and knew right then that I wanted to do what he did. Gary Ghostly, or the Ghost, as he was more commonly called, was the greatest escape artist of our time. He could seemingly break out of anything, as if he was indeed some ghost.

I studied magic books and learned tricks from the owner of a local magic shop. I started by performing for just my friends and then for schools. People began to pay me to perform and I dropped out of school as a teen to pursue my dream of becoming a career magician and escape artist.

This is the only job I have ever held. For much of my life it paid my bills and afforded me some small luxuries and level of fame. Now, I struggled to pay bills and make the rent for my decrepit, one room apartment, in what would be considered the slums of the city.

Granted, I had turned to alcohol many years back, which led to my steady decline and depleted bank account. I became a recluse, a mere shell of my former, charismatic self. I was unable to perform properly after several drinks, but without them, my hands would tremble, hindering my card tricks which made up the bulk of my act. I was required to find the right level of alcohol, which would cease my shaking hands but not impede the rest of my act.

These were dark times for me and if I didn't find more work soon, I would lose my apartment and be cast out onto the street, perhaps having to live in the Junkie Jungle with the other lost souls of the city.

I cleaned myself up to the best of my ability and spent the next week visiting each of the theaters and casinos in the city, all but begging for another chance to perform. Nobody was interested.

"The Great Fazoo? I thought you died forty years ago? Didn't you die?"

"Sorry, we all are booked old man."

"We don't put on magic shows here anymore, just concerts. People don't care about card tricks anymore."

"What was your name again? A Great Baboon?"

"Sorry, Fazoo, your tricks just don't impress this younger crowd."

It was Saturday night and I sat on the edge of my bed, staring at the exposed brick wall within my room. A storm raged outside and water leaked from several spots, thoroughly soaking my torn and stained carpet. Next door on my right, a husband and wife shouted at one another, and to my left, a baby cried ceaselessly. I lifted the bottle of whiskey that I had purchased earlier that day, using the last of my money, to the very penny, and took a mouthful.

Despite my poor living conditions, and my lack of funds, I found that the one thing that distressed me the most about my life was that I wouldn't be remembered as a great magician. To this day, people still spoke of Gary Ghostly. There was books written about him and even a movie was made. Even Vlad Wasili was featured on the covers of some popular magazines and tabloids. But everywhere I went, I heard the same things over and over. Who are you again? I thought The Great Fazoo was dead? Who cares about The Great Fazoo?

All my life, my one dream was to be considered in the same class as Gary Ghostly. That our names would be spoken in concert together, with the same level of respect. I never really cared about the money, just as long as I made a living. Being remembered was the most important thing to me and in that, I failed miserably.

I gulped another mouthful of the whiskey and relished the way it burned my throat on the way down. I closed my eyes and placed my forehead on my knees, listening to the rhythm of the rain, along with the occasional clap of thunder.

"I would do anything, so that my name would be remembered," I spoke aloud, despairingly. "Anything at all."

"Anything, you say?" a voice from within my room said.

I jumped to my feet and quite nearly dropped my whiskey bottle. I had not heard my door open so I was most surprised to find a man standing next to my window; a well-dressed man in an exquisite black suit and matching tie. Outside, the rain came down in buckets and yet this man's clothes were bone dry. He did not live in the building as I was sure I had never seen his face before.

His black hair was slicked back and shiny, most likely having used more than just a dab of Brylcreem. He had a thin dark moustache and a curious-looking triangular tuft of hair on his chin. His skin was a shade of pale and he had sharp features like protruding cheek bones. There was a calmness about him that I found immediately unnerving. He stood familiarly in my room as if he belonged here. In fact, I got the impression that he would probably feel as though he belonged anywhere he wished.

"Who the hell are you?" I demanded.

"I am just a friend that you haven't yet met."

"How did you get in here? I never heard that door open."

"The storm is loud outside and it appears you were distracted. In any case, that's not too important. That I am here now is the main thing."

"You speak in riddles."

I took another drink and sat back down on the edge of my bed. I felt if this man was a threat, he would have done something by now. Anyways, I had nothing to steal and nothing left to lose.

"You seem…down, my friend. What ails you?"

"What do you care?"

"I care about my friends."

"So, we are friends now? I don't even know your name."

"My friends call me, Dee."

"You have a last name, *friend*?"

"But of course, who doesn't? My last name is Eville."

"Well Mr. Eville, I don't need any friends. I can barely look after my own self."

"Then that is exactly why you need a friend. Friends help each other."

"And you just wander around looking for random people to help? What's your game, Mr. Eville?"

"No game. And yes, I like to help people, to our

mutual benefit of course."

"I am afraid that the help I require is far beyond anyone's ability. I have run out of time to achieve what I desire most. I will die poor, alone, and unremembered."

"Very little is beyond my ability. Name your desire and I will see it come to fruition."

"What business are you in?"

"I am an agent, of sorts. I can make dreams come true."

The strange man placed a cigarette into his mouth. He snapped his fingers and flames erupted from the tips to light the cigarette. Once lit, he blew on his fingers and extinguished the flames.

"You are a magician too?" I wondered.

"I am many things. But foremost, I am your friend, and I wish to help you."

"I have always wanted to be remembered as a great magician and escape artist, much like Gary Ghostly. But I am an old man who cannot find work. The Great Fazoo is no longer relevant. The drink has stolen years of my life and now it is too late."

"It is never too late, my friend. I can see to it that you will always be remembered."

I chuckled. "And just how would you pull that off?"

"I happen to know the secret to performing the greatest escape trick the world has ever seen. Were you to perform this particular escape, they would speak your name for centuries to come."

"Why haven't you done it then?"

"Because being remembered as the greatest escape artist is not my dream, it's yours. But I would be willing to share my knowledge with my new friend. Seeing your dream come true is what I desire."

"What do you get out of this?"

"The satisfaction of helping you."

"And that's it? Nothing else?"

"Well no, I would require something of you, but 'tis a small matter."

"Even with the secret of your great escape trick, I can't get anyone to hire me. Nobody is interested in me."

"Leave that to me. As I said, I am an agent of sorts."

"This isn't a joke is it? You can really help?"

"That all depends on you. How badly do you wish to be remembered? What is that worth to you?"

"It's worth everything to me. It's all I have ever wanted."

"Excellent, then we are in business."

Suddenly, Mr. Eville produced some documents from behind his back and handed them to me. That was quite a trick itself, hiding that amount of paper. I glanced through them to find diagrams of the escape trick he had described to me.

"This is all fine and dandy, Mr.Eville, but this seems impossible to escape from. I cannot imagine how that could be achieved and I am familiar with all the tricks of the trade."

"It can be done and I possess the secret. You will be forever remembered after performing this stunt."

"Tell me the secret."

He then produced another sheet of paper. This time it was just one but it was quite a long sheet with plenty of fine print that my aged eyes had trouble reading.

"What is this?"

"This is our contract. It outlines everything that we

have just discussed. That, as your agent, I will secure you with an appropriate venue and share with you the secret of the escape. The contract also states that I am guaranteeing that you will be forever remembered for this."

"You really are going to make my dream come true?"

"Yes, it's what I do."

"Then please tell me, how can I repay you for this?"

He smiled. "Just sign the contract and everything is written there below. We can go over it all together, in detail."

I supposed it didn't matter much what he wanted as I had nothing really to offer him. Most agents took a percentage of the money earned from the show. I didn't care how much of a percentage he wanted, just as long as I pulled this off and people would remember, The Great Fazoo.

"I don't have a pen."

He had one already in his hand, where one didn't exist a moment before. "Here, use mine. Sign by the X, right next to my name."

D. Eville X ______________________

* * * *

Butterflies danced about in my stomach as I stood on the empty stage and stared out at all the empty seats that would soon be filled to capacity. Mr. Eville was true to his word and managed to strike a deal with the owner of the Red Jester Hotel and Casino. They were the direct rival of The Four Aces, where Vlad performed. The owner was quite reluctant at first but changed his mind when we mentioned he would owe me nothing if he didn't agree at the end of the show that it was the best performance he had ever seen. Even if I bombed, he stood to make a pretty penny by not paying me.

For the next week the casino carried out an aggressive ad campaign; the last performance of The Great Fazoo, and the greatest escape you will ever witness.

There was a buzz in the city and I felt important again; a feeling I had long forgotten. I had shaved, cut my hair, and put on my best suit. I fidgeted with a deck of cards while peeking through a curtain as people began to fill the theater. To my surprise, even a few reporters had shown up.

I opened the show with some card tricks. I used a few oldies and a few that Mr. Eville had shown me. I was met with applause. I moved onto some sleight-of-hand, making flowers appear, as well as three live doves. I reveled in the looks of astonishment throughout the crowd, from the young and the old. I was truly The Great Fazoo again and I loved every minute.

After an hour of performing, the audience was given a fifteen minute intermission before the grand finale. As the last of the seats were full again, a long box, quite similar to a coffin really, was lowered from the ceiling. Every member of the audience was invited up to inspect the box and inspect the stage, to be sure that they could detect nothing out of the ordinary, that there were no hidden doors. Once thoroughly satisfied, they each returned to their seats.

Now, it was time. Everything I had always wanted depended on the outcome of this stunt. If Mr. Eville had spoken true, this would truly amaze everyone present.

Two lovely assistants helped me into a straitjacket and tied it tight. Then they wrapped me in chains, across my chest, further pinning my arms to my body, as well as around my legs. The chains were padlocked in place.

I took one final look out at the audience and smiled; basking in my moment of glory. I then stepped into the box and lay down. My assistants secured the lid of the box in place and wrapped it in thick heavy chains. Cables lifted the box into the air, suspending it a good twenty-feet above the stage, in full view of the entire audience. I knew the question on everyone's mind was, how could anyone ever escape from this?

* * * *

80 Years Later

"Go on, Billy, open up that big one next. It is from your mother and me."

Billy, who had just turned nine, tore at the wrapping paper with wild abandon. His eyes lit up at the sight of the gift. "Wow, thanks! A Great Fazoo Magic Kit!"

"Interesting gift," Adam's father commented. "I didn't think kids nowadays knew who The Great Fazoo was."

"How could they not? He was the greatest escape artist that ever lived," Billy's father replied.

"But how do nine year olds know about him?"

"Billy loves magic. He has three books written about The Great Fazoo. And just recently, someone found some old 8mm footage of his last performance and restored it as best they could. It was uploaded online and everyone has been watching it."

"I can't believe that eighty years later, nobody can explain how he escaped. And to top it off, he just vanished? That box was really empty when they lowered it to the stage?"

"It was empty, alright. My grandfather was there at that show. Gramps said they lowered the box to the stage and when it was opened, all that was inside were the chains and straitjacket he was wrapped in. Nobody has ever solved that mystery and The Great Fazoo was never seen again."

"Creepy."

"You are telling me. They said he never even collected his pay. The casino had always said that his money was still there for him to collect, but nobody had ever shown up."

THE TRAGEDY OF KING FINEAS

Everyone knew the tragic tale of King Fineas the world over. It was taught in schools, mostly through reading the version written by the amazing, and long-dead playwright, Samson Schmitt. Schmitt penned a wide variety of plays but seemed to focus on tragic tales from our storied past. Teachers would have their students read the play aloud and act out portions of it. Stage versions were performed in many different countries, but it was not until recently, that a particular reenactment had been grabbing notable attention.

I was a writer for the renowned magazine, *Millennia.* My focus was on reviews. Movies and plays mostly, and with all the recent buzz about the new play, *The Tragedy of King Fineas*, my magazine had taken notice. Surely there had been many other interpretations of the famous Schmitt play but the latest was quite unique indeed.

King Fineas ruled the kingdom of Hallandar a very long time ago. That region of the world, which was located north and east of the Great Desert, was riddled with volcanoes. Ironically, it was the eruption of Mount Fineas which buried the cities and towns of Hallandar. It wasn't until two years ago, that archaeologists unearthed the remains of the capital. Many buildings were still intact, including a good portion of the castle, where King Fineas dwelt.

Some extremely clever entrepreneurs, decided it would be most interesting, and indeed quite profitable, to stage a rendition of the play, *The Tragedy of King Fineas*, right amidst an excavated portion of the old King's castle. Folk had been flocking to the site to watch the play from every corner of the world. The atmosphere was said to be eerie and yet truly magnificent. An awe-inspiring, three-tiered theater, had been built in what was the original throne room. To just imagine, that you are watching the story of King Fineas, right in the exact location where this tragic tale played out.

Now let me be clear, in case you are unfamiliar with the tale, the eruption of the volcano was not the tragedy spoken of, though admittedly, it was an unfortunate event. No, the tragedy that had so enthralled the playwright, Schmitt, took place months before the region was buried under lava and ash.

The kingdom of Hallandar was under threat from the neighboring kingdom of Wakala, and more specifically, King Rudolf, ruler of Wakala. King Rudolf was a cruel dictator, ever wishing to expand his borders. And after swallowing other smaller kingdoms, King Rudolf soon set his sights on Hallandar.

King Fineas was Rudolf's polar opposite. He was a kind and gentle man, loved and respected by his entire kingdom. Hallandar prospered under his rule and never a negative word was spoken about him. Fineas adored his people and strove to make their lives enjoyable, even down to the poorest of citizens. But the love for his subjects would be his undoing.

King Rudolf amassed his armies along the walled-border of Hallandar, calling for the surrender of King Fineas. The evil invader promised that all of the people of Hallandar would be spared, if only the King would give himself up as a willing prisoner.

It was said that Hallandar possessed an impressive army, with more soldiers than that of Wakala's army. The generals of Hallander were supremely confident that they could repel these invaders; they had no doubts. But King Fineas, ever the peace-loving man, had other plans.

Fineas loathed the idea of going to war and having his loyal subjects die senselessly. Even if they were to win, and he had been advised that they surely would, he knew that they could not win without a cost. People were going to die, regardless of their impending victory, and that thought sickened him to the core.

In a most surprising move, and against the protest of his council, Fineas elected to surrender himself to the enemy, in order to save the lives of everyone in his kingdom. He was willing to sacrifice himself, so that not one person would lose their life in defending Hallandar.

King Fineas could not be dissuaded from his decision. He surrendered himself and King Rudolf's men flooded the kingdom and soon occupied the castle. The soldiers of Hallandar lost the advantage of defense, behind the city's walls, and were ordered to lay down their arms.

In a despicable move, and revealing his true colors, the evil King Rudolf forced the foolish and naïve King Fineas, to sit in the throne room and watch as all the members of his council and generals, were executed in front of him. King Rudolf claimed they could not be trusted and were too dangerous to be kept alive. When they had been dealt with, he moved on to prominent and influential citizens, beheading each one as the horrified King Fineas was made to look on.

One particular woman, adept with black magic, was dragged into the throne room for execution. In one last desperate act, before losing her head, she channeled her anger not towards King Rudolf, but towards King Fineas, blaming him for this slaughter. She cursed Fineas to live with the guilt of what he had done to their kingdom for an eternity. She prayed to dark gods that even death would not provide respite to the man who doomed them all.

Fineas was then shackled in a dungeon, unable to even take his own life, which he wished that he could have done. He was to remain there for the rest of his miserable existence to dwell on his foolishness. Then perhaps the gods took pity on the poor King, and Mount Fineas erupted mere months later, burying Hallandar and all the horrors contained therein.

Some folk escaped the cataclysm to spread the tales of King Fineas and what had taken place before the eruption. Hundreds of years later, those tales would spark the imagination of Samson Schmitt. Then another few hundred years after the play was written, would come the very performance from the excavated castle, where this tragedy unfolded.

As I mentioned earlier, this new play caught the attention of my magazine and I was quickly dispatched to the airport, so that I might fly to this destination and review the play myself. Several years ago, I had reviewed one such version of the play that was performed right here in the theater district of the Big City. While I had thought it was quite good, giving it four out of five stars, I was told that no version performed on the planet compared with this latest. I was quite intrigued.

The flight was long but uneventful. I had lunch in a rather bland café and then caught a few hours nap in the afternoon. As the sun set in what was once the kingdom of Hallandar, I readied myself for a night out. Dressed in formal attire, I made sure to grab my notebook and made the twenty minute walk from the recently erected hotel to the castle-turned-theater.

The walk was something of a treat in and of itself. I strolled through streets that were nearly a thousand years old. Construction crews had done a marvelous job at painstakingly excavating the buried capital of Hallandar. I passed buildings that used to house shops and families alike, so very long ago. Every direction I turned, I found tourists taking photographs of these astounding historical structures.

But all of these sights paled in comparison to the restored castle I soon beheld. It was impossible to tell which part of the castle was the original architecture and which was new. No expense was spared in seeing that the castle looked very much like it did in its glory days.

I joined the lineup of people waiting to enter, listening to excited conversations from those around me. For the most part, people were here for the first time and could barely contain their exhilaration. One fellow, about five people in front of me in the line, boasted that this was his third time attending the play, and was just as excited this time, as he was the first. He claimed that words could not describe the performance as it was unlike anything he had ever seen before. He also attested that the lead man that played King Fineas had to be the greatest actor to ever set foot on a stage.

I fed off the emotions of the crowd and was soon growing impatient as the line was not moving at all. I couldn't wait to get inside and witness this event with my own eyes. It wasn't too long though, before I was rewarded, and people began to enter and take their seats.

After showing my ticket at the front gate, I entered a long corridor which was illuminated with rows of torches along both sides. Between the torches hung exquisite paintings, or stood full suits of armor, all original pieces that had been found within the castle, which really added to the atmosphere.

Regrettably, the majority of the castle was off-limits to the public, as they were still doing restoration work. I should like to return one day to tour the rest. So as it turned out, the corridor led straight to the theater itself.

I must say the theater was magnificent. There were three tiers of seats sloping upwards, seating approximately a thousand people at a time, by my guess. Much like the corridor, original works of art dotted the walls, but the real attention-grabber was below. The stage portion of the theater was the castle's actual throne room, and there, in the middle of the stage, sat the real throne of King Fineas.

My jaw dropped at its undeniable beauty. Upholstered with red velvet and inlaid with solid gold and precious gems, the throne was absolutely priceless.

My skin suddenly prickled at the thought that this was the location of all those horrible executions. King Rudolf sat in that very throne, while Fineas stood nearby, forced to watch the ghastly spectacle unfold.

I hadn't even seen the play yet and I was already thinking that five stars would not be enough. The atmosphere alone was worth the price of admission and the plane ticket to get here. Fortunately for me, *Millennia Magazine*, picked up the tab for everything. And speaking of which, my media-status afforded me a front row seat. I would have preferred to be more in the center, as I had the last seat on the right-hand side, though I still had a decent view of the stage. There wasn't really an unfavorable seat in the house.

I was, however, situated close to the stage door, where the actors would come and go, so I could get a close-up look as they passed by. Not much was known of the actors and they had not granted any media outlets any interviews as of yet. By all accounts their performances were outstanding, which was not bad at all for a group of unknowns.

I sat impatiently for nearly three-quarters of an hour, tapping my leg out of habit, waiting for the play to begin. I realized we were waiting until every seat of the sold-out theater was filled, before beginning. As the last person found their seat, the torches lighting the theater were extinguished, casting us into total darkness. There we sat, in unnerving silence, for several long moments. I found I was holding my breath, afraid to even breathe.

I heard the stage door to my right open, though I could still see nothing; my vision had yet to adjust to the gloom. Then suddenly, a spotlight that hung from the rafters, came to life and illuminated the section of the stage where the throne rested. Folk gasped as there was now a figure seated in the throne, draped in a dark robe. The play had finally begun.

THE TRAGEDY OF KING FINEAS
ACT 1, SCENE 1

KING FINEAS: (Discards robe and leans forward in the throne, chin resting on palm) Welcome all, to my home. I am King Fineas, ruler of Hallandar, and this is my tale. Do not weep for me, or pity me, as my fate was brought on by my own foolishness. My compassion for my people was their ultimate undoing. Sit back and journey with us to a time long lost, and bear witness to a story that I am cursed to relive for an eternity.

(Stage goes dark. Enter council members for a meeting with the King. Lights back on.)

I was in awe of the costumes and makeup. Their skin was painted pale white, and with the use of special spotlights, caused it to take on an eerie glow. By the time we were midway through Act Two, I wholeheartedly agreed with the critics thus far, everyone's performance was superb, especially the King's.

Fineas played the part perfectly, his facial expressions were incredible. Even when acting out the portion of the story before the arrival of King Rudolf and his army, Fineas always wore a face of sadness, never breaking character and foreshadowing the doom that was to come. I really felt for the man and hung on his every word. Whatever this actor was being paid, I felt it would not have been enough.

By the end of Act Three, I found myself on the edge of my seat and nearly falling to the floor. I was forced to adjust myself and attempt to lean back and relax, but so enthralling was the play, I was soon back to the edge of my seat.

GENERAL LUKAS: My King, your armies are assembled and awaiting your orders. Let us go forth and crush these vile invaders and send them back to the holes from whence they came.

KING FINEAS: No, my friend. I have given this much mindful deliberation. The thought of even one of my loyal subjects losing their life, tears my heart asunder. I have decided to surrender myself, as this King Rudolf has requested.

(There is a collective gasp from all those assembled in the throne room)

COUNCILLOR ZIMAS: My Lord, you cannot be serious??

KING FINEAS: I most assuredly am. What kind of King would I be, if I was not willing to do everything within my power to keep my people safe? By surrendering myself, I will be ensuring the safety of everyone in Hallandar.

GENERAL LUKAS: But we can defeat them!

KING FINEAS: My mind is set. I will not sacrifice lives needlessly when I have the power to prevent it.

With the arrival of Act Five, the final Act, I noticed the entire theater was on the edge of their seats. Even the odd child, who had been dragged to the play by their parents, had stopped fidgeting and squirming in their seats, and brought their full attention to the play's finale.

Out walked Olga, shackled and being dragged by an armored soldier. The evil King Rudolf sat in the throne, a smug look worn upon his pale face. Beside him, stood King Fineas, rooted in place with horror, as he was forced to watch a procession of executions. No mere crocodile tears streamed down his ghostly cheeks, as was evident by the anguished expression he wore.

This actor was good. All great actors were able to channel some tragic event from their past, to bring it forth from their memories and relive it in that moment, adding such realism to a scene in which they were required to appear sorrowful and heartbroken. This man had mastered that and convinced the entire audience of the horror he was experiencing.

Hands down, this was the most marvelous play I had ever had the privilege of beholding. Even I was moved to tears as Olga cursed King Fineas and he fell to his knees and wept. Curtains dropped and the stage faded from sight.

The theater went dark again as there was a rumbling sound from overhead. The seats rattled and vibrated, in an interesting added effect, signifying the eruption of the volcano, as we all knew was the real ending to this tragic tale. This continued for about a minute until torches flared back to life, illuminating the theater; the play had ended.

Every man, woman and child, got to their feet and applauded the performance, expressions of adoration and wonder plastered upon their faces. I too, stood in amazement, and actually felt a pang of sorrow that it was over; so thoroughly had I enjoyed myself. I had been so lost in the play that I had forgotten to take any notes, but I did not worry, as I was sure I had plenty to say for my review.

Keeping with my initial thoughts of the atmosphere, I felt five stars was not nearly enough and would not do the play any justice. I found myself suddenly wishing I could speak with the actors and get an exclusive interview, especially with King Fineas. Before I even realized what I was doing, I took advantage of a distracted theater employee, and dashed through the stage door.

I had no idea what the penalty might be if I was to be caught. Permanently banned from the theater? A trespassing fine? I felt it was worth the risk to be the first person to secure an interview with the cast. I could even demand a raise, I was sure of it.

I was descending down a flight of ancient stone stairs, where sparsely placed torches afforded minimal light. There was a deep chill in the air and I was soon shivering. It was quite evident that this stairwell, and the underground room it led me to, was the original architecture of the castle, and not restored in the slightest.

I worried momentarily about the structural integrity, but figured that if it was safe enough for the actors, then I should be fine. The barren room I now stood in possessed only one wooden door. Luck was with me as none of the theater employees were posted down here and the door did not appear locked.

I was beside myself with excitement and my mind was assailed with a flood of questions that I had for the cast. I pulled the heavy door open slightly to peer into the room beyond.

The scene before me froze me in place. My jaw hung somewhere down to my chest and I had stopped breathing altogether. In the chamber I now faced, stood the entire cast of the play. This room no longer contained the special lighting of the theater; in fact there was no source of light at all! And yet, the cast still glowed eerily. Costumes were hung on hooks along one wall and I could see that the actor's skin was still a pale white, and upon closer scrutiny, I found I could see right through them!

"Good heavens!" I gasped involuntarily.

Ghosts! The cast members were all ghosts! The curse of King Fineas was true, and here he still dwelt, to relive his tragic tale for an eternity!

BABYSITTING TIMOTHY

Being a teenaged girl living in the suburbs of the Big City, after school employment opportunities were not many. A few of my friends worked at the local grocery store and another at the pharmacy. While looking after other people's children wasn't always so easy, I elected to take up babysitting. At least then I could sit them by the radio to listen to programs, or send them off to bed, affording me time to study or do homework, which was something my friends could not do at their jobs.

I was the primary sitter for John and Jessica, who were brother and sister, and very well-behaved, along with Alice, who lived next door to me. After spending a few evenings with Lester, whose family lived a block away, I had to politely decline further work. I blamed it on an increased workload from school, but in reality, Lester was too much of a handful. He had endless energy and couldn't sit still for more than five minutes at a time. He also hated to go to bed which made for a constant battle that I was no longer interested in waging.

I felt terrible for his parents, who were finding it difficult to find sitters, as word of Lester spread through the world of sitters. I simply wasn't paid enough for the headaches of looking after Lester; it wasn't worth it.

One Thursday evening, my mother called me over to the phone, which had me quite curious as I had never received a call after eight. It turned out to be Mrs. Harrison from two streets over on Oakley Drive. They were going out Saturday evening and their regular sitter was away camping for the weekend.

I hadn't planned to work on Saturday but I could use the extra money that I wasn't counting on. Her son, Timothy, was eight years old and from what I had heard, was a quiet boy. People said he was a little odd but generally kept to himself and certainly didn't cause any trouble. Odd I could deal with, so I agreed.

Saturday evening came and I packed a bag with a few things to help keep me occupied for the night and walked over to the Harrison's house. I was greeted by Mr. and Mrs. Harrison, who I had never actually met in person before, but were quite pleasant. They lived in a typical, cookie-cutter, two-story house, with a long driveway and a perfectly manicured lawn. They had a spacious backyard with several large trees.

They had left some cookies and cake on the kitchen counter so Timothy and I could have a fun snack later on. Since it was Saturday night, I was told that Timothy could stay up later than usual, eleven at the latest. They said Timothy was shy, and indeed, it wasn't until the Harrison's were about to leave, that they managed to coax their son downstairs to meet me.

Timothy was a small boy, small for even his age. He had short brown hair and eyes to match. Indeed he was shy, half-hiding behind his mother's leg, peeking around at me curiously.

"Now Timothy, I don't look so scary, do I?"

He paused and then slowly shook his head, no.

"That's right, Timothy, she is just a normal young girl and there is nothing to be worried about," his mother said. "Now you behave yourself and don't make any trouble for her. You can have some cake and cookies later, but not too late or you won't sleep. You can stay up until eleven." Then Mrs. Harrison turned to address me. "We should be home by midnight. We are going to a dinner party at the Thomas' and I have left their number on the refrigerator in case you need us. You are welcome to use the radio and the record player. Timothy's favorite radio program is on this evening."

"Don't let the aliens get ya, squirt," Mr. Harrison said, messing up his son's hair.

Mr. and Mrs. Harrison then took their leave and I locked the door behind them. People generally didn't need to lock their doors in this neighborhood but I always did out of habit, when at someone else's house.

"So, Timothy, what would you like to do?"

He leaned against the arm of a sofa, shyly averting his eyes and didn't answer.

"Oh come on now, there is no need to be shy with me. Let's turn on the radio then and listen to some music, shall we?"

Timothy shrugged his shoulders and I took that as close to a 'yes' as I was going to get. I walked over to the large mahogany radio and switched it on. I turned the dial until finding a station that was playing some big band music and stopped there. I plopped myself down onto the sofa to enjoy the music. I motioned for Timothy to join me but he continued to lean against the arm of the sofa, not wishing to get too close to this stranger just yet.

I found most children were shy at first and it wasn't always easy to entice them out of their shell. I did, however, learn that talking about their favorite subjects generally helped.

"Your mother said your favorite radio program is on tonight, which one is that? I wonder because I also have a favorite on Saturday nights."

Timothy looked up and I knew I now had his attention. "Invaders from Space," he softly answered.

"Wow, imagine that, that is also my favorite program," I replied, stretching the truth a little.

I had listened to the program a few times before; I just wasn't as interested in aliens from outer space as I was with the adventures of the orphan, Beatrice, or the explorer, Jungle Johnny. But to help break the ice here, Invaders from Space was my new favorite.

I had not heard any of the recent episodes, but fortunately for me, I recalled a conversation between two of my classmates during a lunch break only a few days ago.

"I wonder what Commander Foxx is going to do tonight? I don't think the other military leaders believe him about the alien threat," I cleverly asked.

Timothy's face brightened and he stood up straight. "Commander Foxx's men believe him. I think they will secretly take some planes and intercept the aliens all by themselves."

"Ooooh, I hadn't thought of that. But will that be enough?"

"Commander Foxx is the best fighter pilot in the whole world!"

I nodded. "Yes, he sure is. I guess no alien ship could stand up to him, eh?"

"Do you think Commander Foxx is real?" Timothy asked.

"Well no. It's just a radio program. Commander Foxx is just an actor doing the voice." Timothy seemed saddened by that so I quickly added, "But sometimes these characters are based on real people. They probably got the idea for Commander Foxx from a real pilot."

"I hope so."

"Why is that?"

"Can I have a cookie now, please?"

"Of course you can. Come on, let's go to the kitchen for a snack before our program starts."

I breathed a sigh of relief as Timothy seemed to have come out of his shell, which made my job much easier. We sat at the kitchen table and each had one homemade chocolate chip cookie, along with a small sliver of carrot cake. We washed it down with a tall glass of milk, then returned to the living room and prepared for the program that was soon to start.

Timothy and I sat on the carpeted floor, directly in front of the radio, and I was pleased that he did not try and sit as far away as possible; he was becoming comfortable around me. He didn't seem very odd to me, just a typical shy boy.

We listened intently to this week's episode of Invaders from Space. Just as Timothy had predicted,

Commander Foxx was unable to sway the minds of his superiors that a threat from outer space was imminent, so secretly gathered his loyal men to his side and took off with borrowed fighter planes. The episode, as was typical of these programs, ended with a cliffhanger; an alien attack was nearly upon us and Commander Foxx and his men were the only ones who knew.

"Aliens aren't really from Mars, like in this program," Timothy finally spoke, once the episode was over.

"Oh no? I thought scientists figured Mars was the most habitable of all the other planets? Where do they come from, then? Jupiter? Saturn?"

"Xaalox-9."

"Xaalox-9?" I chuckled. "And just where is that?"

"It's the third planet from the star, Syrealius."

"Oh it is, is it? How do you know that?"

"Do you wanna see my telescope? It arrived in the mail last week but I don't think it works very well."

"Sure, why don't you show me? Maybe we can find Xaalox-9 with it?"

"I doubt it, it's too far."

Timothy ran upstairs to his bedroom and promptly returned with a small telescope, no larger than a soda bottle. I felt sorry for the boy in that moment. He ordered the telescope from an ad in the back of a funny book, where it claimed you could view the planets with it. In a cruel joke, small stickers of planets were placed on the lens so that you saw planets anywhere you looked. I can only imagine how many budding young astronomers had their hearts broken when this piece of junk arrived in the post.

I tried to hide my amusement. "Well I don't think you need this thing anyways, it sounds like you are very familiar with the planets out there."

"What do you think would happen, if General Zasslar attacked Earth?"

"Who is that?" I had to wonder.

"General Zasslar is the military leader of Xaalox-9. He commands a great fleet of ships."

"Oh he does, does he? Well then, I guess we would need Commander Foxx to save us."

That sad expression returned to his face once more. "I thought you said Commander Foxx wasn't real?"

"Well Foxx might not be real, but I said he is most likely based on a real person."

"I really hope so. Xaalox-9 is a dying planet and the aliens there need a new home to conquer."

Timothy sure did have a fantastic imagination, thanks to programs like Invaders from Space. For the next little while I listened to music as Timothy sat on the floor and drew pictures of flying saucers with his crayons.

It was soon eleven o'clock and I reminded Timothy it was time for bed. He didn't complain at all and gathered his drawings, along with his telescope, and ran up the stairs to his room. The Harrison's should only be another hour at most, so I retrieved a book from my bag and settled in on the sofa to pass the hour reading.

I soon realized I had left the radio on and should turn it off, so as not to keep Timothy awake. I switched it off and returned to the sofa, when I heard something from upstairs. It sounded like someone was talking. I first wondered if maybe Timothy had also turned on a radio upstairs but as I moved to the base of the stairs to listen more closely, I found that it was Timothy's voice I heard.

Perhaps he was playing with his army men, as I knew

that was also something he enjoyed. He really needed to get to bed though; I didn't want the Harrison's to think I was allowing him to stay up too late.

I ascended the stairs and found his room was the first door on the right. It was an easy guess, from the drawings of space ships and green aliens that were taped to the door. From inside I could hear his voice clearly and it sounded like he was having a conversation with someone.

I knocked first and then entered. "Now Timothy, you are supposed to be in bed already, not playing."

Timothy was standing near his window, which was slightly open. He hadn't yet dressed for bed and was holding a tin can to his ear. Attached to the closed end of the can was a string that stretched from the can all the way out the window. I imagined another can at the other end of that string, as I had seen other boys create these devices in an attempt to communicate with each other, usually linked between tree-forts.

"This is much too late to be chatting to your friend next door, your parents wouldn't want you up this late. Now run along and change and brush your teeth before they get home and you get me in trouble."

"Alright," he said, placing the can on the floor and running off to the washroom to brush his teeth.

I approached the window and my eyes followed the string up the side of the house where it was indeed attached to another can which sat on the edge of the roof. The open end of this can was strangely attached to the lid of a garbage can, giving it the appearance of a homemade satellite dish, like those I had seen photos of.

I was a bit surprised, expecting the string would stretch over to a neighbor's window, or perhaps to a tree-fort in the backyard. I was about to close the window when I thought I heard a sound from the can resting on the floor.

Curiously, I picked up the can and placed it to my ear. A voice from inside the can caused me to squeal in fright; I threw it to the floor and ran from the room.

"Commander Timothy? *ZZZZRT.* Commander Timothy, are you *ZZZZRRRT* still there? I hope you are ready for our arrival tomorrow. *ZZZZRRRRRT.* For the *ZZZZRRRT* glory of Xaalox-9, I look forward to testing our army against yours. General Zasslar, out."

THE UNREMEMBERED SOLDIER

My eyes shot open at the sound of a loud explosion and I grabbed my Thompson machine gun which rested across my lap. I tried to orient myself in the darkness of the forest and there was just enough light from the moon for me to realize there was no immediate threat. The shelling was taking place somewhere to the north. It wasn't our concern; not yet anyways.

I looked about and noticed several of the other soldiers sound asleep and completely oblivious to the sounds of the distant battle. A few men snored away. Those are the ones I envied, as I cannot remember the last time I had a decent sleep. The ground was uncomfortable and there was always the constant threat of the enemy creeping up on us in the dark.

We were deep in enemy occupied territory and they knew this terrain well. They also knew we were coming as we had routed several of their companies three days previous. I couldn't tell if the shelling from the north was from us or them but prayed for the well-being of my comrades-in-arms.

I noticed a few other men nearby were as wide awake as I was. At first I thought to strike up conversation but then abandoned the notion; these men had not been so keen to make friends with me. It wasn't that these men were not friendly, quite the opposite in fact, they treated each other like blood, like brothers. I understood they were only being cautious; attempting to minimize the chance for heartache.

I was the newest member of this platoon, having joined up with them only a week ago. These men had seen plenty of action already, and as a result, had seen many good friends die. A bloody battle loomed before us, so I knew the other soldiers did not wish to get close to me before the coming fight, in the event that I did not survive. Then I would just be some random dead solider, a tragedy still, but not a beloved brother. So I understood their coldness and took it in stride.

I am a demolitions expert and was appointed to this platoon for a mission of great importance. There was a bridge about a day's march away from where we were currently camped. It was a key location that was held by the enemy and used to move their tanks and troops across. We needed to hold this side of their territory until more of our reinforcements could arrive. In order to achieve this, we were required to destroy that bridge. Without those damnable enemy tanks, we could most likely hold the land we had thus far taken.

I jumped as another distant explosion echoed

through the trees of the forest. One might think that a demolitions expert would not be so unnerved by the sounds of explosions but I was always unsettled when I was not the cause of it.

This was the closest I had been so far to actual combat and I can admit to feeling frightened by it. I had voluntarily enlisted, for it was the right thing to do, but I was unprepared for the feeling of dread one felt in the field of war. The grief these other men carried around with them was worn in plain view, as plain as their uniforms. I couldn't even begin to imagine the horrors they had seen. But I would be a party to the further horrors they would soon see, of that I had no doubt.

The next morning we were up and moving. We marched single file and spread out, keeping distance between each soldier so that one grenade, or one mine, could not cause several casualties.

I managed to keep pace with the others despite being more heavily laden. Like the others, I carried my gun, along with adequate ammunition and several grenades. On top of the backpack we carried with extra clothes and supplies, I carried two other heavy satchels filled with explosives; the tools of my trade.

Before joining the army, I worked for a large construction company in the Big City. There, I was trained in explosives in order to demolish old buildings to make room for new ones. When the military caught wind of that, I immediately began training with a demolitions unit. I trained for only six months before being given my current mission; to destroy that bridge.

Later that afternoon, my platoon stopped for a rest near the burned ruin of a barn and sent three scouts out to be sure the area was secure. I pulled an apple from my pack and decided I could use a snack to replenish some of my depleted energy.

"How long 'til we reach the bridge, ya think?" I asked one of the other men.

He glared at me and then walked away to join two others. Their voices were hushed but I could hear every word.

"What's his name anyways?"

"Who knows, I don't care to know it."

"Seems like a nice enough guy."

"You wanna know his name, you go ask him then. You really want another name to haunt you when he dies taking that bridge tomorrow?"

"Good point. I don't need to know his name."

I sighed and crunched away at my apple.

An hour or so later, our platoon leader announced the area was safe, or as safe as it could be, given where we were, and that we would camp at this farm for the night. The bridge was not too far away now and we would reach it tomorrow by mid-morning. He wanted us all to get a good rest in preparation for a tough fight.

Sleep did not come to me when the sun finally fled the sky. With the darkness of the night came renewed shelling to the north, and this time, it was it much closer. We were informed that our Delta Company was attempting to soften up the enemies defenses near the bridge before our morning arrival.

The sounds of mortar shells exploding soon mixed again with the snores of the men around me who somehow managed to find deep sleep. I would find no rest here in the ruined remains of the barn, so I picked up all my gear and headed out into the fields of the farm, looking for a quiet place to lie down out of earshot of the slumbering soldiers.

The sounds of their snoring traveled far and I soon found myself at the very edge of a field where the farm met the thick forest. I dropped my bedroll, when a curious sight caught my attention from the corner of my eye. A few feet away, I noticed some sort of mist rising up from the ground.

Cautiously, I approached. I risked pulling out my flashlight and still held my gun at the ready in my other hand. With the aid of my light, I noticed a small fissure in the ground where smoke trickled out. It was definitely a fire that produced this smoke, but from underground? How was that possible?

I leaned in for a closer look when the ground suddenly gave way beneath me. I cannot tell how far I fell exactly but I landed with a crunch and screamed out from the intense pain in my right leg. The shaft was not wide, nor smooth, and the rocky sides tore at my skin during my descent. I must have bled from several wounds but none compared to the pain I felt in my leg; I was sure it was broken.

Luckily for me, my flashlight landed within reach and I grabbed it to assess my situation; it was not good. The surface was too high up and I knew I could never climb back, especially in my current condition. Worse still, nobody knew I had come out this way and would have no idea where to look for me.

I cursed myself for wandering away then inspected my current location. I was now lying in a tunnel that was just tall enough to sit up in. The tunnel branched off into two directions and that curious smoke still emanated from somewhere down the eastern tunnel, to trickle up the shaft and out into the open air above.

I was fortunate, in a sense, that I had only dropped my bedroll when investigating the smoke. When I fell I was still carrying my equipment pack and weapons. I tied a bandana around my nose and mouth, since much of the eastern tunnel was filled with smoke, and began to crawl in search of its source.

I gritted my teeth as every movement I made sent sharp waves of pain throughout my leg. I came to the horrible realization that even if I managed to find my way out of this mess, I would be of no use to my platoon in tomorrow's battle.

The tunnel was certainly not smooth and did not seem to be made for travel, but it did appear to have been dug out by someone for a reason. Some chimney of sorts, I figured. Once I noticed a strange light ahead, I turned off my flashlight and approached more cautiously, trying to make as little sound as possible.

After crawling another twenty feet, I found this tunnel led straight to a strange chamber, and at first, I had to wonder if perhaps the fall rendered me unconscious and I was simply dreaming. My eyes stung and watered from the smoke that billowed up from a fireplace directly below my position. This tunnel looked out over the chamber from near to the ceiling, about twenty-five feet up.

The large chamber was clearly manmade with smoothed-over walls, floor and ceiling. There was electricity in this room and it was illuminated by several lights that hung from the ceiling. The most curious thing was the large machines which dominated the walls of the chamber. They were all sorts of shapes and sizes with strange gauges, buttons, knobs and colorful lights.

Disturbingly, wires from these machines were connected to several long tables which were occupied by men. I then made the shocking realization that these men were all dead. They were soldiers, dressed in the uniforms of both allies and the enemy. What on earth was going on here in this morbid underground bunker?

I decided to crawl back to the other tunnel to see if it led to a similar chamber but found that it was a dead end. My heart sank as there was only one way for me to go; that ghastly laboratory.

I returned to the chamber and was thankful that the fire was nearly out and very little smoke filtered into the tunnel. I was considering how I was going to drop down to the floor when someone suddenly entered the room. I ducked down trying to remain out of sight.

It was an extremely tall man with a bald head. His skin was nearly as pale as the white lab coat that he wore. He moved about the room, turning dials on different machines and flicking switches. The machines hummed to life and he whistled to himself while he went about his work. He was so nonchalant, despite the dead bodies that occupied the room with him.

The man picked up a beaker, which was filled with a glowing green liquid, then poured it into a funnel that protruded from the top of a machine. He pulled a lever and tendrils of electricity ran down the wires from the machine to one of the tables that held a body. Wires and tubes had been inserted into the nearly naked body and it started to twitch as the electric currents ran through it.

My mouth hung open at the gruesome spectacle but

the odd man watched with excitement; his hands clenched with nervousness.

I could not fathom what he was hoping to achieve until a moan shot forth from the dead man's mouth and the body actually sat up. I could barely contain my yelp at the horrific sight. The tall man's face lit up with joy and he danced about the room laughing maniacally.

"I've done it! I've actually done it!" he said with an accent I couldn't quite place.

He walked over to the table to stare at the man that now sat up. The former soldier sat there silently with a blank expression, his eyes a milky white. Strangely, I noticed his chest did not move; the man did not draw breath and so was still very dead. But as the man in the white coat walked around the table, the dead soldier's head followed him. A chill ran down my spine.

"You are the first of my children," he said to the dead soldier, "the first of many. The lifetime I have spent in research has paid off. This war was exactly what I needed to provide me with the specimens to work on. As your two armies continue your senseless fighting, the bodies of the dead will pile high. Soon, very soon, my immortal children will number enough that neither army will be able to stop us and we will be the true victors. I will take over this pathetic world and all will bow down to me."

I wished right then that I was unconscious and dreaming but I was quite sure that I wasn't. This mad scientist had somehow raised that dead soldier to some mockery of his living self; a zombie of sorts. He planned on creating an army of zombies using dead soldiers and I could not imagine the havoc he could wreak with them. How could you kill something that was already dead?

"Come my child, walk with me. We shall return shortly and awaken your brothers."

The zombie somehow understood the words of the man and rose from the table. It shuffled slowly on stiff legs and followed the man that beamed with pride from the chamber.

As the shuffling sound faded and the room fell silent, I knew exactly what I needed to do. I was still in possession of all my explosives and figured my best course of action was to destroy this room. I was not sure how long I had before that man and his "child" returned, so I needed to act fast, or as fast as I could, given my current injury.

I knew once I dropped down from the tunnel there was no going back up, so I decided to first attach explosives to the ceiling while I was still up here and able to reach. I figured it best to collapse the room as well and bury anything that wasn't completely destroyed by the blasts.

Once finished, I dropped my packs and machine gun to the floor below, right next to the fireplace which had now burned itself out. I gave myself a shot of morphine from my med pack, then hang-dropped from the tunnel to the floor.

I still gasped with pain and rolled around for several moments, before regaining some measure of control and suppressed the pain as best I could. I quickly returned to my task at hand, planting explosives connected with a long wire on each of the machines. I could use my remote detonator to blow the room from the safety of the hallway the mad scientist had left from.

Satisfied that I had rigged the room to the best of my

ability, I limped over to the fireplace to retrieve my gun. A voice from behind had me spinning around, my heart racing.

"Where did you come from?" the mad scientist shrieked, the horrifying zombie stood to his left, staring at me with those dead white eyes.

"I know about your plans and I cannot allow you to proceed with them," I answered.

The man looked around the room and only then did he notice the explosives that I had planted. He took note of the detonator I held in my left hand and his eyes went wide with horror.

"You cannot destroy my life's work! Do you even understand the gravity of what I have accomplished here? I have done what no one else has ever achieved. I have brought the dead back to life."

"That thing there," I indicated to the zombie by pointing with my machine gun, "is not alive. That is some mockery of life. That is just a monster."

The man growled. "You are a fool. You know nothing. Get him, my child. Feast upon his flesh."

The former soldier shuffled towards me, its mouth open and moaning, causing my skin to shiver. I unloaded all thirty rounds from my gun, and despite the terror that gripped me, more than half of those bullets found their mark.

Many of the rounds found the zombie's chest and two found his face. I staggered back in shock as the zombie paused only a moment and then continued towards me. No blood flowed from the wounds and the monster showed no ill effects whatsoever.

Behind the zombie, the mad scientist laughed. "Did

you think you could stop my child with your weapon? What good are bullets on the flesh of the dead?"

What good indeed? I thought. My options had just run thin. I threw down my machine gun and quickly drew my sidearm. Instead of aiming for the zombie, I pointed my pistol at the mad scientist but he dove out of sight behind one of his many machines.

In one last futile attempt to stop the monster, I unloaded my pistol into its body but found the result the same. On it came, despite the multitude of wounds. It was intent on feasting, with my flesh on the menu.

I sighed aloud when I realized I had only one choice left to me. I would use the detonator and blow the room as planned. I would destroy the machines and hopefully the monster and scientist too. If the explosions didn't stop the zombie, perhaps the collapsing ceiling would.

My life was about to end in this room and nobody would ever know of the sacrifice I made to save the world from this man and his monsters. Nobody would hail me as a hero and nobody would remember my name.

KABOOM!!

TOMBS OF THE FALSE

I will never forget, it was in the morning of April 1st, when I received the phone call, and at first, I had to wonder if it was merely an April Fool's prank played by one of my chums. The call had been indeed legit, but now looking back, I almost wished that it had been only a joke.

At the time, I had been quite ecstatic to have been chosen to lead an expedition into some newly unearthed tombs located within the Great Desert. The entrances lay buried deep beneath the sands for god knows how long. By all accounts, the architecture and symbols found on the sealed doors were completely alien and unique, when compared to anything that had been previously discovered on Earth. To say that I was excited to visit this site was an understatement.

It seemed that the dedication to my studies had finally paid off. I had graduated from the most prestigious university in the Big City and prided myself on the knowledge I possessed of ancient civilizations and languages. Naturally, I was the perfect choice.

My only distress at that time was that I could not choose my own team. I was appointed a partner by my superiors, a shifty and shady individual, of whose background and education I knew nothing about. In fact, everyone I consulted with had no idea of his past either.

The skeletally thin, mustached man, claimed to be an experienced archaeologist, though through the use of subtle querying, I found his knowledge to be quite lacking. Though I certainly had my doubts about this dubious character, it was not my place to say anything further and question my superiors.

After months of planning, Sebastian and I touched down in a makeshift airstrip that lay just outside the southern tip of the Great Desert. It was such a relief to land without incident as it was only recently that a plane crashed in the desert, killing all on board except for one woman who had miraculously survived.

A camp had been erected where locals who would serve as our guides through the desert awaited our arrival. I remember well that stifling heat as I exited the plane. The Great Desert was always hot, but it was now July and the heat was near unbearable for a city-man like myself. If Sebastian found it distressing, he never complained about it. It seemed that his eagerness to get to these tombs eclipsed his feelings of discomfort.

We were both anxious to begin our journey, and after a quick bite to eat, we gathered our hired help and set off into that desolate wasteland. The tombs had been discovered about a day's walk from the encampment. So we pitched tents when night fell and then resumed our dreadful march as that unforgiving sun beat down upon our heads once again.

There came a point when even my excitement did little to lift my spirits; the oppressive heat had thoroughly sapped my endurance. Sebastian spoke little and of that I did not mind. I had still not taken to my traveling companion and the less we said to each other the better.

Right at the point when I was about to plead to our guides to take a momentary pause, we spotted the tips of white tents peeking over the top of a distant sand dune. I was about to chalk it up as a mirage, a trick of my delusional, sunbaked mind, when our guides began to talk excitedly amongst each other in their own language and urged us to pick up our pace.

Not long after, we arrived at the appropriate spot. A large section of earth had been excavated, leaving a deep pit which was accessible by ladders only. The sun was nearing its time to set but there was still enough light for us to make out two strange stone doors positioned near the floor of the pit.

My excitement and energy soon returned and Sebastian and I were not willing to wait for the arrival of morning. We found ourselves descending the ladders with lanterns in our hands.

Through my studies in university, I was quite familiar with all known languages and symbols that had so far been discovered, but the hieroglyphs that had been carved into these doors were completely foreign to me. My heart skipped a beat as I realized we had truly found something completely new to the world.

The Great Desert had been home to a marvelous, ancient civilization, that had built the famous pyramids.

They had used hieroglyphs that were somewhat similar to what I was now beholding, though these still appeared slightly alien to those others.

"Let us open these doors and explore, shall we?" Sebastian suggested.

"What of the rest of our team? Perhaps we should wait?"

We had arrived two days before the remaining members of our team who would be charged with the task of cataloguing and recording everything that could be found within the tombs.

"You really wish to wait two days now that we are here standing before these very doors?"

"Well…I,"

"We won't disturb anything or remove anything. Let's just peek inside, the suspense is killing me."

I had to admit the temptation weighed heavily on me as well and Sebastian's suggestion seemed sound; we would just peek around and not disturb anything. I nodded in agreement and we began the task of inspecting the doors more thoroughly to determine how they could be opened.

They were thick stone slabs and would have weighed a ton. Where these stones came from and how they were brought here was another mystery entirely, much like the construction of the great pyramids.

We required more lanterns to continue our work as the sun was now fully disappeared and the desert was engulfed with darkness. After the better part of two hours, our efforts were finally rewarded, and by sheer luck, I might add. I noticed something out of the ordinary with a hieroglyph which depicted a door. As I ran my finger over it, I noticed a faint rectangular border around it. Curious, I pressed the symbol, and to my surprise, it receded back into the door. It was a button of sorts and soon the entire door groaned as it shifted back into the earth.

The walls of the pit we stood in shook and we were soon showered with sand. I feared we might be buried in a terrible avalanche when it suddenly stopped. I shook my head, attempting to remove the bulk of the sand from my hair, then stood rooted in place, as I realized the door had fully opened and a dark passageway now greeted us.

Sebastian and I looked to each other in wonder, and without any need for further conversation, we each picked up a lantern and proceeded inside, albeit with the utmost caution.

I took the lead, but not without a healthy level of nervousness, as I was well aware that some tombs were booby-trapped. Needless to say, the going was slow while I inspected the floors and walls to the best of my ability, each step of the way.

Fortunately for us, the ceiling of the black passage stood six feet tall, and since each of us were a few inches shorter than that, we had little trouble navigating the tunnel. The air was cool and dry but there was a smell. I couldn't quite find the words to describe it but we could almost taste it. It was faint, not overpowering, though it was clearly present.

The tunnel continued without turning and stretched on beyond our limited vision by lantern-light. As we traveled at a snail's pace, I glanced to my pocket watch and found that it had nearly been an hour. The walls of the passage were quite smooth and featureless. We found no further markings or symbols as we went.

I should have been thoroughly exhausted after trekking through the hot desert the entire day, but I felt none of that in the tunnel as my excitement and curiosity had effectively chased away any feelings of weariness.

I was beginning to worry that this tunnel would stretch on without end, when at the very limits of our vision, we noticed the passage opened up into a dark chamber. We paused, and again, Sebastian and I looked wordlessly to each other. We nodded and then continued.

We descended four stone steps, and upon entering the chamber, I turned left and Sebastian turned right. We were attempting to getter a better feel for the size of what turned out to be an enormous room.

I should first mention the immediate sense of horror I felt after discovering the ghastly truth of the floor that we tread upon. It felt uneven and I quite nearly tripped before I crouched low for a closer inspection. I gasped out loud but it did not seem to startle Sebastian, as he had already made the same discovery as I. The entire floor, for as far as we could see, was made up of bones. Initially I had wondered what type of animal they had belonged to, until a grim sight just about stopped my heart from beating. I spotted a skull, a *human* skull. And not just one as I soon learned, but hundreds, if not thousands.

This was not simply the tomb of some long-dead king or queen; it appeared that it was a mass grave of some sort, unlike anything previously found in this region. I must say it was quite uncomfortable, walking about and feeling bones crunch underfoot, but there was no way around it.

This also explained the indescribable smell I had noticed upon our entry. I had not put the pieces together earlier but it was in fact the undeniable smell of death. Still though, even in this chamber of bones, the smell was not overpowering, but it did indeed linger, and was detected on my tongue along with my nostrils.

Praising my foresight, I attempted to wash the taste from my mouth using the water bottle I had brought with me. It helped, somewhat.

"Where is the treasure? All I see is bones?" Sebastian wondered aloud, untroubled by the mass grave.

I looked around as we had yet to determine the actual dimensions of this tomb and gasped a second time when I observed a curious sight in the gloom ahead.

"Look, what is that?" I pointed in the appropriate direction.

Something glowed faintly, roughly thirty feet away from the edge of our light source. It was an eerie, pale white, and was just far enough away that we could not make out any of the details.

"Perhaps there is a shaft nearby leading to the surface," Sebastian suggested.

I scoffed at the notion. "It is night time. There would be no light coming from the world outside and it could not be reflecting off our lanterns."

My curiosity for this new object momentarily made me forget about the grisly scene underneath us. The two of us crept forward for a better look. We soon ascertained that the object in question was an ivory pedestal, standing just over waist-height. It appeared to be carved out of stone and bore no other features, save for two odd imprints of hands, found on the smooth surface of the circular top. The imprints were just large enough that most any human could have placed their hands comfortably within them.

The pedestal glowed slightly, but as to its source, I could not even begin to speculate.

"What do you suppose is the purpose of this?" Sebastian inquired.

"I cannot even hazard a guess. I have never seen anything quite like it before."

"Where is that humming sound coming from?"

I cocked my head and listened intently, and then I heard it as well. It emanated from the pedestal. There was a very low humming sound, almost electrical in nature, as if the pedestal had been plugged into an energy source, which of course was sheer lunacy.

"It originates from the pedestal," I told my partner. "A river running underneath us, causing the vibrations? I have no other explanation."

We left the strange pedestal for the time being and once again spread out with the goal of mapping this particular chamber. We found that it was indeed massive and circular in design. The glowing pedestal was situated directly in the center and the entire floor of the macabre room was covered with human remains. I could not even guess at the number of people that were buried in here.

The chamber possessed a high, domed ceiling, and had no other exits except for the one from which we had entered. There were however, many more hieroglyphs etched into the walls, similar to those we found on the doors. If we had been smart; we would have left right then, and never returned.

I pointed out one particular group of hieroglyphs which depicted a person placing their hands into the pedestal's imprints. Sebastian wondered if one of us should try and do just that but I heartily disagreed. I suggested more study needed to be done to learn the purpose of the strange object.

Much later, as I stared ceaselessly at the alien symbols attempting to discern their meaning, I noticed that my partner had become oddly silent. I glanced around to find him standing directly in front of the pedestal. Before I had time to shout any form of protest, Sebastian placed his hands directly into the carved imprints.

His scream was like nothing I had ever heard in this world. It was not just simply a scream of agony, or sheer fright, but there was something else to it…understanding? It was almost as if placing his hands on the pedestal revealed some horrifying truth that resulted in instant madness.

Sebastian's torture was not to last for too long though, as his body was suddenly engulfed in flames so intense, I had to avert my gaze. When it was safe to look again, all that remained of Sebastian was a pile of bones, the jaw of his skull still open wide in a silent scream of horror.

It took me quite some time to pick myself up off the floor and make my way back to camp. I was shaken to the core by what I beheld. I did not leave my tent for two days until the rest of our team arrived. I sent a message immediately to my superiors that their presence was required as soon as was possible.

By the week's end, our tiny little camp was teeming with activity. Archaeologists, scientists, media and even soldiers to secure the site. Even after I had explained the demise of Sebastian many times over, it took one more fool to place his hands on the pedestal before I was believed. Thankfully, I was not present in the tomb to witness that spectacle a second time.

For six months, myself and a group of the world's leading experts in ancient languages, studied the hieroglyphs from the chamber of bones, as it was aptly named. We had finally begun to have an understanding of their meanings, and if we were correct, the pedestal was a form of punishment for liars. Nobody could say who built it or how it worked, but any false person placing their hands upon it, was instantly punished.

Further investigation into Sebastian's past, revealed that he was not who he had said he was, much as I had thought. He was selected by an unknown source to be one of the first to enter the tomb, with the plan of stealing priceless treasure before anyone else even knew it was missing. This was determined by correspondences that had been found between himself and another equally unscrupulous individual who had not yet been identified. Sebastian had been leading a false life, and thus, had been punished by the pedestal.

Soon, world leaders were beginning to take great interest in the pedestal and were now in discussions for using it in a court, to determine someone's guilt or innocence. A liar would be immediately found out and dealt with, eliminating the need for prisons.

When all others had given up studying the pedestal and hieroglyphs, and moved onto other projects, I continued on, convinced there was more to this than we first thought. There were a few symbols that had so far eluded our understanding.

Two years after the discovery of the tombs, and mere months before the pedestal was to be used for the first time in court, I made a startling discovery. I determined that one of the hieroglyphs depicted a dark god, or devil more like it; a strangely tentacled being. It would appear, by my understanding, that the pedestal was a tool of this devil to gather souls from which it fed on. I wondered now if Sebastian was granted that revelation the moment before he died, which had led to that inhuman scream that still sends shivers down my spine.

I attempted to share my discovery with my superiors and beyond, right up to world leaders, but they were not interested. The mysterious pedestal was going to save them much money and that was all they cared about.

What happened to the souls afterwards was not their concern. I shuddered to think of what we had just unleashed on the world.

MY HAUNTED CHAMBERS

A tribute to Robert W. Chambers and The King in Yellow

My eyes fluttered open, as beams of sunlight penetrated the gaps of my dark curtains to bathe my face with its heaven-sent warmth. It did little to wash away the grogginess that clouded my head and I sat up, momentarily disoriented.

My heart rate decreased as I soon realized I was in my bed, within my own chamber. How many hours had I slept this time? Two? Maybe three at the most?

The ghost visited my room again last night and I had been paralyzed with fear. I do not mind admitting that I cowered underneath the covers, praying that it would leave me alone. It stood at the foot of my bed, as it usually did, watching me. I cannot say how long it stood there, for it felt an eternity to me. Eventually though, when I had hazarded to peek, it was gone, but sleep did not come quickly.

I rose from my bed and stretched the stiffness from my limbs, before opening the curtains fully to light my chamber. It was amazing the effect a little light could have by chasing away the shadows and putting me at ease. Let it be known that I am no coward but what could one do with a ghost, a spirit of the netherworld, except to cower?

Shaking my head, I put thoughts of the ghost aside and gazed out my window. I had a wonderful view from the tenth floor of the keep's tower. Sparkling with the light of the sun was the waters of Lake Hali. Giant and dangerous birds-of-prey floated serenely on the momentarily calm surface of the lake, heads scanning ceaselessly for their next meal.

Directly below my window sat rows upon rows of armored chariots, awaiting the call to defend the keep from unwelcome adversaries. All seemed in order with the world outside, it continued on with little concern about the events within the keep. Those vicious birds cared little for ghosts roaming the halls; they were blissfully ignorant of such horrors.

My stomach grumbled and reminded me that I had not eaten much as of late. I turned my attention to my chamber door and noticed the maid had left my morning meal on the floor as she had been instructed. Due to recent events, my door was locked at all times, and until I was sure it was safe to do so, I never left my room. Only Cassilda possessed a key to get in and she only used it when dropping off my meals. She never stayed and we never spoke.

I picked up the tray of food to inspect what I had been left. Scrambled eggs again, it seemed, along with some overly cooked toast with a raspberry jam.

As was my routine, I sat on a stool next to my lazy dog, and fed him bits of my breakfast to ensure that it was not poisoned. He was an obedient dog and never barked or made any noise, keeping a silent watch over my chamber. He remained silent all through the night as well, which led me to believe that the ghost was invisible to his canine eyes. I felt bad about feeding him some of my food first, putting him at risk, but it was a necessary evil as I had many enemies.

The tyrannical lord over these lands was now dead by my hand, but I am positive that he has loyal followers that wish me ill. They hide amongst common folk, blending in and scheming away. But I am smarter than they are, I remain one step ahead.

After assassinating the cruel lord, I named myself the new ruler and took over residence of the tenth floor of this tower. For my own safety, I immediately locked myself within, fearing retaliation. The lord was known for his cruelty, banishing many folk from the realm, and he personally made rounds, violently demanding taxes from people. I had seen enough.

He was not so tough and not so brave, as he pleaded for his pathetic life. It did nothing to help him and I joyfully drove that knife into his black heart. I had liberated the people of this realm and put an end to his tyranny. As things settle down, I will prove to the people that I can be a just and good ruler. They will accept me and everyone will live happier for it.

The dog appeared to be his usual self, so I was satisfied the meal was safe and ate the rest and quieted my angry stomach. I washed it all down with some warm water, then remembered that I had a meeting with two of my advisors.

I found the two men already seated at the council table, as Cassilda had been instructed to allow them, and only them, into my chambers. I promptly took a seat and rested my elbows upon the table, linking my fingers together.

The heavy man to my right had reddish-brown hair, with a streak of white running through the center. His cheeks were always puffy and had the appearance of a chipmunk, which had filled his mouth to capacity in order to bring food home to store for a long winter.

The man to my left, I had to be wary about. There was something unsettling about him; he appeared almost reptilian, in a way. He had a cold silent demeanor, with a longish nose and pointed teeth, resembling fangs. He had yet to provide me with reason for alarm but I felt I needed to exercise caution within his presence.

"Gentlemen, thank you for coming," I said. "Last night, I was visited again by the ghost. I know not why it chooses to haunt me. Whether it's the spirit of that vile lord, or some long forgotten tenant of this ancient keep, I cannot say."

Both men remained silent as they usually did at the mention of the ghost. I was not sure if it was purely out of fright, or if they simply thought me mad and imagining the whole ordeal. I decided to change the topic and put them both at ease.

"Moving forward, I would like to lower taxes for the people of this realm, undoing the misery imposed by the last lord. I want the people to like me, to love me even. Perhaps a parade is in order, when I feel the threat against me to be over and I can venture forth among the people."

My two advisors offered nothing of value this day and I dismissed them, growing irritated by their silence. I spent the rest of the afternoon sitting alone by my window, hypnotized by the rolling waters of Lake Hali.

Minutes turned into hours and day became night. Before I even realized it, the moon was high in the sky. I trembled slightly at the darkness that now engulfed my chambers, knowing the ghost would soon arrive. I dove into my bed and drew the covers to my chin, my eyes darting around frantically, attempting to make out shapes in the shadows.

In a corner, my dog slept, sensing nothing amiss within the room. But I knew different. My chambers were haunted and I could not have been imagining it. The dread I felt was very real and I did not believe that my eyes were deceiving me. The ghost must have wanted something, but what? Why visit me? Did these chambers once belong to it, and each night it returned, only to find someone else sleeping in its bed? Or was it indeed the cruel lord who I had murdered, come back to make my life miserable in revenge for the deed I had done?

Whatever the reasons, I needed it to stop, somehow. I could not continue on living this way; fearful of the night and not getting my much needed sleep. It was taking its toll on my body and my health. Eventually I would be driven mad; of this I had no doubt.

Clouds passed in front of the moon, sending forth more shadows into my chamber. My imagination created horrible shapes, posing in the darkness. They leered at me, mocked me, fueled by my fear.

Then I heard it. At first a distant shuffling sound, the

source of which was out of sight. A shape formed in the darkness and grew larger as it approached the foot of my bed. I pulled the covers over my face and froze, fearful to even draw breath. Silly I know, to think that lying completely still would somehow make me invisible to the ghostly presence in the room.

Drawing some measure of courage, I decided to peek, nearly crying out with fright, as the ghost once again loomed over my bed, staring down at me with those empty black pits for eyes.

Like the ghosts from children's tales, it was dressed in a long white sheet. A break in the clouds allowed enough moonlight to trickle through my window, causing an eerie glow to the already frightening spirit.

"What do you want of me?" I said, finally finding my voice. "Leave me alone! I have done nothing to you!"

The ghost waved its arms in the air and it suddenly seemed to me that it was attempting to communicate, though I could not understand it.

"Go away!" I shouted. "Leave me be! I beg you!"

To my horror, the ghost moved around the side of my bed, coming closer. Frantic, I kicked my legs out, trying to keep it away from me. It reached for me with a ghostly hand and I recoiled, feeling a stinging sensation on my right arm. I cried out without even realizing that I had done so. My vision grew blurry and then I knew no more.

I bolted upright in my bed, my body covered in a cold sweat. My heart raced and I soon realized that night had turned into day. Midday too, by the position of the sun outside my window. I slept the night through and the morning it seemed, as well. It was not a restful sleep though; I had had a terrible dream.

I got out of bed in search of some water as my mouth felt horribly dry and my head felt incredibly cloudy. Thankfully, Cassilda had left a fresh pitcher of water for me, along with my breakfast that had long ago turned cold.

Feeling a little refreshed, I sat on the edge of my bed, trying to recall the night's events. I remembered the ghost had visited again. I remembered shouting at it before it touched my arm. Its touch stung me, and then I must have passed out, for I don't recall anything after that, aside from my disturbing dream.

I shuddered as I thought of that dream. The cruel lord had sought me out and found me, standing alone by the shores of Lake Hali. I just knew it was the lord, even though his face was hidden behind a pallid mask. He was draped in a tattered yellow robe and was laughing at me. A most sinister, skin-shivering laugh. As he approached, I awoke, though that laugh still haunts me, even knowing it was only a dream.

Thoughts of the ghost soon chased away my musings over the dream and my focus was back to the nightly problem that I was having. The ghost had touched me, actually touched me, and I felt it! I was beginning to wonder if maybe this spirit was more solid than I would have first believed. Tonight, I figured, I would attempt to put that theory to the test. Provided that fear did not get the better of me again. And of course, before it could touch me. Its touch had caused me to black out, fall asleep. I would need to be quicker this time to surprise it.

I spent the rest of the afternoon and most of the evening staring out my window in silent contemplation. I did not wish to speak with my advisors and I had even passed on eating, as I possessed no appetite this day. At some point, Cassilda had refilled my pitcher of water, though, I do not recall her coming and going. I appreciated that as my mouth had been extremely dry since awakening.

I watched the moon slowly ascend in the night sky before deciding it was time. I picked up my dagger, which I seemed to have left on my meal tray, next to a stale piece of bread, and then slid into bed, pulling the covers to my chin.

Try as I might, and I did indeed try, I could not prevent my heart from racing. I was awash with nervousness, as though I had bathed in the stuff, were it real and tangible. My skin had probably turned a shade of pale that matched even the ghost, while I lay there waiting.

I could not be sure if it was mere minutes, or whether it was hours, but the ghost predictably arrived. A faint shadow in the darkness at first, then enlarging into the ghostly specter I had come to recognize.

Involuntarily, I stopped breathing, staring into those black pits for eyes; frozen in fear I was. Again I got the feeling that it was trying to say something to me and communicate in some unholy manner.

When I did not respond, as I had done the previous night, it moved around the side of the bed, gliding towards me. Under the covers my right hand gripped the handle of the dagger, knuckles turning white as my hand trembled with terror. It loomed over me, looking me in the face. My god those eyes! They were empty voids, like I was staring into oblivion!

I could take it no longer. I steeled my courage and lunged forward, driving my dagger blade towards the chest of the ghost. And…nothing. I had accomplished nothing. I was such a fool to believe that cold steel could actually harm some spirit of the netherworld. It continued to look at me, completely unconcerned about the weapon that I held.

Like the night before, it reached for me and my arm instantly stung. Again I recoiled and my vision became blurry. I dizzily collapsed to my bed and my room, the bits of it that I could make out in the darkness, began to spin.

I closed my eyes and drifted off to sleep. And there in my dreams awaited the evil lord in the pallid mask, laughing at me once more.

* * * *

Dr. Vassef left the room, locking the door behind him, and placed his syringe back onto his cart. Before proceeding to the next room, he straightened his white smock and walked over to a phone that was mounted on the wall. He dialed a familiar number, then waited.

"Hey, were you asleep yet?" he asked.

(pause)

"Ok, good. You won't believe what this patient just did."

(pause)

"He just threatened me with a banana of all things. Can you believe that? A banana!"

(pause)

"Yeah he was holding it like a knife," he chuckled.

(pause)

"I know, I know, I am always careful. He is actually a small man, kinda frail. He was an artist, I believe, a painter from Paris. He is the one I told you about, he murdered his landlord."

(pause)

"No, nobody still knows why. His apartment was a disgusting mess when the police went in to arrest him. Weird paintings all in yellow paint were all over the place."

(pause)

"He has had some family drop by and leave a few gifts. Just some stuffed animals. He tries to feed food to the stuffed dog and he has a chipmunk and a crocodile sitting at a table. He talks to those ones sometimes about his plans to rule some place called Carcosa."

(pause)

"Really he just spends most of his day sitting by his window, staring out at the duck pond and the parking lot."

(pause)

"Oh yeah, one curious thing they did find in his apartment was an old book, ancient in fact. Could have been written hundreds of years ago, with no credited author. It was actually a play, oddly enough, titled, *The King in Yellow*."

(pause)

"No, I never heard of it before either. The police turned the book over to Dr. Tannis, he was going to look through it for any possible clues. Strange thing is, nobody has seen or heard from him now in three days. His family has filed a missing person's report."

(pause)

"Crazy, I know!"

(pause)

"Hey I saw that book on Tannis' desk still when I started my shift tonight. I should bring it home and we can both take a look at it. Seems creepy, you'll love it."

(pause)

"Ok, you get to sleep now. Leave the chain off the door for me in the morning."

(pause)

"Love you too."

(pause)

"Yeah, yeah, don't worry, I won't forget the book."

(pause)

"Bye."

DINNER WITH ARTHUR VANDERFROST

For several years, it was my life's goal to receive a dinner invitation from the wealthy and influential, Arthur Vanderfrost. It was a gloomy Tuesday afternoon when a messenger found me having lunch alone and handed me that most glorious envelope, sealed with the unmistakable wax seal, of Mr. Vanderfrost. The symbol consisted of a scale, flanked by a crow to the left side and a downwards pointing dagger to the right; the Vanderfrost family insignia.

Everyone in Ravensbridge, along with the surrounding regions, knew that symbol well. Arthur Vanderfrost was the most powerful man in the city and was even rumored to be pulling the strings of Mayor Ableton. He came from a large family but was the last remaining member; never having married and never had any children.

He looked quite healthy and vibrant for a man rumored to be somewhere in his seventies. He was tall, standing a few inches over the six-foot mark, with a lean body. His hair, and he still had all of it, was of the purest white, along with his neatly-cropped thin beard. He had penetrating blue eyes with a deep, very recognizable and commanding, base voice.

Mr. Vanderfrost dressed in the finest clothes; the best that money could buy. He never left his colossal home without his trademark blue overcoat and black top hat. The man could walk perfectly fine but always carried a cane that was capped with the solid gold head of a cat, with genuine rubies for eyes. He was very fond of cats and the snobbish animals roamed all over his property and were said to live inside his home as well.

His fortunes were vast and it was believed he had amassed an endless store of coins. Indeed he no longer needed to work but it seemed that the more money one had, the more money one wanted. He continued to trade and import goods into the city with no sign of slowing in his advanced years.

Once a year, Mr. Vanderfrost hosted a grand dinner party within his home, inviting only the city's wealthiest, along with those he did business with. It was quite an honor for someone to receive an invite and made that someone the envy of all their peers, who did not. It was the only chance that most people had of ever getting that close to the man and spend an evening with him.

My hands trembled as I held that invitation; my goal having now become reality. I didn't even bother to finish my lunch. I dropped a handful of coins onto the table; much more than was actually required. I didn't care, though; I needed to rush home as I had much to do before the party which was to be held in two days' time.

I bought a new suit; something more worthy of being in the company of the city's highest class, along with a new hat. I spared no expense, even when considering that I would most likely only wear these on that one evening. I felt it was well worth the money.

The next two days passed in a blur and my excitement had reached a fever pitch. I was up at the crack of dawn and spent much of the day pacing back and forth, awaiting the setting of the sun. It seemed that Mr. Vanderfrost was interested in my proposal to import an exotic red wine from the Far East. I had learned that he was quite enamored with red wine and was rarely seen without a glass of it at his parties.

My research had paid off and my letter must have grabbed his attention. Whether he wished to actually speak business with me tonight or not, I could not tell, though I did not care; attending the party was all I had really wanted.

At the appointed time, I took a deep breath, slung a satchel over my shoulder, and left my home to enter the hired carriage that had just arrived to pick me up. Despite the speed in which the last two days had vanished, my carriage ride seemed to last an eternity. In reality, it was only a mere twenty-five minutes to arrive at the gates of Vanderfrost Manor, but to me, the horses felt as though they were moving at a snail's pace. I couldn't get there fast enough.

I could barely contain my rising impatience as I was forced to wait in a long line of carriages, each pulling up to the front gates in turn to drop off their privileged occupants.

I tipped the driver upon my eventual exit from the carriage and stood with awe in front of the open, wrought iron gates. There was a steady flow of magnificently dressed men and women passing me by to enter the majestic manor grounds. An elderly man, obviously a member of the house staff, checked invitations as people passed.

Here I was, about to step onto the property of Arthur Vanderfrost, after spending so many years looking for my way in. This was the one and only night these gates stood open to welcome those who were not normally granted access at any other time. Many were the tales of those who attempted to gain uninvited entry to the manor, no doubt for nefarious purposes, and were never seen again. Those who thought to relieve Mr. Vanderfrost from some of his considerable wealth seemed to shorten their life span quite significantly.

I had most certainly chosen the right course in securing a proper invitation, signed by Mr. Vanderfrost himself, no less. While the exquisite wine which I had used to attain his attention did not actually exist, my enthusiasm for meeting the great man was very real.

I limped into the manor grounds using my own cane for support. My cane was custom-made and intricately carved with eastern symbols. It had been in my family for centuries and passed down when the previous owner no longer had any use for it. I only brought it out for special occasions and tonight was most definitely one of those special occasions.

There was nothing at all wrong with my right leg but the limp helped add credence to my story that the journey east to obtain this rare wine had been fraught with many dangers. Some embellishment to my false tale only gave it more life.

The manor grounds were breathtakingly beautiful. The grass was impeccably manicured and bushes and hedges were meticulously trimmed into all kinds of fascinating shapes. A large stone fountain dominated the center of the front lawn and was known to be a favored gathering spot for all sorts of birds, who were currently absent from the fountain, due to the late hour and the unusual amount of guests milling about.

Statues also carved from the same smooth stone as the fountain populated the grounds as well. They depicted all kinds of mythical creatures and were made with such fabulous detail. My favorites, thus far, being the statue of the Sphinx, as well as one of a Hydra, a five-headed dragon.

The sun had retreated to the west and brilliant, ornate lanterns, provided the illumination needed to navigate your way around the manor grounds in order to admire its beauty. My mouth hung open as I perused the gardens, spotting several species of plants and rare flowers that I had never seen before in my life. That was quite a thing, considering the many remote places I had traveled to around the world. It was evident that Mr. Vanderfrost was a connoisseur of many fine things.

After marveling at the many wonderful sights displayed outside the home, I felt it was time to enter the immense manor itself and behold the treasures that must be contained within.

I followed a procession of guests through the impressive double-doored main entrance to stand in the spacious front foyer. My eyes were immediately drawn to the incredible chandelier that hung from the ceiling which consisted of at least one hundred candles. A middle-aged woman in a violet gown to my right was as equally impressed.

"My goodness, Herbert, have you ever seen anything as beautiful?" she asked of the man beside her.

"Aside from you, my dear, no I have not," he correctly answered.

I moved further into the home, inspecting various paintings that decorated the walls. There was family portraits as well as stunning scenery; all painted with astonishing artistry. I imagined that some you could not have even put a price on.

Similar to outside, extraordinary statues and sculptures could also be found displayed in the foyer and hallways branching off. A wondrous staircase led upwards to the second floor of the house but was roped off, indicating that it was off-limits to the dinner guests. I was hoping to see more of the enormous house but it appeared that we were contained to the main floor, which was still quite a large area indeed.

I stepped into a library where I noticed other guests mingling and sipping drinks served by the house staff. A pretty woman in the black and white garb of the staff approached me carrying a tray of drinks, red wine of course, and bid me to take a glass. I graciously accepted the offer and carefully lifted a frosted glass of superb quality.

I took a sip and did my best to hide my grimace. Despite playing the part of someone who imported exotic wines, I had no real love for the drink. For show, I continued to sip and pretended to enjoy it while disguising my distaste.

"Quite the collection of books, wouldn't you agree?" a voice directly behind me asked.

I turned to face a large man dressed in a costly black outfit. Hints of grey were visible in his dark hair and long beard. He wore a monocle in his right eye. In his left hand was also a glass of red wine, which he sipped with much pleasure.

"Why yes indeed, his collection is vast," I replied. "Most impressive. Must have taken the family a century to amass so many."

"Mr. Vanderfrost is quite taken with reading. A wealth of knowledge, he is. He is a scholar of ancient history but I have yet to find a topic that he is not familiar with."

I nodded and took another sip, forcing an expression of enjoyment.

"I don't believe I have seen you around before, good sir," the man commented. "I am Donovan Brouwer and I manage the bank here in Ravensbridge."

"A pleasure," I nodded. "I am Edgar de Jaager. I import rare and exotic wines. I have managed to procure a very special vintage that Mr. Vanderfrost may be interested in investing in. I am hoping to add him as a business partner so that we can begin importing this splendid wine to the good people of Ravensbridge."

"Wonderful, Mr. de Jaager. I always enjoy a good drink. I look forward to that."

I nodded again and Mr. Brouwer moved off to mingle with the next closest guest. I wanted to keep my conversations with others to a minimum; not wishing to explain my false credentials for being here to many.

Something brushed my leg and gave me a start. I glanced down to see one of the many cats that Mr. Vanderfrost was said to own. In fact, I noticed several in the room. They must have followed their owner, as there, standing at a far door to the library, stood the tall, and elegantly-dressed, Mr. Vanderfrost. I sucked in my breath.

A heavy-set man also noticed the arrival of the cats but not of the party's host.

"Such dreadful creatures," the man said, indicating to one of the cats. "Wicked little buggers, actually, and quite dumb. Can't train them like a good dog."

The man must have noticed the change in expressions of those around him and the blood drained from his face as he turned to regard our gracious host.

"Cats are quite intelligent, my dear, Mr. Voort. They are difficult to train because they simply choose not to listen. They are cunning, independent, and see themselves as superior to all other beings, not willing to submit to anyone. A quality I find most admirable."

"Ah, well, yes," Mr. Voort stammered. "My apologies for my rude remarks. I have simply had too much wine."

"I am sure."

Then to my surprise, Mr. Vanderfrost looked straight at me and strode across the room in my direction. My heart raced at his approach. For a split-second I had to wonder if he had come to realize the falseness of my story and was about to confront me, but my imagination was running wild and he could not have known.

"Mr. de Jaager, is it?" he inquired calmly, in his deep voice.

I paused momentarily, not believing that I was

standing this close to the man. "Yes, yes it is."

"One of the doormen told me you had arrived and provided me an ample description. Enjoying the wine?"

"Yes, yes indeed I am."

"I apologize that is most likely not as exotic a vintage as you are used to, but it's the best that Ravensbridge has to offer." Then he added, "Though we will have to change that, won't we?"

"Yes indeed, we shall."

"Excellent, I will look forward to talking business with you a little later." Then he raised his voice and addressed everyone in the room. "Dinner is about to be served, please, everyone, find your appropriate seats."

Mr. Vanderfrost turned and strolled from the room, breaking the trance that I felt I was under. I was finally given a chance to converse with the man and I couldn't spit out more than one sentence answers. I felt almost locked in his hypnotic gaze and struggled to find an appropriate reply. I shook my head and exhaled, then followed other guests to the dining hall.

In my mind, I had envisioned the lavish sprawl of food that someone of Mr. Vanderfrost's wealth could provide, and the layout before me exceeded my wildest expectations. First of all, the sheer enormity of the dining table was mind-blowing, as it must have sat eighty to a hundred people. Someone sitting at one end of the long rectangular table wouldn't even be able to see those seated at the other end.

The variety of food was simply amazing. There was everything one could think of, from seafood, to fruits and vegetables, to meat dishes and pastries, and the staff kept bringing more. There was also a frosted glass of red wine beside every plate.

The seats were numbered and I quickly checked my invitation to find that I was surprisingly close to Mr. Vanderfrost, a mere ten seats away from the host himself. I took my seat and attempted to refrain from gobbling my food like a savage, given that I was extremely hungry. I had refrained from eating all day, waiting for the dinner which I planned to thoroughly enjoy.

I was most curious to watch Mr. Vanderfrost throughout the dinner. He didn't touch an ounce of food, electing to watch, and to listen, to those seated closest to him. He did, however, sip on a frosted glass filled with red wine. He was a highly intelligent and calculating man, and it was evident to me that he was reading his guests, discerning their strengths and their weaknesses to further aid him in future business dealings.

"Ghastly thing, all those bodies being found. Appears Mr. Shletzborg is the newest addition to that growing and mysterious list," someone nearby commented.

I nearly choked on some pheasant. This was hardly the place or the time to speak of such gruesome things. The man could have waited until later, or at the very least, when dessert was served, but not during dinner. Murder was not a topic to be enjoyed with food.

The expression on Mr. Vanderfrost's face told me he also disapproved of such talk while others were eating. His penetrating eyes met mine again and he raised his glass.

"This time next year," he announced, "I hope we will all be enjoying a rare wine from the Far East, courtesy of Mr. de Jaager."

I cleared my throat before replying. "We need not wait until next year, for I have brought a bottle along with me for you to sample."

I attempted to gauge the reaction from our host but there was none. He sat there stone-faced; his expression never changing.

"Shall I pour you a glass?"

"I fear if I drink much more this evening, I will not be able to perform my duties as a proper host."

"Just a sip, then," I said, rising from my chair.

I opened the satchel which I had stored under my chair and pulled out a clear bottle, half-filled with an inexpensive red wine that I had purchased right here in Ravensbridge. I grabbed my cane and limped my way over to the head of the long table where our illustrious host was seated.

I poured some of the wine into an empty silver goblet and sat the bottle on the table in front of Mr. Vanderfrost. I took a step back and fixed my eyes onto the bottle.

"Perhaps our great mayor would like the first taste?" he said, motioning to Mayor Ableton, who sat directly to his right.

"I certainly would not mind that, pass it here, my friend," the mayor replied.

As Mr. Vanderfrost reached for the goblet, I pulled my cane in half, revealing a sharpened wooden tip that was concealed within. To the horror of those present, I drove my weapon into the left side of Mr. Vanderfrost's back with all my strength. The sharpened end slid right through the man to exit from his chest, perfectly piercing his heart.

Jaws hung open in shock. Terrified guests were rooted to their seats unable to react otherwise. Then, as if that spectacle was not enough to unsettle them, Mr. Vanderfrost let out an otherworldly shriek and melted right before their very eyes. In the blink of an eye, all that remained of our host was a puddle of disgusting goo, along with his clothing.

"I believe there will be no more missing people in Ravensbridge, with the…departure of Mr. Vanderfrost," I said, breaking the deathly silence that followed his destruction.

Arthur Vanderfrost had been very careful in keeping his identity a secret. I found no mirrors present anywhere within the main floor of his home. Even the glasses that were used to serve drinks were frosted and provided no reflection. I wasn't completely sure he was the monster I sought, until placing my own bottle in front of him and noticing he cast no reflection in the glass of the bottle.

I tipped over the glass he had been drinking from and immediately noticed the difference in texture from the liquid that poured forth. Our host had not been drinking wine like the rest of us, he had been drinking blood.

Mr. Brouwer was seated near the head of the table and was the first person to find his voice. "Quite a show. I get the impression that you are not, Edgar de Jaager, an importer of exotic wines."

"Indeed sir, you are correct. I am Sigmund Helgaard, Vampire Hunter."

THE WEEPING WILLOW

It was midafternoon on a Friday and I was in the office typing up a report. For the first time in quite a while, I had no pressing cases that required my attention over the weekend and I had planned to visit a cabin near Lake Everest. That was the plan anyways, until I was approached by Detective Milton.

"Hey, Kane. You got a minute?"

"I have several, but how many I have to spare depends on what for."

"Well…I am working on this missing person's case and…"

"Milton, it's Friday afternoon and I am going to the cabin this weekend. Gotta run to the supermarket and grab some food for the grill as soon as I am done with this report."

"Please, Kane, I am stumped. This rich woman has disappeared and I know the husband must be behind it but I've no evidence. It's been a month now and I've got nothing on the guy. His wife has just vanished."

"She has not run off with another man?"

"No, it would not seem so."

"You've searched his car for traces of blood, in the event that he moved a body?"

"Completely clean."

"The house?"

"No traces."

"The husband stood to gain much by her disappearance?"

"Much indeed. Her ailing father is the owner of The Four Aces Casino. She is an only child and heir to that fortune. The husband is a nobody with several fraud charges."

"Quite suspicious, I would have to agree with you. Why can't these criminals just make it easier on us and leave the smoking gun on the table, huh?"

"Yeah, you're telling me."

"So, she had no reason to run away? There were no prior signs of distress?"

"A note was left behind."

"You have this?"

"Yes."

"Let me see it."

The young detective searched through the papers of an overflowing folder until he found what he was looking for and handed it over.

You have never treated me like the adult that I am. How long did you think to continue with such behavior until you drove me away? I am more than capable of making decisions on how to govern my own life and I do not need you sticking your nose into all of my affairs. I love you and I always will, but you are smothering me to the point where I can no longer breathe. Of this latest matter, I shall not back down, and you have left me no other choice than to leave this house for good. Perhaps one day you shall see the error in your ways and regret your attempts of controlling every aspect of my life. I am sorry to say that this is good-bye.

Ethel

"It looks to be the handwriting of a woman, very neat and orderly. Have you confirmed that it is her writing?" I wondered.

Milton nodded. "Yes, I have compared it with several other letters she had written, along with grocery lists. I would say without a doubt that this was written by her."

I scratched my head. That ruled out my forged letter theory to cover a murderer's tracks. Maybe this Ethel did run away after all. There were plenty of places for someone to hide away in the Big City, especially someone with money.

"Where do they live?"

"A large house on Canadine Avenue, over in the Midwest section of the city."

"Yes, I know exactly where that is, I have to pass by there to get home." I sighed. "Alright, look, give me the address of the house and I will stop by there on my way home. I'll speak with the husband and see what I can find out."

"Thanks Kane, I appreciate it, really I do. I got no read on the guy. He is a fraudster with practice in the art of deception. I owe ya a coffee."

"Yeah, yeah."

Once I had finished my report about a half hour later, I decided it was time to leave. Milton had given me the address and the name of the husband. Questioning a man about his missing wife was not how I had planned to spend my Friday afternoon but I didn't mind lending a hand to Milton.

Detective Milton was only promoted from the police force last year. He was fairly young, as detectives go, and inexperienced. Previously he had worked in the bowels of the city, the Junkie Jungle and other such neighborhoods. He was used to dealing with a certain type of criminal; the drug dealers, the gangsters, not so much the clever and sophisticated kind. Gangsters weren't generally concerned with hiding bodies. Their murders were brazen and meant to send a message.

But the city was full of intelligent killers; those that went to great lengths to hide evidence and concoct the perfect stories. Those were the most dangerous ones. This Wallace Wells certainly seemed to have every motive to eliminate his wife. Nobody was perfect though; they all made mistakes.

I grabbed a hot coffee along the way, despite the summer heat, and was soon cruising down Canadine Avenue scanning for the correct house. Some of the houses on this street were virtual mansions, with some gated. There was a lot of money in this area. It was not generally the type of neighborhood you would find a two-bit hood, like Wallace Wells, living in.

I located the house and parked on the street directly in front. It certainly wasn't the biggest house in the area but neither was it the smallest. With the failing health of

Ethel's father, she had apparently already inherited most of his wealth. The land was well-kept and was most likely the result of hired help.

The long driveway was occupied with three expensive cars. I worked honestly and could never afford to drive any of them. Rubbed me the wrong way when someone like Wallace came by this dishonestly. Of course the man was innocent until proven guilty but my gut already told me the verdict. Now it was just a matter of finding out where he slipped up.

I tightened my tie but left my jacket in the car; it was just too hot. I approached the front door and knocked. I didn't think someone like Wallace would work and hoped that he would be home. After a minute I knocked again.

The door opened and I was greeted with a rather skinny man in a bright red smoking jacket. He had greasy black hair and a thin moustache; reminding me of someone who sold used cars. He appeared to be in his forties, which would make him about fifteen years younger than his wife.

"Whatever you are selling, I don't want or need any."

"I am not selling anything, I am looking for a Wallace Wells. Is that you?"

"Yes, that is me. Who are you?"

I pulled out my badge. "I am Detective Edward Kane and I just wanted a moment of your time to discuss your missing wife."

"I have already spoken to enough detectives, Mr. Kane. I don't know what else I can tell you. Unless you have any leads there isn't really anything further to discuss."

"Well that's just it, Mr. Wells, there has been a

possible sighting of your wife just outside the city. I am now helping with the investigation and wanted to ask you something about the letter she left behind."

His eyes narrowed. "Alright, do come in."

He led me to an extravagantly decorated sitting room where it appeared he had been reading the newspaper prior to my arrival. Next to the paper rested a still-smoking pipe which he promptly scooped up and took a puff.

"Do you smoke, Mr. Kane?"

"No. I have enough bad habits that I don't need to pick up any new ones."

"Well then, what is this you say about a possible sighting of my dear Ethel? I miss her terribly."

"I don't mean to raise your hopes just yet, but someone meeting her description was sighted yesterday in a train station outside the city."

"Interesting," he said, before puffing on the pipe again.

I pulled out the letter that Milton had given me. "I had a question about this letter, though."

"I would be happy to help."

"Ethel mentioned something to which she wouldn't back down from. What was that all about? You were arguing about something in particular?"

"Why, yes, 'tis a silly thing really, and one I do come to regret now. Ethel wished to take some courses at one of the universities. At first I thought it ridiculous, given her age and all. On top of that she is extremely wealthy already so it seemed like a dreadful waste of time."

"She became very upset by this, I take it?"

"Oh yes, much more than I had anticipated. I realize now that it wasn't my place to tell her what she can and cannot do. I fear my pigheadedness has driven her away for good. If I could only rewind time and apologize for my behavior."

"This makes sense, Mr. Wells. The sighting was at the Oakvale train station, and as we know, Oakvale is home to one of the top universities."

"Yes, yes indeed! She must have gone there to continue with her plans. Oh, Mr. Kane, you must find her."

"I will do my best," I said as I stood to leave. "I know you must be worried sick about her, along with her father. How is he doing by the way?"

His expression soured. "I wouldn't know. We do not speak, him and I."

"Oh, I am sorry to hear that. Well, try and enjoy the nice weather this weekend, Mr. Wells, and I will keep you informed of my progress."

"Thank you, and please do."

The supermarket would have to wait. I figured a trip to visit Ethel's father was now in order. If her father and Wallace Wells did not get along, then it was quite possible to learn some valuable information from her father, who would have nothing to hide.

Her father lived thirty minutes in the opposite direction of where I was headed but I had involved myself now and needed to see this through. I agreed with Milton, Wallace was involved with the disappearance in some way, but how? I didn't buy the whole university disagreement.

Heavier than usual traffic, due to being a Friday, made my trip to Ethel's father's place take longer than expected. Forty-five minutes later, I arrived at the apartment building and shortly thereafter was knocking on the door of a penthouse suite.

A young woman dressed as a maid answered the door.

"Good afternoon, Miss. My name is Detective Kane and I was wondering if I could speak with Samuel Davis for a moment."

"Mr. Davis is in poor health, Detective Kane, and he is resting."

"Please, I will not be long. It's concerning his daughter."

"My daughter did not run away, Detective!" Mr. Davis roared, after I was brought to his room and introduced by the housekeeper.

He was then wracked with a fit of coughing for his exertion. The frail elderly man lay in a bed and was hooked up to an oxygen tank. The sight reminded me of just how mortal we all are. Here was one of the richest men in the city, but that wealth could do nothing to help him now, as he was bed-ridden and wasting away.

"Tell me about Wallace Wells, if you may."

"He is a no-good scoundrel. A liar and a thief, pure and simple. I was against their getting married from the very beginning. But my Ethel couldn't be swayed. She threatened to run away and disown the family if I didn't allow her to make her own choice."

Hmm, very interesting, I thought. I pulled out Ethel's letter and showed it to her father. "Mr. Davis, have you ever seen this letter before?"

The housekeeper fetched his glasses upon his request and he glanced over the contents of the letter. "Of course I recognize that letter, she wrote that for me when I told her she could not marry that crook. I told her that he was only after our fortune but she wouldn't listen to me."

"So this letter, when was it written?"

"Nine years ago. Just before she ignored my protests and married him anyways."

"Thank you, Mr. Davis, you have been most helpful."

When Detective Milton first told me that Ethel had left a note behind prior to vanishing, my first thoughts were that it must have been a forgery. Milton was convinced that it was her handwriting and indeed it had been; only the context was all wrong. Wallace had somehow gotten ahold of the letter written years ago to her father and kept it handy. He cleverly informed police it was written only recently and referred to an argument between the two of them over her plan to continue her education. As I said earlier, everyone slips up.

I decided to call it a night and head home. Sadly the cabin would have to wait, as I now planned to visit Mr. Wells again in the morning with some developing leads. Milton was going to owe me more than a coffee for this.

"Detective Kane, you are back again so soon?" Mr. Wells said, as he answered his door at precisely eleven o'clock the following morning.

"Yes, I have received word that someone matching Ethel's description has now been seen on the campus of the Oakvale University. I was wondering, Mr. Wells, did Ethel have a study? Or any kind of room where she kept personal books and items?"

"Why, yes, she did have her own study with a library of books."

"Might I take a look around, if it's not a bother? Perhaps I might find some clues as to what program she might have enrolled in at the university, to aid in our locating her. Or perhaps you have an idea?"

"By all means, you can look around. I only know that she was interested in business, seeing as how she would be shortly taking over The Four Aces Casino."

We proceeded up the stairs and down a long hallway to a cozy little room with a large window facing the backyard. There was one tall bookcase against a wall filled with all kinds of books covering a wide variety of topics. There was a writing desk and a leather chair, facing the window, so Ethel could enjoy the lovely view while sitting there working away on whatever she might have been doing. The room smelled pleasantly of pot pourri.

"I am not sure what kind of clues you might find here, Detective. As you can see, she had a wide range of interests when it came to books."

"One never knows, Mr. Wells, sometimes we find the most helpful clues in the unlikeliest of places. That is a lovely photo of Ethel there on the wall. Was that fairly recent?"

"Yes, in fact that was taken only a week before she vanished. I thought it only appropriate to hang it here in her favorite room."

"Where was that photo taken?"

"Right here in our backyard. I took it myself."

The photo depicted Ethel in a long flowing dress, standing in the grass. Other houses could be seen in the distance behind her.

I walked over to the window to regard their sizable backyard. The grass was emerald green and the only things that occupied the large space was a patio table and chairs, near to the back door, and a weeping willow tree that was placed almost directly in the center of the yard. The tree was not yet very tall which told me that it was not too old.

I paused for a moment in thought and then turned back to the photo of Ethel. Curiously, the photo that was taken only recently, did not contain the weeping willow tree.

"I have always loved those weeping willows," I commented. "They are strangely beautiful, in a creepy sort of way."

"They were Ethel's favorite."

"Thank you for your time, Mr. Wells, I must be going."

"You didn't look at her books."

"Perhaps another day. I just remembered an appointment that I must get to. I can show myself out, good day."

When I arrived back at home I got on the phone and called Detective Milton. "If I were you, I would get over to the Wells' place with a team and dig up that willow tree in the backyard. I believe you might find what you are looking for. Yes, yes, you are going to owe me more than a coffee."

I was a little disappointed that I was not able to make it to the cabin this weekend. I tried to make up for it on Sunday by going for some ice cream and a walk with a lady friend.

After dropping her off, I took a minor detour on my way home and turned onto Canadine Avenue. I was not too surprised to find several police cruisers parked out front, with much activity in the driveway. I spotted Detective Milton speaking with a couple of officers so decided to park my car and head over.

"Kane! What a surprise. You won't believe what

happened."

Poor Ethel, I thought. I had a feeling she was buried beneath that tree. "Found her, did you?"

"Sadly, you were correct. But there has been a twist."

"Oh?"

"Come around back and see for yourself. A complete mystery, this is."

I followed Milton through the house and out the backdoor to the yard. There, around the willow tree, stood several officers gawking at a body that hung from the branches of the tree. I could see that a portion of the ground around the tree had been dug up.

As I got closer, I realized the body hanging from the tree was that of Wallace Wells, and he was quite dead. Strangely, several branches were wrapped around this throat in some bizarre death grip.

"We found what was left of her body beneath the tree," Milton informed me. "The roots had actually grown right through her. But now, who could have hung Mr. Wells up like that? We had an arborist come by this afternoon, you know, one of those tree experts? She said it was near impossible for anyone to wrap those branches around his neck without them snapping. She said it was almost as if the tree itself had grabbed him and is refusing to let go. It's the darndest thing."

Yes, I thought, the darndest thing indeed.

"What do you suppose happened here, Kane?"

"Justice."

APRIL SHOWERS

As storm clouds gathered in the dismal sky above, I thought it best to turn into the ramshackle gas bar that was fast approaching on my right side. I wasn't familiar with this backwoods road but I did know that there wasn't another service station for another eighty miles. In fact, there wasn't anything at all for another eighty miles.

My car was beginning to pull to the right as one of my tires was becoming dangerously low. I figured I had best have an attendant fill it with air before continuing on my trek. The sun would be setting shortly and I didn't want to have to make any more stops until I reached my destination.

I am a reporter for the *Heavensville Sun* paper, and I was rushing to be the first to interview a witness in one of the bizarre cult murders that happened only two days ago. Until now, nobody had caught any glimpses of the suspects involved with a string of abductions and murders which all pointed in the direction of some loathsome cult.

This witness, one, Gerard Stone, claimed to have seen four men wearing black masks and driving in a dark-colored pickup truck, only a half-mile from where the last person was abducted. He had been very cooperative with the police so far but had yet to speak to any of the media. One of my coworkers demonstrated his investigative skills and came up with Stone's home address, so now I was attempting to secure the first interview.

"What can I do for you, Miss? Shall I fill it up?" asked the white-haired gas bar attendant.

"Yes please. Fill it up and also check my tires if you would, I believe one of them is dreadfully low."

"It would be my pleasure."

I figured I would arrive in Tanners Run too late this evening to call on Mr. Stone, so I would just check into a motel, visit Mr. Stone in the morning, and hopefully make it back in time for a family gathering tomorrow night. It was my Aunt Matilda's birthday and my Uncle Gus was a professional chef, which meant it was going to be a meal that I did not want to miss out on.

"You are right, Miss, your front right tire has a nail in it. So far it would seem the nail has plugged the hole and you are only losing air slowly. To be on the safe side, I could change the tire for you, if you like?"

"I am afraid my spare is flat."

"I could call over to the next station and see if they have the right tire, I don't believe I have the one you need here. I am sure they would."

"How long would that take?"

"Oh, maybe about an hour at most, to get the tire brought over here and put on for you."

"Hmmm, no thanks, I don't want to wait that long but I appreciate the offer."

"Well as I said, it's a slow leak, it could be fine for another day or two."

I smiled and nodded, then grabbed my purse to pay the man and clumsily dropped my wallet, spilling cards onto the ground. The man was kind enough to gather them all up for me and hand them back. He did, however, notice my name on my driver's license and smiled.

"Interesting name."

"Yes, my parents had a sense of humor it would seem."

"Much obliged for the tip and you drive carefully now, Miss Showers."

"Thank you for your help and yes I shall."

Oh wonderful, I thought, as I attempted to adjust the radio dial after pulling back onto the road. It appeared the reception out here in the middle of nowhere wasn't very good at all. I tried all my favorite channels, along with a few not so favorite, and all I got was static. I did not relish the idea of a long, lonely drive, without music, or at the very least some news.

I decided to hum and whistle to myself, listening to imaginary tunes in my head. I wondered what my cat was doing at this very moment without me around to supervise. I had a sneaking suspicion that she got into much hijinks when I was not around and just played the innocent sleepy-head when I was around. Plants and ornaments had a tendency to be in different positions each time I returned home from a short trip. Of course, Mayla always wore that innocent face.

I found my grip on the steering wheel was getting

tighter, the darker it got. The clouds blotted out all the light from the moon and the stars, and of course, there were no street lights along this lonely road. My headlights did not afford me much distance and I was forced to decrease my speed as the road took many sharp twists and turns.

A thick forest, as black as pitch, lined both sides of the road, and according to the map, stretched on for the better part of my trip. Deer darting across the road suddenly became a concern of mine. I had heard tales of the tremendous damage they could cause to your vehicle if struck, and I would be absolutely mortified, to top it off, if I had ever ran into an animal.

I began going over the questions I had planned to ask Mr. Stone, to distract myself from the unsettling drive. I was curious to know if he had gotten the license plate number of the truck he had seen. So far none of those details had been released by the police.

Suddenly, and without warning, my car pulled violently to the right and I swerved off the road. Fortunately for me, I was able to apply the brakes in time to prevent myself from running headlong into a large tree. My heart was beating so fast it felt as though it were about to burst through my chest.

With my hands still trembling, I fumbled to open the car door and step outside to assess any damage. I cursed myself for not putting fresh batteries in the flashlight I kept in the glove box; the others had died months previous.

My headlights offered the only source of light, making it difficult to properly inspect all angles of my car in the gloom of the night. It appeared to be alright, well, aside from the flat tire. Of course I would be made to pay for my impatience at not wanting to wait for a new tire. The evil nail had done its worst, effectively ruining my tire and making it undriveable.

I cursed myself for the second time at not waiting until morning to make this trip. In my haste to get to Mr. Stone before anyone else in the media, I made a rash decision. I dreaded the thought of having to walk back to the service station in this frightening darkness. I had been driving for nearly thirty minutes, which would translate into a two hour walk, I figured, at the least. But I didn't know what else I could do; I certainly couldn't just sit around and hope that someone would drive by on this isolated road. Who knew how long that wait could be?

Despairingly, I turned my car off, locked the doors, and trudged off in the direction I had come. All I could hear was the sound of chirping crickets all around, until the hoot of an owl gave me quite a start.

"Whoooooooooo," I heard it call.

"Me, that's who," I answered. "Just a foolish woman who didn't heed the advice of the gas bar attendant."

After roughly twenty minutes into my miserable trek, my heart skipped a beat at a glorious sight up ahead. Two headlights off in the distance joyfully announced the approach of a vehicle. With luck, perhaps I could convince this person to take me back to Heavensville. I would certainly be willing to pay them if that's what it took.

As the vehicle got closer, I felt a knot form in my stomach and a sudden nervousness overtook me. I had no idea who this person could be. I decided it might be wise to step off the road and not draw attention to myself.

I scampered off the road and ducked behind the first

tree I found. It was too late though, I soon realized. The driver must have spotted me as the vehicle began to slow. Several voices could be heard telling me it was not a lone driver. The engine made a deep rumbling noise, which to me, sounded like a truck. My suspicions were soon confirmed as I noticed it was a pickup truck, with two people inside the vehicle, and two others sitting in the back. The license plate read, DRKNSS.

The vehicle crawled past my position and now I could hear their voices quite clearly.

"I coulda swore I saw someone on the road."

"You're right, I saw it too."

"Looked like a woman."

"What would a woman be doing walking this road at this time of night?"

"Who knows, but I mean to ask her."

"Let's just go. Hank is waiting for us at the Lion's Pub and you know Hank doesn't like to be kept waiting."

"Hank won't care if we bring him company for those that we have locked in the pub's basement."

That last comment caused the hair on my arms and neck to stand on end. My gut was telling me these men were dangerous, very dangerous. I squinted for a better look then involuntarily squealed aloud as I noticed the men were all wearing black masks. A flashlight momentarily blinded me.

"It is a woman! There behind that tree!"

"Come on out you pretty thing. We won't hurt you…much."

I took off in a blind run into the impenetrable darkness of the thick forest. Within minutes I must have bled from a half-dozen cuts and scrapes to my face and arms but I did not care and I did not stop.

Behind me I could hear the voices of the four men as they took up the chase while hooting and hollering. They were taunting me and telling me that I could not escape. They were saying that running will only make it worse for me and that I should just give up.

I knew immediately these were the men that Mr. Stone had witnessed and they must have been connected to the cult abductions and murders. I came looking for an interview concerning this case and wound up becoming a part of the story.

It was dark, so dark, and I had no idea where I was or which direction I was headed, but I just kept running. And so did the men, no doubt following the sounds I made of snapping twigs and crushing leaves underfoot. As fast as I was running, which under the circumstances I felt was quite fast, their voices were getting closer and closer, but I dared not look back.

Then an unfortunate thing occurred, which I supposed should have happened earlier but didn't; my foot caught on the thick root of a tree and down I went striking my head against a stone. Bright lights danced in front of my eyes and a sharp pain shot through my skull as I attempted to lift my head.

"Quickly girl, over here, and don't make a noise."

To my credit, I did not scream out as that voice whispered to me a few feet away to my right. I could not see the person but there was something about the tone of the voice that I felt I could trust. In any event, I possessed no other options as bobbing flashlights and the voices of the four men were nearly upon me.

Despite the searing pain in my head, I crawled dizzily

towards the whispered voice. A dark figure sat crouched in a natural ditch and I soon joined him.

"Lay still and don't say a word."

I was completely out of breath and it took every ounce of effort to try and control my breathing and stifle the noise. I heard my pursuers very close by. They had stopped, noticing that they could no longer hear me running.

"Where are you woman? Where did you go?

"Come out, come out, wherever you are."

"We have all night to look for you, we will find you."

I trembled uncontrollably in fear, while the shadow of the man kneeling next to me remained still and calm. For once, on this dreadful evening, I was afforded a bit of luck, as the men moved off in other directions, away from the ditch where we hid. They continued their taunting but their voices were becoming more distant.

I allowed myself to exhale and breathe a giant sigh of relief. I was certainly not out of danger yet but was given a moment's reprieve.

"What is your name?" the stranger in the dark asked of me.

"April."

"Alright, April, we need to move from here. Are you still able to walk? Are you hurt?"

"I hit my head, I can feel it bleeding, but my legs are fine I can walk."

"Good, come along then. Follow me and make as little noise as possible."

"Who are you?"

"My name is Henry, now let's go."

I had a dozen more questions to ask Henry, foremost

being, what was he doing out here by himself at night, but they would have to wait for now. As we rose from the ditch I was able to get a better look at the mysterious man. He didn't stand much taller than me and had a slim build. He wore brown pants and a thick brown coat. On his head was a fur hat with a raccoon's tail hanging from the back of it. He had a bushy brown beard and kind blue eyes. I thought he looked very much like a hunter and then that was confirmed as he picked up a long musket-style rifle.

"You have a gun. You can shoot those men then, if you have to."

"I hunt animals, April, and then only out of necessity. I do not hunt people."

"They are not people, they are monsters."

"Regardless, let's hope it doesn't come to that. Now let's move."

Henry crouched low to the ground as he moved away from the ditch and I followed suit. He would stop often to make sure that I was still close behind. We could no longer hear the men or see their flashlights and I hoped that was a good thing.

I was relieved when we emerged from some thick bushes to find a clear pathway. Enough of the moon was peeking through the clouds so that I could make out a trail that cut through the forest.

"We will follow this trail and it will lead you out of the forest. There is a ranger's station where you will be safe."

"Thank you, Henry."

"This is a strange place for a woman to be wandering around by herself at night. Did something happen to your metal wagon?"

"My what?"

"Your means of transportation."

"You mean my car? I got a nail in my tire, it's flat. What are you doing out here?"

"I live here."

"Here? Like in this forest?"

"Yes, here in the forest. It has been my home for a very long time."

We heard voices approaching and we stepped off the trail, crouching behind a bush. We could see two flashlights and they were coming straight for our position.

"We can hear you, missy. Just give yourself up."

"We know you are close."

"Quickly April, pick up that stone and throw it over them," Henry whispered.

"What?"

"Throw it so it lands behind them."

I did as Henry instructed and threw the stone with all my strength to land it a fair distance behind the two men. They whooped with excitement and spun around, running off in the opposite direction, thinking their quarry was close at hand.

Henry and I immediately sped down the trail away from the men, not stopping until the forest thinned and ahead of us was a clearing. In the distance, I could make out the lights of a small cabin, the ranger's station. I almost could not contain my elation. We had managed to elude those vile murderers, and best of all, I had their license plate and the name of the pub it seemed they used as their base of operations.

"Henry, I cannot thank you enough…Henry? Henry?"

I looked about for my rescuer but he was nowhere in sight. "Henry, where are you?"

I dared not linger for too long searching for Henry, lest those men come this way and find me. I dashed across the clearing and pounded with both fists upon the door to the cabin.

A man dressed in a ranger's uniform opened the door wearing a shocked expression. I am sure they were not used to visitors frantically knocking on their door at this hour of the night. I was brought inside and found there were two men on duty, and to my relief, several rifles hung on the wall.

I told the rangers of the men who pursued me and that I suspected they were involved with the recent cult murders. They immediately radioed the police and officers were on their way.

"I would never have found that trail and escaped those men if it were not for Henry. I want to be sure that he is hailed as a hero and gets a reward for saving my life."

"Where is this Henry now?"

"When we reached the clearing, I turned and he was gone. I don't know where he went."

Then I noticed a most curious sight. On the wall hung a painting, depicting a man who looked very much like Henry, standing next to a log cabin with his rifle in hand.

"That's him, that's Henry."

The rangers looked to each other, seemingly unconvinced. "That's the man who led you out of the forest? That's your Henry?"

"Yes, he was dressed exactly like that and even carried that rifle."

"That is Henry McAbbott. The trail you used to exit the forest is the famous McAbbott trail."

"He told me he lived in the forest, that's him!"

"Henry McAbbott was one of the first pioneers in this region. Miss Showers, Henry has been dead for one hundred and thirty years."

JUNGLE JOHNNY

Some of you may choose to think my words false, that I have imagined this tale or embellished it to the point of ridiculousness. I can assure you that is not the case. Sadly, I possess no photographic evidence but I was present for Johnathan White's last adventure on that dreadful island. My name can be found in the ship's ledger and the magazine that I work for can vouch for having sent me to travel with Jungle Johnny.

Why have I waited so long to tell this tale, you ask? Simply put, I have just arrived back to civilization after months lost at sea. I am no seaman, nor am I versed in the ways of nautical navigation. Aside from the odd fishing trip as a young lad, I had not spent any time on a boat. I hardly consider the daily ferry commute from Glorchester to Avindale as boating experience. Indeed, I am fortunate to have found my way back to land before my food stores were completely depleted.

Now that I am returned, I am obligated to apprise the details of Jungle Johnny's fate, along with the members of his crew. That I am even here to impart this information onto you is no small matter. I could have easily met my end on that selfsame island, though for whatever the reason, and maybe that reason is to tell this tale, I was spared a ghoulish fate.

Many of you are familiar with the Jungle Johnny of film and radio fame. I mean, who hasn't seen one of the many fine Jungle Johnny movies, where he was portrayed by the strapping young actor, Claudio Hart? And how many of you may have huddled around a radio, listening to the Jungle Johnny program, voiced by the remarkable, Stewart Rayne?

At the risk of damaging his reputation, Johnathan White, the real Jungle Johnny and the inspiration for those films and programs, was not the most pleasant of men. He was not the handsome and amiable fellow of fame, and certainly was not the brave and fearless leader most of us had thought.

I found the man to be brutish and his demeanor most unendearing. This revelation may come as a shock to most but I am sure those of you who have actually met the man, would wholeheartedly agree with that sentiment.

But I must apologize, my goal here is not to bash the character of perhaps the world's greatest explorer, I am simply here to relate the events that I am unfortunately the sole witness to.

I was first introduced to Jungle Johnny in Port Rock. His small ship was docked there while restocking their supplies. My initial feeling was one of slight disappointment. I realize Claudio Hart was just an actor but the two looked nothing alike. Jungle Johnny was a large man, though not muscle-bound like his counterpart in the pictures. He had a protruding stomach and a scruffy beard. Granted, the man was now in his late fifties, but he certainly did not care much about keeping up appearances.

Nor did he care much about making new friends. I found him quite rude and dismissive. A cantankerous fellow who was not overly pleased at having me join them for their next excursion. While I had mixed feelings myself about joining them and sailing into potential danger, the thought of discovering some new species of primate was admittedly exhilarating.

Some fisherman had stumbled upon an uncharted and unexplored island only recently. They reported witnessing a strange type of white ape, roaming about the beach. They claimed it looked something similar to a gorilla, only slightly smaller and possessed hair of the purest white. They dared not land on the beach for fear of these apes and what they may be capable of. They did, however, snap a photo, albeit fuzzy, but their claims appeared trustworthy.

Now it was the duty of Jungle Johnny, the famous explorer, to visit this island and bring back one of these white apes for study. In the past, Johnny had been responsible for the capture of many wild and rare animals from all over the globe. From the biggest of cats to the most dangerous of reptiles, Johnny had hunted and captured them all. An expert hunter, if you will; seemingly fearless.

The Jungle Johnny of the films wrestled tigers and bears with his bare hands. He once knocked out a gorilla with a punch, to save the lead female in the film. I highly doubted that the man I met was capable of any of those feats, though he was successful at what he did.

The magazine I worked for was interested in getting an exclusive story of this adventure, and the seemingly inevitable capture of this new species of ape. Thus, I was dispatched to Port Rock to rendezvous with Jungle Johnny before he set sail. I caught up with him, and his crew of five, while they were loading the last of their supplies onto the ship, and we set sail the following morning.

Disappointingly, the ship was not large enough for me to have my own cabin and I was forced to bunk with the other members of the crew. They were not the friendliest lot, mimicking the poor behavior of their captain. I did make some headway, mind you, with Borga, a black-skinned man who was said to be an unparalleled tracker and an expert marksman. He had been in the employ of Jungle Johnny for nearly thirty years and provided me much insight into some of their previous adventures.

Nickolas and Tomas were clearly sailors and did most of the work on the ship. They poorly hid their distaste for me and would not speak with me unless it was to tell me to move out of their way.

Kenneth was also an expert marksman and spent the majority of his time on the ship cleaning a variety of rifles. Horacio was the youngest of the men, only in his twenties, and the butt of much amusement and jests. From what I gathered, he was the "pack mule", as the others referred to him. He would be overburdened with packs and supplies and do his best to follow the others and keep up.

Thankfully, I was left well enough alone and was not assigned any extra duties while aboard the ship. Most often

I was making notes while speaking with Borga, and other times I was doing my best to elicit information from Jungle Johnny, which was no easy task by any stretch of the imagination. He tended to grunt his replies quite frequently, avoiding the use of actual words whenever possible, at least in my company.

That made for an uncomfortable trip. Though after two and a half weeks of sailing, and three unsettling storms, Tomas shouted that he had spotted land. The crew had little solid information to go by in locating this mysterious island. The coordinates provided by the fishermen had not been accurate and we were forced to change course several times. Though luck was with us and it appeared that we had found our island.

I was a little nervous, though quite relieved to have land once again in my view. It was no secret that many sailors had gone missing in this area of the ocean. So I was happy to learn that we had not become hopelessly lost.

I leaned over the rail of the ship as we approached the island, searching for any signs of the white apes that were previously spotted roaming the beach. At this moment, the beach was devoid of activity, and I supposed I felt that was a good thing, since we were almost ready to disembark.

Nikolas dropped the anchor a good hundred yards from the beach, then he and Tomas stayed with the boat as the rest of us paddled to land on a bright yellow dingy. Borga and Kenneth were the first on the beach, rifles in hand and on high alert.

I remember feeling surprised, thinking that Jungle Johnny would have proudly strode first onto the beach, chest puffed out like the brave explorer of the big screen.

Instead, Johnny remained in the dingy with myself and Horacio, until given the signal by Borga that all was clear. He doubled checked that his shotgun was loaded, then exited the dingy and proceeded to the beach.

"Come along, writer," he called back to me. "We have an ape to catch."

Horacio motioned for me to go first and then he followed, dragging the dingy onto the beach. I noticed Borga kneeling on the ground, inspecting strange footprints in the sand.

"Ape tracks," he said. "The fishermen were right. Looks as though several passed by here only recently. It would seem they are slightly smaller than we are, if my guess is correct."

"Excellent. Smaller means a good shotgun slug should take them down," Johnny said, tapping his gun.

"Are we not to capture one alive?" I inquired.

"If it's possible we will take one alive. We have no idea how vicious these animals can be. We also get paid quite handsomely by scientists for a dead specimen to study."

I was mortified. Here we were, on the verge of making contact with a completely new species of ape, and their plan was to kill one for no other reason than to sell it to a scientist. Claudio Hart would be rolling over in his grave. The Jungle Johnny of the movies did not even carry a gun. He would have been repulsed by the actions of his real self.

The midday sun beat down on us and the humidity of the jungle was near suffocating. When I wasn't wiping sweat from my forehead, I was swatting flies and mosquitoes, which could fly about at times in thick swarms.

Borga led the way, hacking at vines with a machete. Kenneth followed, with Jungle Johnny a good distance behind him. I was next, and poor Horacio did his best to keep up, hauling several packs and satchels filled with our supplies. I felt bad for the fellow. The going was tough for me and I only carried a pad of paper and a few pencils. I had to admire his dedication though; he marched on without a single word of complaint.

Soon, the three men in front of me were stopped and huddled together in conversation. I overheard Borga mention that the tracks disappeared, meaning the apes had taken to the trees. I glanced nervously upwards, expecting one of the hairy white beasts to descend on me at any moment. At the boat I was offered a pistol but had turned it down; dreadful things they were. Now though, I wondered if that was not the wisest of decisions on my part. I did not wish to harm anything, but at the same time, I did wish to get home in one piece.

It wasn't long before Borga was hacking at vines and trudging forward yet again, ever mindful of the trees. I was overwhelmed by an uneasy feeling of being watched. Surely we were being watched by several things simultaneously, as colorful birds and small monkeys were visible in the branches above, but this was a different feeling, almost as if there was an intelligence behind it. I know it is difficult to describe but I felt it all the same.

We had been moving deeper into the dense jungle for nearly three hours, though to me it felt as though it had already been days. We came across a clearing with a small pond and Jungle Johnny decided we would stop here for a time.

My heart threatened to leap straight out of my chest as Borga picked up a large snake that was as thick as my thigh and tossed it out of the way. Thank the lord it just decided to slither away and pay us no further mind. The sight of it alone was still enough to upset me and I was ever wary of my surroundings as I took a seat on the stump of a fallen tree.

Four of us had all taken a seat to rest our weary limbs. It took Horacio crashing into the clearing and finally collapsing with exhaustion, before I realized he had yet to join us. The poor lad, the others just laughed.

Jungle Johnny announced that the sun would soon be setting and that we would camp here for the night and resume our hunt in the morning. I had no complaints about that. My stamina was spent and I had no desire to be stumbling around this unforgiving terrain in the dark.

A little later, Borga got a small fire going and we were cooking weenies on sticks. There had been no further appearances of any slithering serpents, though I was still not at ease, and continuously glanced over my shoulder in an attempt to thwart their plot of creeping up on me. The bugs, however, I could nothing about. They were everywhere and beyond bothersome.

In my time on the boat, I had come to see Borga as a reasonable man. While everyone was occupied with their meals, I decided to take up conversation with the hunter.

"Borga, my good chap, you do not seem like the type of person who would wish to hunt and kill a new species of animal."

"People pay."

"Yes, people pay for a lot of things, that doesn't make it right to sell them what they want."

"When people stop paying, then that is the day I stop hunting."

"We are talking about an ape here, not some wild turkey that you would hunt and eat. This is a primate."

"An animal is animal."

"You are incorrect. Apes are highly intelligent. Why, we are not even sure yet of just how intelligent they could be. It's quite possible they are just as smart as we are."

Jungle Johnny laughed, a great belly laugh, with genuine amusement. "Listen here, writer. All animals are stupid. If they are as smart as us, then why do they live here in the jungle like savages? Why are we, humans, the dominant species on this planet? Why, because we are the smartest by far. These apes have eluded us today, but we are more intelligent, and by tomorrow, we will have one of these stupid creatures in a cage."

"Now it will be in a cage? You are not going to shoot one?"

"Had we spotted one of them today, I would have mostly likely had it shot. But they have proven elusive thus far. So tomorrow we will set a trap. A trap that works without fail, because all animals are stupid."

I decided not to press the debate. These men were thick-headed and any further conversation would only raise my ire. I did look over to Horacio, who merely shrugged his shoulders, denoting an indifference to the topic.

I found no sleep that night, so horrified was I by the thought of creepy crawlies. And they had not just been haunting my imagination, for I had seen a large hairy spider which had me standing and pacing for much of the night. I began to hope that we would catch one of these apes in the morning so we could get back to the ship, and thus, off this island.

With the arrival of morning came the suffocating humidity. We trekked for another hour, deeper into the jungle, until we found another substantial clearing.

"This is perfect," Jungle Johnny declared. "We will set our trap here."

I found a suitable log to place my rear and watched the four men go to work. I watched them, while again, I was assailed by that strange sensation that we too were being watched. I tried my best to shake those thoughts and retrieved a snack from one of Horacio's many packs.

The trap was fairly simple in design and one I had seen used many times on the big screen. On the ground of the clearing they placed a sizable net, which was then concealed with large green leaves. Ropes were tied to nearby trees and several bunches of bananas were placed in the center of the net for bait.

"There you go, writer," Johnny said, addressing me after they finished. "No guns needed. The stupid apes will not be able to resist those bananas. As soon as one gets to the center of the net, bingo, it will close around the ape and it will be ours. Works every single time."

Johnny then indicated to a group of tall trees with long thick branches. He thought that would be the best location for the five of us to lie in wait and remain out of sight.

Borga was up the tree first, securing a knotted rope to the trunk, making it much easier for the rest of us to climb up and join him. Of course I inspected the area thoroughly for snakes and spiders and breathed a sigh of relief that there were none. There were plenty of ants, but ants, I could handle. I tried my best to get comfortable and settle into what could prove to be a long wait.

Roughly twenty minutes into our vigil, I found myself glancing around nervously, when something shiny caught my eye. It was a fairly short distance away, behind us in another much smaller clearing. Something was reflecting the sun, something…metallic?

Borga had noticed it as well and was soon grabbing a pair of binoculars off of Horacio. He shook his head in disbelief and handed the binoculars to Jungle Johnny.

Johnny smiled ear to ear. "Gold! Look at all that gold!"

"Gold?" I wondered.

After Kenneth and Horacio had both taken a look, the young lad gave me the binoculars. I peered through the lenses and Johnny had indeed been correct. In the smaller clearing behind us, was a pile of gold coins. A wooden chest sat nearby, tipped over.

"Probably left here by pirates, long ago," Kenneth commented, barely able to contain his excitement.

The four men suddenly cared very little for the trap we had set and could not climb down out of the tree fast enough. It was the first time on this trip that I witnessed Jungle Johnny take the lead. In fact, in a most childish move, he even tripped Kenneth, who seemed to be passing him and might have made it to the treasure pile first.

I sat on the tree branch, watching the men hoot and holler as they reached the treasure and began scooping up gold coins with their hands. Johnny, who generally wore a scowl, laughed and even danced about with glee.

Unfortunately, their joy was not to last. I remember

watching the event unfold in utter disbelief. From under their feet, a large net suddenly wrapped itself around the four men, and ropes tied to nearby trees hoisted the net a good thirty feet into the air. A trap, just like ours. The gold was used as bait in the same way that we had used bananas.

A rumbling sound shook the tree I sat in and my heart stopped beating altogether at a sight that stole my breath. A monstrous, white-haired ape, marched into the small clearing. The ape, whose hair bordered on silver, stood about thirty feet tall and glared into the net which hung at eye level. It licked its lips as it regarded the trapped morsels within.

Soon, a second gigantic ape walked into the clearing, carrying two others that were much smaller, just a little smaller than us. Babies, I soon figured. The small apes the fishermen had seen, and the small tracks we had found on the beach, were the babies.

I positioned myself out of view and trembled as the first ape untied the ropes from the trees, then slung the net over its back with its speechless prisoners trapped inside. The two apes then plodded off into the jungle, and I know how strange this must sound, but I could swear they were giggling.

It took half a day before I found the courage to climb down out of that tree and make my escape. Thankfully, I grabbed one of Horacio's packs, the one that contained water, before dashing off in a mad run. I followed the trail that Borga had hacked all the way to the beach.

To my dismay, I now noticed several giant footprints in the sand. They led to the water, then back into the jungle. I did not even bother with the dingy and swam my way back to the boat and climbed the rope ladder that still hung down the side. I found the boat empty and knew the apes had taken Nickolas and Tomas.

I raised the anchor and managed to figure out how to start the boat. As I mentioned before, I know nothing of nautical navigation and just picked a direction, any direction away from that nightmarish island.

As I sailed away, I kept hearing Jungle Johnny's voice in my head, talking about stupid animals and how that trap always worked without fail.

THE PANHANDLER'S WILL

"Good afternoon, everyone. As most of you may already know, my name is Markus Shaw. Many years ago, I sat in this very same auditorium where you all sit now, as a student, like yourselves. And now, I am a huge success."

And that was the honest truth. I had been invited to come speak to these students from my former school, to show them that with hard work and dedication, they too could be as successful as I. I had grown up in the same neighborhood as them and had attended the very same school.

I knew the teachers present didn't care much for hearing this fact but I never bothered attending college. Several years after graduating from the high school that I was currently addressing, I started my own small printing company. Clients came easily and soon I was having trouble keeping up with the demand. I was forced to expand and even hire staff to help me. Over the next fifteen years, I moved the company location five different times, requiring a bigger warehouse with each new move.

I got into the stock trade and made some extremely wise decisions. Now I lived in a penthouse suite, in one of the most favorable areas of the Big City, with my gorgeous wife, Veronika.

Ahhhh Veronika, what more could I say, but she was the kindest and most beautiful woman on the planet, with her long raven-black hair. Veronika and I had met through a mutual friend, back when my company was still young. I was not yet wealthy, the opposite in fact. I was quite penniless in those days, having invested everything I owned into my budding company. Veronika didn't care about that though.

She came from a simple family and didn't require much to keep her happy. Her smile was radiant and infectious, lighting up any room she entered. She was a social butterfly, having the ability to strike up conversations with anyone at any time. She was genuinely interested in other people's stories and helping those in need.

Oh, if I could have only been like her, but I just didn't have the time. My company demanded most of my attention, as it had right from the very beginning. But my uncompromising dedication is what has led to my success. And as they say, the more money you have, the more money you want. I continued to pour my heart and soul into my company and it continued to prosper as a result.

After finishing my hour-long presentation, I left my old high school and hoped that I had been an inspiration to those young students. It was important that they heard that nothing had been handed to me in life; I worked for every copper coin.

Speaking of copper coins, I fished my hand around inside my pocket, looking for any spare change, as I approached the front of my apartment building. As per usual, Old Stan sat on the ground, his back resting on the brick wall of the building. He was like a permanent fixture in the neighborhood. Day in and day out he sat there, always wearing a glowing smile, despite the poor hand that life had apparently dealt him.

I couldn't exactly guess at Old Stan's age, much of his face was concealed behind a scruffy, greying beard, but I would place him somewhere within the seventies range. A frail, skeletal body, lay buried underneath layers of sweaters and a thick parka, which he seemed to wear no matter the season, along with a grubby blue toque, invariably affixed to the top of his head.

Like my adorable wife, Old Stan would talk to everyone, but then, I guess you would have to when attempting to elicit spare change from each person that passed you by. He did love to talk and could continue on endlessly unless you found a way to disengage yourself from the conversation.

"Good afternoon, Mr. Shaw," he said, his face aglow at my approach. "A fine day isn't it? Perfect weather for a walk, I see."

"Hello Stan, yes it is a very nice day indeed," I answered, dropping a handful of coins into an empty tin cup that sat on the ground directly in front of him.

"Ah, bless ya, Mr. Shaw. You are always so kind to this old man."

I smiled and nodded, then proceeded past to the lobby door.

"Oh, I almost forgot, Happy Anniversary to you as well. Lucky fella you are to have a wife like that Mrs. Shaw. Lucky man indeed," he said.

I paused before the lobby door. Good lord, it was our anniversary and I had completely forgotten, being so focused on my speech at the school. Old Stan said something else but I did not hear it as I rushed into the building towards the elevator. What would I do? I had no gift and no time to run back out to the shops.

The elevator ride was painstakingly slow, as one of the annoying children from the second floor of the building thought it would be amusing to push all thirty buttons. I could have pinched him for that but it did give me more time to contemplate my predicament. Then the simple solution came me and my problem was solved. Who didn't like money?

"Happy Anniversary, my dear," I announced upon entering our suite.

"Ahh, you remembered. I didn't think you would," she replied delightedly.

"Of course, how could I forget the day that I married the world's most wonderful woman?" Then I presented her with several hundred dollars in cash, a most impressive stack of bills. "Here you go, I want you to get whatever you like with that, but it has to be for you. Don't go giving it to the poor and don't buy anything for the apartment, it's all for you."

"Oh, how thoughtful. I don't know what to say."

Money always did the trick. I kissed her and offered to ring for some food to be delivered.

Several months later, I exited the building lobby one morning in search of a cab to hail. I owned my own car, of course, but most times it was easier to just walk to your destination, or grab a cab, within this area of the Big City.

"Good morning, Mr. Shaw," Old Stan called over. "Off to work, are ya?"

"Yes, Stan," I replied, cursing inwardly as I had forgotten to bring some change down with me in my rush.

"Anything big planned for tonight, for Mrs. Shaw's birthday?" he asked.

Unbelievable! Her birthday had completely slipped my mind. I had spent the last several days stressing over three different meetings that I had scheduled for today. How could I be such a fool?

"You know what she would really like, I bet…is…."

"Sorry Stan, we'll have to talk later," I cut him off as a cab pulled up in front of me. I simply could not be late for my first meeting of the day.

The meetings went better than I had even expected and I managed to secure three new large clients for the company. The day was a great success. I had sent my assistant, Olivia, out that afternoon to go and purchase my wife an extravagant diamond ring for her birthday, the biggest the store carried.

That night I slipped it on her finger over dinner. "It was the biggest diamond in the store," I said. "Olivia picked it out and assured me that its style was the latest craze."

"Yes…well…it's lovely, thank you," she replied.

I knew how much all women loved diamonds. Only the best for my most amazing wife.

"I was thinking we could do a dinner cruise tomorrow night. They have just started a new one down by the Third Street harbor," she suggested.

"Tomorrow is no good, my dear. I have to meet Maxwell about signing the new contracts."

"Of course, I understand."

She always understood, she was the best.

Business was booming and once again I was considering the purchase of a larger property for the company to keep up with the rising demand. This evening, Veronika and I had planned to go to the picture show. A new one was just opening by Otto Friedhelm and was starring Maude Levine. It was a werewolf picture that was already receiving much buzz. Veronika expressed great interest in seeing it and making a night out of it. I spent most of the day pouring over papers and contracts in my office at work, and when I glanced down to my pocket watch, I realized I would be late in picking her up.

Dammit, I thought to myself. I still had much to do before I could leave. Then I was struck with an exquisite idea. Veronika always enjoyed riding in a limousine. I would ring for one to be sent to pick her up and take her to the show. That would cheer her up undoubtedly and she probably wouldn't even notice that I wasn't there.

Later that night, when I got home, she was already in bed asleep, so I did not wish to wake her. She slept quite long into the morning and had not yet awakened by the time I decided to head out and grab a coffee with a business associate. This day, I made sure to grab some loose change before stepping out.

"Good morning, Stan," I said to the old man, dropping some coins into his cup.

"Ah, good morning to you too, Mr. Shaw," he replied. "I hope Mrs. Shaw enjoyed the show last night?"

"She told you about that, did she?" I asked.

"Oh yes, she was quite excited about the night out you both had planned. She was out here waiting for you to come by, so we got to chatting."

"Yes, I got held up at work. I imagine she was quite excited to ride in that fancy limousine, eh?"

"Well, I am not so sure I would have used the word excited."

"Overjoyed, perhaps?"

"Well…"

"Markus! Over here, Markus!" someone shouted.

The friend I was meeting for coffee, Franklin, was attempting to flag me down from the opposite side of the street.

"Sorry, Stan, we'll talk another time."

When I returned home later that afternoon, Veronika had just woken up. She complained of some headaches and said she just wasn't feeling too well. For the next several days she slept much and I worried for her health.

"You know what you need?" I said one morning over breakfast. "A good vacation. You can do nothing but sit on the beach all day and read a good book. How does that sound?"

Her face brightened, a sight I had not seen in some time. "Really? That does sound nice."

"Yes, really. I will buy you a plane ticket this very afternoon and book you the finest hotel available."

"Oh, you won't be coming then?"

"Dear, you know I cannot leave work in Harold's hands for more than a few days, no telling what mess I would return to. But you go and have a wonderful time. I will spare no expense to see you happy."

She smiled, women loved to travel.

I remember it clearly; it was a cold winter's day, when I was sitting in my den with a warm fire burning in the hearth. I received a peculiar telephone call, asking me stop by a lawyer's office later in the afternoon to speak with a Mr. Halstead. Curious to see what this was all about, I attended at the appointed time.

"You must be Markus Shaw. Please, have a seat," the well-dressed, middle-aged lawyer, with the bushy moustache said to me.

"What is this about, Mr. Halstead?" I asked. "Is someone suing my company over something?"

He chuckled. "Be at ease, Mr. Shaw, nobody is suing you. This has to do with Stanley Wright."

"Stanley Wright? Who on earth is Stanley Wright?" I had to wonder.

"Well you must have known him, your name is the only one listed in his will."

"His will?"

"Yes."

"Stanley Wright is dead then?"

"Oh yes, most regrettably. You wouldn't have been called here if he wasn't."

"What did he die of?"

"The doctors weren't too sure. One suggested he died of a broken heart. Personally, I believe it was the elements that finally got him, living on the streets as he did."

"Stanley Wright lived on the streets?"

"Oh yes, for many, many, years."

"Ohhhhhh...you must mean Old Stan?"

"I believe some called him Old Stan, yes."

"Hmmm, I did find it strange that I had not seen him in front of my building for several days. Stan had a will? I didn't think he owned anything."

Mr. Halstead produced a small wooden box and sat it on the desk in front of him. "It's not much," he said, opening the box. "There was just this silk handkerchief, and a sealed envelope, a letter, I believe."

He handed the items to me and I held the handkerchief awkwardly between the tips of two fingers. I couldn't imagine the germs that could be found on a panhandler's hanky. Oddly, it looked fairly white and unused, with several blue butterflies stitched on both sides as a pattern.

I thanked Mr. Halstead and promptly left his office. As I approached my building, a feeling of sadness overcame me while I looked to the now empty spot, where Stan had sat for years. It would feel strange not seeing his face every morning when I left and every evening when I returned. Though, I supposed, I would save more money now, not that I needed it.

I sat in my den, which doubled as a library, with the hanky and Stan's envelope resting on top of an opened book. I was curious about what Stan would have had to say in a letter to me. Probably thanking me for all the money I had given him over the years. Lord knows he could have probably afforded to stay in a hotel instead of living on the street.

The smell of scented candles filled the room and I was enjoying some music on the record player when Veronika entered. Dark rings were visible under her eyes; she had not been sleeping well lately.

"What are you doing?" she asked.

"Oh, nothing, was just looking through some old books," I said, closing the book to conceal the hanky and the envelope. I knew how much Veronika was fond of Old Stan and didn't want to upset her tonight with the news of his demise.

I returned the book to its proper place on the shelf and took Veronika by the hand, leading her to the kitchen where I could pour her a glass of wine.

Her next birthday came and went, and I disappointingly did not remember it until two days later. I joked to myself that I needed Old Stan around to remind me of these important events. I made it up to her though with an astonishing, custom-made diamond necklace. What a piece it was. It was certain to make all women jealous.

Now, that dreadful week in July had been one of the busiest for me at work. A few nights I was even forced to sleep in my office so I was admittedly inattentive at home. In hopes of cheering up Veronika, I booked her a trip to a world famous resort and spa at some exotic southern island for the week; a most expensive trip. Sadly, she had not felt up to going.

The Friday of that week was the worst day of my entire life. The scene in front of my building will forever be etched into my mind, playing itself out continuously in my dreams, both while sleeping and during the kind you had throughout the waking day.

A crowd of people was gathered around the lobby door as police attempted to clear a path for the medical crew. They were pushing some unfortunate person on a stretcher towards the waiting ambulance. The significance of this scene before me was not yet evident, until one person in the crowd pointed at me with a most distressed expression and said to a police officer, "That's Mr. Shaw."

The officer approached me, his face pale, visibly uncomfortable at having to be the bearer of bad news. "Mr. Shaw, let's take a walk."

I was told that it was a deadly mix of alcohol and drugs which had finally led to Veronika's untimely departing of this life. Alcohol and drugs?? That was not the Veronika I knew. She enjoyed her wine but certainly not to excess. And drugs? How on earth did she even acquire such horrible substances?

The officer said a great deal more after that but I heard not a word of it. My mind was already on a downward spiral to the very pits of despair. I did remember the man grabbing me by an arm to help keep me on my feet, as my legs had given out and I nearly crumbled to the street.

The next few weeks, even months, were a blur. It was difficult to tell what was real and what was a dream, as I spent most of the waking hours heavily intoxicated and never leaving the apartment. Even after a year had passed, my grief was still too much to bear. I longed for some memento, something personal that had belonged to Veronika, so that I might hold it, and in so doing, perhaps feel as though she was near. But alas, I had none, save for the treasures made of gold and diamonds that I had purchased, but she had not worn too often.

I was neglecting my company and in my absence, the imbecilic Harold, was running it into the ground with poor judgment and empty-headed decisions. My stocks also suffered at the hands of my disregardance. By the end of the second year, all that I had spent my lifetime building, was in ruin. There were repeated knocks at my door, which I had ignored, and many letters were then shoved underneath.

It took police officers breaking down my door, before I learned that I was being evicted from the apartment, my funds having completely run out. I was given two days to pack up what I could and not an hour more.

On the second day, in one of my rare, semi-sober moments, I stood in my den with a fire burning, packing away some books into a box. That's when I found it. One particular book slipped from my grasp to tumble and lay open on the table beside the box. Looking down, I spotted that odd handkerchief with the blue butterflies and the sealed envelope that was left to me in Old Stan's will.

The fire was burning low, so I tossed the hanky into the hearth, having no foreseeable need for an old panhandler's hanky, and then opened the envelope to find a handwritten letter inside.

Dear Mister Shaw,

I hope this letter finds you well. Weller than I, since if you are reading this, then I have finally left this miserable existence and hopefully have gone to join with Harriet. I wanted to thank you for all the years of kindness and the coins you had always so thoughtfully given to me. I was once very wealthy, like yourself, but the grief of losing my wife, Harriet, was too much for me, and I subsequently lost everything. So unfortunately, I have nothing left to leave to anyone in a will, save for some advice, and this I leave to you. I can say I was very blessed to have met your lovely wife, Veronika. What a kind and gentle soul, so full of compassion for everyone. It was many a day, that Veronika stood and spoke to me about life, when everyone else would rush past, pretending not to see an old beggar on the street. I know I always put on a smile for everyone who walked by but I was not a happy man. One day, Veronika had caught me in one of my weak moments. She offered me the handkerchief, which I have left for you, in order to dry my tears. So lovely an item it was, I could not use it, but I kept it and treasured it, as it was a gift of great kindness. You see, it was her favorite, made by her mother and given to her as a child. Veronika has a passion for butterflies and loves them very much. Are you aware of that, Mister Shaw?

I was not.

I see the fancy jewelry you have purchased for your wife but these expensive trinkets are not what she truly enjoys. You need to take the time to learn these things, things like butterflies. Veronika wears a distant stare now; she is losing her love of life. Yes, you are a busy man, but do not let your work get in the way of your personal life. Do not allow yourself to lose Veronika, as I had lost Harriet. It is not too late, Mister Shaw. So my advice to you is, get to know Veronika, the real Veronika, before she forever slips from your grasp and you spend the rest of your life regretting it. Do not become like me.

* * * *

A chill December wind blew down from the north and I shivered slightly as I leaned against the wall of a building. A well-dressed man in a long brown overcoat walked down the street swinging a briefcase. He was approaching my direction.

I put on my best smile. "Excuse me, sir, can you spare any change?"

ONE LESS HUNTER

The fog rolled in from the water of the harbor in thick waves, substantially limiting my visibility. Dark clouds had already hidden the moon and stars behind a heavy blanket and now the fog was blotting out the light from the street lamps.

This evening had proven to be quite uncooperative and was seriously impeding my search for Erwin Baardwik. I had spent the better part of a year tracking the man to this town which was comprised mostly of fishermen.

This was now my second night in town and I had yet to set my eyes on Baardwik, but my extensive information gathering had led me to firmly believe that he was indeed here. He was most likely using an alias, as I had learned that the man rarely, if ever, went by his real name. And therein was my biggest challenge. I had never seen Baardwik in person and had to rely on second-hand descriptions of the man.

Thankfully, he possessed a scar which ran down the right side of his face from his temple to his jaw. That provided me with considerable aid when inquiring about the man and if anyone had seen someone matching that description.

In Belborn he went by the name Christian Kranz. In Red Valley he was Demetrius Kloeten. In Cantos he was Albert Peeters. But each of those men was tall, dark-haired, and bore a scar that ran down the right side of their face.

In each of those places, someone went missing and was never found. The monster that was named Erwin Baardwik left a trail of death everywhere that he went. Now he was here in Vandenbourg and I needed to find him before he chose his next victim. I just hoped that I was not already too late.

A bell tower that was obscured by the fog gonged to announce the tenth hour. The evening was still fairly young and I was positive that Baardwik must have been about. The monster moved around and hunted only at night, which suited me just fine. I understood the dangers that the night brought on but did not fear them as others did, or should.

Vandenbourg was not a big town and only had a few places that catered to a night life. I chose to visit the largest of the pubs this night, as I felt that would have been Baardwik's choice as well. I had to get into the monster's mind and think like him. The largest pub simply meant more people to choose from for his next potential target.

Despite the low visibility of the night, I successfully navigated my way from my room at the inn to the pub known as *Robin's Rest.* I paused at the door for a moment only and then entered.

My senses were immediately assaulted by a cloud of pipe smoke which left the pub in a haze that was no different from the fog outside. I possessed a sensitive nose and my eyes were soon watering from the sheer amount of smoke.

The spacious taproom was extremely busy. Most of the patrons looked like the gruff sailors that made up most of the population. Given the port here in town, strangers were not uncommon in Vandenbourg, arriving in various ships. So fortunately for me, nobody paid me much attention as I entered. A few gazes shifted my way but they did not linger and soon returned to their own business.

I wondered where I might sit as all the tables and chairs were taken, when a large man seated at the bar vacated a stool and stumbled for a side door. He appeared to be in a hurry and looked as though he was about to lose his dinner and everything he had been drinking thus far.

I quickly moved in and took his seat at the bar. The man to my left guzzled a large mug of ale, spilling more onto his long disheveled grey beard than actually went into his mouth. To my right was a hard-looking man with a flat nose, doing his best to impress the equally as hard-looking woman beside him.

Life in these types of towns was tough and produced a tough breed of folk. It didn't seem like the type of place for Baardwik to hunt for another victim, but then so far, his victims did follow a certain pattern. Some were old and some were young. Some had been male and some had been female. His lack of a preference only made my job here more difficult.

I rested an elbow on the bar and casually scanned the

faces in the room. Not all were locals. It was a simple thing to pick out the visitors by their attire, just as my long black overcoat announced my status as a stranger to town. I sighed as nobody fitting Baardwik's description stood out.

The busy barkeep eventually made his way over to me and I ordered a mug of ale for the simple reason of blending in. I did not drink but did not want to appear out of place while waiting to see if the monster showed his face.

Twenty minutes passed when a tap on my shoulder startled me. I was so focused on one end of the room, and with the volume of voices around me, I had not even heard the approach of the large man whose seat I had taken.

He appeared less intoxicated from the time he had stumbled out. I supposed most of the alcohol in his body now coated the ground of the alley beside the pub. He was large with a substantial gut. His forearms looked as thick as tree trunks and he frowned from beneath a bushy black beard.

"I believe you are sitting in my seat," he growled.

"I did not see a name on it when I sat down."

"A smart guy, eh? A smart-mouthed city guy, by the looks of you."

"I just came in for a drink, I am not looking for any trouble."

"Well trouble is gonna find you if you don't get up off that stool."

"There is a seat over in the corner," I pointed to a recently vacated chair. "How about you just go over there."

"Because that is not my seat. This one is."

I could have easily got up and went over to the other chair but I had an immense distaste for bullies. I found it too difficult to ignore their behavior.

"No, I think I am comfortable right where I am," I said.

"I was hoping you were going to say that," he smiled wickedly.

He grabbed the left shoulder of my coat with his meaty right hand and he possessed an iron grip. Undaunted, I stood and brought my own right arm around in a circular motion, my wrist slamming into his. My fingers wrapped around his thick wrist as best they could and I slid my body to the side of him, while twisting his arm at the same time.

I used his size and strength against him, bringing his arm around painfully behind his back. He howled as he was forced to take a knee. Before he could spit out a curse, I snapped his arm, breaking it at the elbow. He fell to the floor with a roar that now had every face in the pub focused on us.

"Sorry for the trouble," I said to the barkeep.

I tossed a few extra coins onto the bar and casually walked out, leaving the obnoxious man rolling about in agony. It was not my intention to cause such a scene but I decided it best to continue my search for Baardwik elsewhere.

He could have been in any of the other pubs, or in none at all. He could very well be out prowling the fog-shrouded streets. The next closest pub was only a block away, so I first paid a visit there, and when Baardwik did not appear to be present, I decided to tour some of the dark alleyways.

I found the usual drunks and homeless populating many of the alleys. I stumbled across a few shady dealings and drew perturbed stares but I would run into no further trouble this night.

However, in the last alley I had decided to walk through, I did find something out of the ordinary. I spotted a small pool of blood, with drops leading to the far end of the alley. While following the trail I noticed one woman's shoe. I began to wonder if maybe I had been too late. Perhaps Baardwik had already chosen his next victim.

I followed the trail to the street and that's where it ended. Obviously, I couldn't be certain that this was Baardwik's doing, as street fights and bar brawls were common in this town. The shoe made me wonder, though it could have been lost by a drunk.

As dawn approached, I knew Baardwik would be retiring to wherever he was hiding out, so I decided to do the same. I would continue the search tonight, when the monster would be hunting again. I suddenly realized how hungry I had felt but the hour was too late now and I did my best to ignore the pain.

I awoke on the third evening and immediately set out from the inn. It wasn't as foggy this night which would make things a little easier. Anger filled me with determination as I thought of the woman that Baardwik had murdered in Red Valley. While I had not known her personally, she was by all accounts a decent woman. Beautiful and intelligent. She owned a chain of well-to-do clothing shops and was highly respected.

I spat on the ground when I considered that terrible loss of life. There were many inns in this town, given the amount of ships that came and went, so I decided to hit a few more and make some inquiries.

I had no luck with the first three but then I entered the fourth, *The Red Herring Inn.* It was a four-story building that looked out over the harbor. I found a tiny, mouse-like man, seated behind the reception desk reading an old book.

"Hello stranger, need a room?" he asked, putting his book down.

"No, sorry. Just some information if you have a moment to spare."

The innkeeper frowned so I produced a large silver coin to brighten his mood, and it worked.

"I am looking for a man who may have checked in within the last several days. His name is Erwin Baardwik, though I doubt he would have used that name."

The man leafed through a ledger that sat on the desk then shook his head. "No, nobody by that name has checked in here. At least not within the last month."

"He is a tall man, a little taller than me. He has dark hair and a scar that runs down the side of his face."

The description elicited a curious reaction from the innkeeper, though he shook his head, *no.*

"Please, good sir, it is of the utmost importance that I find this man. He is a danger to your town."

He visibly paled, which told me that he also must have believed this to be true, but out of fear, shook his head again. This man knew something and I wasn't about to leave without finding out what that was.

I changed my tone and stared menacingly into his eyes, leaving him no doubt that I was quite serious. "You will tell me what you know. This man needs to be stopped and I am the only one in this town capable of it."

Sweat formed on the innkeeper's brow and his lips twitched as he fought some internal struggle. Despite his apparent fear of Baardwik, I won over.

He glanced about nervously and lowered his voice. "Three days ago, a tall man with a scar checked in. He is in room 410. He unnerves me something terrible. He demands not to be disturbed at all during the day and he is out all night."

"I would like to get a room beside his."

"W-well, 409 is already occupied and 411 is booked for an early morning arrival tomorrow."

I placed a small pouch of coins onto the desk and made sure to jingle it before putting it down. The innkeeper's eyes lit up as he undid the pouch and peered inside.

"I-I-I will make other arrangements for that guest. You may have 411," he stammered as he handed me the room key. "P-please, sir, I don't want any trouble in here."

"Then pray that I am on time."

I silently ascended the steps to the fourth floor and with extreme caution, approached the door to room 410. I placed an ear against the door and listened intently for any noise from inside. There was nothing. As quiet as a church on Monday.

Once I was positive that Baardwik must have been out, I carefully tried the doorknob which of course was locked. I pulled out two small pieces of wire from a pocket within my coat and quickly set to work on the lock. The building was old and the lock unsophisticated. In mere moments I was inside the room, quietly closing the door behind me.

A quick scan of the room confirmed I was alone. The

only other door in this room led to a privy, and that door was open, revealing that it too was empty. Some clothes were strewn about on the floor and a black hat hung on a wall hook. The hat did match those that Baardwik tended to favor and a pair of pants on the floor would indeed have been his exact size.

A black leather bag lay open on a writing table near the window, so I walked over for a peek inside. I spat again in disgust as the bag was filled with the various tools of Baardwik's revolting trade of dealing death. I had indeed found my man.

At a glance, it did not appear that any fresh blood coated his implements of murder. The fact that he was still here in town told me that he must not have taken a victim as of yet. He would be out there, at this very moment, prowling about.

He could be anywhere, I figured, and decided to head over to my room next door and wait. I should be able to hear his arrival with these old thin walls and I knew he would be back to his room sometime before dawn.

If there was one thing I possessed an overabundance of, it was patience. I sat on the edge of the bed in my room, unmoving for hours, until I was finally rewarded with the sound of voices next door. It was a man and a woman speaking in hushed tones. Baardwik had returned and brought company with him.

With the stealth and agility of a cat, I was into the hallway in a flash, standing before the monster's door. There was a conversation going on within the room but I could not make out the details. I pressed my ear against the door hoping to gauge the monster's intentions.

I jumped back as the woman inside the room

suddenly let out a blood-curdling scream. I cursed myself, I was too late. I was positive that I was too late. I tried the door but Baardwik had locked it behind him.

With all my strength, I kicked the door down, taking the hinges right off the aged frame. Barely able to contain my rage, I stalked inside.

The woman lay sprawled on the floor near the window and a tall, dark-haired man, with a scar that ran down the right side of his face, spun around to glare at me in surprise.

"Who the hell are you?" he demanded.

"My name matters little, but I have come a long way to find you, Erwin Baardwik."

He did well to hide his shock at the mention of his real name but I noticed the subtle change in his expression. He narrowed his eyes as his mind raced through all the possibilities of who I might be.

Baardwik backed up, moving closer to the writing table, closer to his bag of deadly weapons. As he moved further from the body of the woman, I noticed the wooden stake protruding from her heart.

"You monster!" I roared.

In my fury, two of my teeth elongated into razor-sharp fangs and I dove at Baardwik with inhuman speed. He managed to reach the writing table but it was too late. I sunk my fangs into his neck and tore a hole in his throat.

Baardwik choked and sputtered for air as I dropped him to the floor and laughed at him.

"You have hunted your last vampire, Baardwik. No longer will you murder my kind."

With one hand, I lifted the dying human into the air and then finished the job I had set out to do.

ABOUT THE AUTHOR

Jeremy was born in Scarborough, Ontario, Canada. He started creating his own characters and writing his own stories by the age of 9. He is a boxing fanatic, having been an amateur boxer and is now a professional boxing judge. In his spare time when not watching boxing, or reruns of Lost in Space and Rocket Robin Hood, Jeremy tries to find time to write some of the many stories floating around in his head.

Made in the USA
Middletown, DE
07 April 2019